"It's a great picture, eve creepiness."

Could he hear the way her breath caught when his hand brushed hers as he took the phone back? Or the shakiness of her slow exhale?

As he slid the phone into his back pocket, his arm grazed hers. She didn't pull away, and a few seconds later, the back of his hand rested against her hand. Hannah shifted hers slightly, and his fingers threaded through hers.

"This feels like a great place for a first kiss, doesn't it?" he asked quietly, and Hannah looked up at his profile, her pulse racing.

Her body trembled, and she knew Rob could feel the shaking in her hand because his fingers squeezed hers. But she ignored the voices in her head urging her to think about what she should do, and instead let her heart—or her body, at least—take the lead for once. "It's a perfect place for a first kiss."

When he turned to face her, resting his free hand at her waist, every thought in her head that wasn't about desperately wanting his mouth on hers was silenced.

Rob's hand slid halfway up her back. "For our first kiss."

"Yes." It came out as a whisper, and then his lips were on hers.

Dear Reader,

Years ago, I wrote a book filled with things I love—two people falling in love amid family shenanigans, s'mores, ATVs, camping and a lot of laugher. *Exclusively Yours* became the first book in the Kowalski family series, and that family was beloved not only by readers, but by me. It wasn't easy to say goodbye to them.

In the years since, I've explored new families and places, but a piece of my heart will always belong to the Kowalskis. Readers have since asked for more, but it was never the right time—until now. In the Kowalski brothers series, the siblings decide to buy the campground that's home to so many fun childhood memories. Shenanigans ensue, including Rob Kowalski trying not to fall for one of their campers. Hannah Shelby's looking for a quiet place to mull over a major decision, and a handsome guy with blue eyes and a great sense of humor has the potential to turn everything upside down.

I'm thrilled the next generation of my favorite family is falling in love and finding their happily-ever-afters. Whether you know the Kowalskis already or you're about to meet them for the first time, I hope you enjoy *A Kowalski to Count On*.

Stop by my website at www.shannonstacey.com for my latest book news or to sign up for my newsletter. And I love connecting with readers, so you'll also discover links to where I can be found on social media.

Happy reading!

Shannon

A KOWALSKI
TO COUNT ON

SHANNON STACEY

Harlequin

SPECIAL EDITION

Harlequin®
SPECIAL EDITION™

ISBN-13: 978-1-335-40217-2

A Kowalski to Count On

Recycling programs for this product may not exist in your area.

Harlequin Enterprises ULC
22 Adelaide St. West, 41st Floor
Toronto, Ontario M5H 4E3, Canada
www.Harlequin.com

Printed in Lithuania

MIX
Paper | Supporting responsible forestry
FSC® C021394

A *New York Times* and *USA TODAY* bestselling author of over forty romances, **Shannon Stacey** grew up in a military family and lived in many places before landing in a small New Hampshire town, where she has resided with her husband and two sons for over twenty years. Her favorite activities are reading and writing with her dogs at her side. She also loves coffee, Boston sports and watching too much TV. You can learn more about her books at www.shannonstacey.com.

Books by Shannon Stacey

Harlequin Special Edition

Blackberry Bay

More than Neighbors
Their Christmas Baby Contract
The Home They Built

Sutton's Place

Her Hometown Man
An Unexpected Cowboy
Expecting Her Ex's Baby
Falling for His Fake Girlfriend
Her Younger Man

Carina Press

The Kowalski Series

All He Ever Needed
All He Ever Desired
All He Ever Dreamed
Love a Little Sideways
Taken with You
Falling for Max
What It Takes

A Kowalski to Count On

Visit the Author Profile page
at Harlequin.com for more titles.

To every reader who's loved a Kowalski over the years.
Thank you, my favorite readers of doom,
for changing my life.

Prologue

Today had been one of the most exhilarating, terrifying and also greatest days of Rob Kowalski's life. Signing his name on several bottom lines had put him in enough debt to make him sweat, but he'd signed his name alongside his brothers' and now they were all in debt together. And they owned a campground.

Now that it was done, it felt damned good.

Or maybe that was the sugar talking. They'd decided to celebrate closing on the Birch Brook Campground with a campfire, complete with s'mores, and he might have overdone the marshmallows.

Rob looked at his brothers over the top of the fire they'd built to fend off the early March chill—and to provide flames for toasting the marshmallows, of course. The four of them had always been chaotic, whether they were getting along or fighting, but they were his brothers and he hated the distance that had come with adulthood. Not a physical distance, really. None of them had moved far from their parents. But they were busy, and it often took a family dinner or holiday for all four of them to be in the same place at the same time.

There would certainly be some intense togetherness in

their near future, and right now, it felt good as he looked around at his brothers. Danny had been very clear he'd be a silent partner thanks to his financial contributions, and while he had no interest in the day-to-day running of the campground, he'd help get it off the ground. And Joey and Brian, who'd be learning about pool chemicals and sewer hookups and astronomical insurance premiums right alongside him.

"This is the most reckless thing we've ever done, and that was already a high bar," Brian said, his eyes reflecting the flames they'd all been staring into.

Rob shook his head. "It can't be reckless, because we have a business plan. Reckless people don't write out business plans."

"Even if that business plan was written on the back of a Jasper's napkin?"

He nodded. "*Especially* if it was written on the back of a Jasper's napkin."

They all knew any agreement written on the back of a Jasper's Bar & Grille napkin was considered legally binding in the Kowalski family.

Three of them had been hanging out at their uncle's sports bar—Danny had been away on a book tour at the time—catching up after a busy few weeks of not seeing each other, when Brian had mentioned the campground where their family had spent so many summer weeks was closed down. It was for sale and languishing on the market because the previous owners were of an age that made it difficult to keep up with the property. The brothers had reminisced, laughing over the summer antics of their youth, before lapsing into silence as they each mourned the loss.

We should buy it.

Rob couldn't even remember which of them had said it aloud, but it didn't really matter. All it had taken was another pitcher of beer, a napkin and a pen, and the three of them were ready to scrap their existing life plans—such as they were—in favor of ones that sounded like a lot more fun.

Kowalski Brothers Business Plan:
1. Buy the Birch Brook Campground*
2. Work hard
3. Play harder
* Ask Danny for money

As business plans went, it probably wouldn't show up in any college curriculums, but it had worked…so far. As of eleven o'clock this morning, they owned the campground. The true test of their agreement would be when it actually opened for business and they found out if it would put money *into* the pockets of Kowalski Brothers, LLC instead of just taking it out.

"This campfire would be a lot more fun if we weren't sitting in snow," Danny said, propping his boot-clad feet on the large rocks surrounding the fire ring.

"It's not like your ass is actually on the ground," Rob pointed out, since he was the one who'd remembered to sneak into their parents' garage and "borrow" four folding camp chairs. "Also, it's still early March. Snow was pretty much a given."

"It's gone at home."

Rob shrugged, but didn't bother arguing since he got the feeling Danny was complaining just to hear himself complain. His brother knew as well as anybody that winter came early and stayed late in the northern part of New Hampshire.

"You need to spend more time outside," Joey told Danny. "You've become an inside cat."

The yellow Lab lying next to Brian's chair picked her head up at the mention of a possible *cat*. Brian had found a wooden pallet and covered it with a wool blanket and dog bed he'd brought from home so Stella would be comfortable, which made Rob smile. His brother hadn't thought to bring a chair for himself, but the dog was living large.

"If I'm outside, I'm not at my desk," Danny pointed out. "Books don't write themselves."

Rob kept his mouth shut because he didn't know how much—if anything—Danny had shared with the others about his struggle to write anything at all lately. Buying this campground was undoubtedly a distraction he didn't need, but they hadn't been able to do it without him adding a substantial amount to the financing pot. Now they'd have to wait and see whether he managed to keep to being a *silent* partner, or if he was going to welcome rolling up his sleeves and using the work to be done here as an excuse to avoid his *actual* work.

"It's supposed to be warm next week," Rob said. "The rest of this will melt off by next weekend."

"It's been a long day," Brian said, pushing himself out of his chair. Stella lifted her head again, but she didn't get up. Rob knew she'd wait to see if any of the other humans moved, because if Brian was hitting the bathroom or grabbing a snack and then coming right back, she wasn't about to give up the warm, comfy spot she'd nestled into.

Then Danny stood and folded his chair. "Last one in gets the camp cot."

That got Joey moving, but Rob took his time. As the youngest, he already knew he was getting the camp cot because there weren't enough beds in the fixer-upper house that had come with the campground. With three older brothers, he'd gotten used to making do with whatever was left.

Rob knew the argument for the queen bed would get

heated—Joey was the oldest but Danny had put up the most money—and he didn't want to hear it. Instead, he took his time dousing the campfire, using the pile of snow they'd dug out of the ring so they could fill it with wood. Then he took his chair and the chair Joey had knocked over and left in his rush to get to the house and set them on top of Stella's bedding. Then he put that pile in the shed with Danny's and Brian's chairs.

Before he went inside, he took a last look around the quiet, empty campground he now owned a quarter of. His finger itched for his camera's shutter button, but he'd already taken at least a hundred photos today.

This was it. This was the day his life changed and he stopped being the irresponsible youngest Kowalski boy who'd had three different jobs in the last four years and just wanted to take pictures. Today he became a business owner, and his partnership with his brothers would give him the opportunity and freedom to finally take his photography to the next level. Maybe he wouldn't be able to support himself with his camera, but he wanted to be taken seriously.

His family didn't take him seriously. They never had, but that was going to change.

They had less than two months to get this campground ready for the campers to move in and there was a lot of work to be done. If everything went according to plan, Danny would go back to his desk and write more books. And Joey would spend most of each week in the southern part of the state with his wife and stepdaughter, leaving Brian and Rob to coordinate their schedules and do most of the heavy lifting.

But if there was one thing Rob knew, it was that when it came to the Kowalski family, things very seldom went according to plan.

Chapter One

Two months later

With a groan, Rob sat up and swung his legs off the ancient twin bed. Figuring out long-term accommodations and buying a decent bed were leapfrogging up the to-do list. They'd been so busy getting the campground ready for campers, they hadn't had the time or energy to worry about themselves.

Today was the official opening day for their incoming seasonal campers, so all four of them had spent the night in the small house. And while he'd graduated from a camping cot to the twin bed, it—like most things in his life—had been a hand-me-down and the mattress barely met the definition of the word anymore. The house had two small bedrooms, one of which was mostly taken up by the queen bed and a dresser. It had only taken a couple of nights back in March before Brian won that bedroom. Or Stella did, really. If she didn't have room to stretch out next to her human, she grew restless and none of them slept well.

They'd managed to get two twin beds into the other bedroom, though Rob and Joey had to share a dresser. Once they'd been able to turn the water on to the bathhouses, Danny had used the small cabin whenever he stayed over.

But the old, broken-down beds in the cabins had been thrown away and the new ones hadn't arrived yet, so he was stuck with the couch in the house. It was in about as good a shape as the mattresses.

He'd floated the idea of buying a used camper—or borrowing their parents' very nice one—and taking one of the sites for their own use, but Danny had shot him down. Unless Rob wanted to pay the full seasonal fee for the site, he could sleep in the house with the others.

A few more weeks, he told himself as he shuffled to the only bathroom. Once the campground was fully open to the public and they'd gotten the rhythm of it, he and Brian would be the only ones actually *living* there. Joey would show up for weekends, more than likely. And Danny even less.

First, though, they had to get through today, he thought as he joined his brothers in the kitchen.

He walked in just in time to see Brian closing the fridge with a snort of disgust. "I'm not sure what it says about us that we did the shopping and we have a stockpile of camper light bulbs and an apocalypse-worthy stash of toilet paper, but we have nothing for breakfast."

"I brought coffee, sugar and milk when I came up last night," Danny said. "What else is there?"

"Eggs, maybe," Brian suggested. "Bacon. Toast. Home fries."

"Humor's totally lost on you."

"Oh, that was humor? I guess I missed that because it wasn't funny."

It was too early for brotherly bickering—Danny was the quietest while Brian was a button-pusher, and they had a long history of not getting along—so Rob decided to distract them with the promise of food none of them had to cook. "Let's go to Corinne's because we're going to burn through some calories today."

Corinne's Kitchen was the only restaurant within a reasonable driving distance. Luckily, the food was good and the prices were decent, because they'd become regulars over the last couple of months. That hadn't been part of the plan and the meals couldn't be paid for with the campground's credit card even if they talked about the business, as per Danny, but when you spent an entire day digging trenches to upgrade the electrical system, you just wanted somebody to set a plate of already cooked food in front of you.

"Who's buying?" Brian asked, opening the door to let Stella out.

Joey snorted. "I vote for separate checks. I've seen you eat."

Twenty minutes later, they were ready to go, but had to wait while Brian let Stella inside so she could have the first of her many daily naps while they were gone. Then they headed for two of the vehicles, but Rob stopped, phone in his hand.

"Wait. We need a photo." As if he'd pressed a sound effect button, all three of his brothers groaned in unison. "Just one, in front of the sign, to commemorate the day."

"You say just one, but it'll take you an hour to set up the shot," Joey protested. "I want breakfast."

"And more coffee," Danny said.

"Five minutes. And you know Mom and Dad will want a picture. Especially Mom. She'll be disappointed if she doesn't get a picture to post and brag about on Facebook."

As expected, *Mom* was the magic word and though there was some muttering and rolled eyes, his brothers gathered in front of the Birch Brook Campground sign, making sure they didn't block the letters.

Rob wanted to run into the house for his equipment bag

so he'd have his good camera and tripod, but he knew if he did, there was a good chance they'd get in their vehicles and leave without him. Instead, after using the stand built into his phone's case to prop it on the hood of Danny's car, he framed the shot. Then he joined Brian on one side of the sign, so they were evenly split, and pulled up the remote shutter button on his smartwatch.

"On three," he said, and counted them down.

They didn't even give him a chance to see if the auto-focus had gone awry or if any of them had their eyes closed. Rob barely had time to retrieve his phone from Danny's hood before his brother was in the car, with Joey sliding into the passenger seat. It surprised him they didn't run over his foot in their rush to get to breakfast—or with Danny driving, to get to the coffee.

Brian pulled up so Rob could jump into the passenger seat of his truck, and after fastening his seat belt, he checked the picture. He wasn't too worried about it because he could always retake it when they got back. But over the years, he'd learned that when taking a photo like this, the most emotion was in the first shot. With each subsequent take, it became more about the picture than the moment the camera was capturing.

And what a moment he'd captured, he thought as the photo filled his phone screen. All four of them were relaxed and smiling, with the same air of *yeah, we really did it* he'd felt. It was probably the best picture of the four of them he'd ever seen, and he pulled up his messages and scrolled through until he found the one labeled *Family Group Chat of Doom*. That one was pretty much the entire Kowalski family, including his grandparents and all the aunts and uncles—even the cousins in Maine—and he knew it would blow up their phones. He didn't mind because it *was* a day to celebrate. Also, it would annoy Brian, which was always a bonus.

Their favorite table was available, and Kenzie Pelletier—the owner and the only full-time server—didn't bother to ask before bringing four mugs and the pot of coffee to their table.

"Today's the big day, right?" she asked, setting the mugs in a line and filling them before handing them out.

"Yep," they all said at the same time, and she laughed.

"Congratulations. And a big day needs a big breakfast, so I'll give you a few minutes while I deliver those plates in the window."

Rob wasn't sure what he wanted, but that plate of French toast waiting in the pass-through window for her to pick up looked good. Everything at Corinne's Kitchen was good, though. Frank, who was Kenzie's dad—Corinne was her mom, but she'd passed away—couldn't cook a bad meal as far as Rob was concerned.

Their phones all buzzed for what was probably the fifteenth time in the last ten minutes. During the season, most of their guests would arrive on Fridays, but they'd decided to make Saturday opening day so fewer campers would show up in the dark. That meant most of their family was off from work and able to chat.

"I would look at a menu," Brian muttered. "But I guess I'll read six thousand text messages instead."

"You could have waited until after breakfast," Joey pointed out.

"We'll be busy after breakfast," Rob shot back. "And you don't have to react to every single one. Let everybody congratulate us and then when it peters out, do a quick *thanks all* and move on."

"It's a good picture of us," Danny said, picking up his menu. "Thank you for taking it."

"It *is* a good picture," Joey admitted, and even Brian nodded.

While the others moved on to pondering their breakfast orders—seriously, Danny and Joey had been arguing about the difference between a cheese omelet and scrambled eggs with cheese melted on top since Rob was in diapers—he tuned them out. He was definitely having the French toast.

A truck pulling a camper turning into the parking lot distracted him, and he tilted his head to get a better look out the window. The driver could be going anywhere, of course. There were a lot of campgrounds in northern New Hampshire, not even counting the private land some owners kept campers on. But it was still an exciting reminder they were actually going to welcome their seasonal campers to Birch Brook today.

Then the door opened and a woman walked in. Rob forgot about French toast and Birch Brook and pretty much everything but her.

She was a few inches shorter than him—Rob, of course, not only being the youngest Kowalski brother, but the shortest at five-nine—and wearing jeans and a plum Henley shirt that hugged her curves. Her long, dark hair was pulled into a ponytail, and when she looked around and her gaze met his, he could see that her eyes were just as dark. And the door that closed behind her didn't reopen, so she was alone.

No wedding ring, either.

He could feel his heart beating in his chest as he looked into her eyes. Then he gave her his most charming Kowalski smile.

Because her GPS had informed Hannah Shelby she'd be turning right too late to actually brake safely enough to *make* the turn, and it took her a few miles to find a space big enough to turn the truck and trailer around, she ended up in the parking lot of a little restaurant called Corinne's Kitchen.

And since a glance at the clock told her it was too early to check into the Birch Brook Campground, where she'd be spending the next three months, Hannah put the truck in Park instead of turning it around. She was down to her emergency stash of granola bars, anyway. Since she didn't particularly like granola bars, ending up here seemed like a sign she was due for a breakfast somebody else cooked.

As the door closed behind her, she glanced around, looking for a place to sit. That's when her gaze tripped over the man who was looking at her. He was a handsome one. There was no doubt about that. All dark, tousled hair and sun-kissed skin. Bright blue eyes that practically sparkled with warmth and good humor. And he had lips that curved into a smile that took her breath away.

Hannah didn't mean to return the smile. Even though it was early in the day, she was tired from a predawn start and tense driving, and she wasn't in the mood to encourage the attention of a stranger. But she couldn't help it. There was something about him that made her smile back before she went to the counter and took a seat.

She set her bag down on the seat next to her and pulled out the paperback she was currently reading. Because she could see the table with the handsome charmer through the corner of her eye, she was thankful to have the story to focus on so she wouldn't surrender to the urge to turn and see that smile again.

The server, whose name was Kenzie, according to the battered plastic tag pinned to her shirt, brought her a menu. "Do you want coffee?"

"Yes, please." The one she'd gotten for the road had been awful and prepared wrong—she *never* wanted hazelnut flavoring, for the record—but coffee places were hard to find in the northern part of New Hampshire, apparently. And she hadn't wanted to deal with finding a place to pull the truck and camper in without having to back up more than necessary.

The need for caffeine was strong, though, and so she'd spent the entire drive sipping the disgusting coffee, swearing, and then sipping it again. She really hoped Corinne's Kitchen served a good brew because she intended to drink her fill of it.

When Kenzie returned with her coffee, Hannah was ready to order. "I'd like two scrambled eggs, with bacon and wheat toast, please."

"Sure thing. Do you want home fries or beans with that?"

"Home fries, please." She'd been in this part of the country before. Getting her master's degree in history from the University of New Hampshire had been her way of exploring Boston without actually staying in Boston, and one of the first things she'd learned was that a lot of New Englanders ate baked beans with their breakfast. While she'd wanted to immerse herself in a historically rich part of the country, that was one of many local customs she'd chosen to skirt.

The coffee was delicious, and if she'd been alone, she would have moaned with the pleasure of it. But she wasn't, so she just took another sip and savored it in silence. It was probably a good thing it was piping hot or she might have embarrassed herself by chugging it as if she was at a frat party.

After setting the mug down, she flexed her fingers, which ached from strangling the steering wheel for the last hour. She'd pulled her parents' camper before. And she'd driven her dad's truck often enough to be comfortable doing so. But towing all the way across the country—especially alone—was new.

And the logging truck that was determined to go faster than her despite being behind her had been the cherry on the stress sundae. With nowhere to pull over and let him pass, she'd had to cope with his menacing presence in her mirrors, pushing her to the limits of her speed comfort zone. If she'd known she was going to make such good time due to the pressure, she would have slept in a little longer.

Kenzie walked out of the kitchen balancing a tray laden with plates, and Hannah watched the French toast pass by with a pang of regret. It was a dish that was either regrettably forgettable, woefully undercooked or exceptional. Since she didn't like to gamble when it came to enjoying her first meal of the day, she rarely ordered it, but that French toast looked exceptional and before she'd even received her own breakfast, she knew she'd be back.

The four men at the other table laughed a lot. She wished she could tell which voice and which laugh belonged to the guy with the charming smile, but she guessed it wasn't the guy who kept grumbling about text messages.

Hannah kept her eyes on her book, though, holding it open with her right hand while she ate with her left. It took her several tries at reading the same paragraph before the story grabbed her enough to displace thoughts of those blue eyes, but eventually she lost herself in the reading.

Until chairs started scraping behind her as she took her last bite. The urge to look was strong, but she simply pushed her plate back and held the book in front of her. Then she took another sip of her coffee, which was a good distraction because she forgot Kenzie had just topped it off and it was hotter than she'd anticipated.

And speaking of things that were too hot, the man with the smile slid onto the seat next to her bag and nodded toward the paperback in her hand. "You have great taste in books."

The domestic suspense set on a remote island was definitely geared toward the female market, and she wondered if he'd actually read it. "So far, so good."

"I probably wouldn't have picked it up, but my mom recommended it and by the time I got to the part where she finds the knife in the bottom of her bag—and I can see you're past that, so no spoilers—I was hooked."

How was she supposed to resist a guy who had a great smile, read books *and* whose mother was in his book rec trust circle? But she found herself nodding anyway. "I don't usually love an unreliable narrator, but it's very well done."

"I'd love to know what you think of the ending. Maybe we could get together when you're finished and talk about it? Maybe over dinner?"

Her sister often joked that the surest way to kidnap Hannah would be in a food truck that also offered a lending library, so as pickup lines went, dinner and book talk would probably—under different circumstances—be a winner. "I'm just passing through, so it's not likely our paths will cross again."

Disappointment dimmed his expression slightly, but his smile rallied. "That's too bad. I think you and I would have made a good book club."

Oh, he was good. Hannah almost wavered. She was going to be in the area for three months, after all, and there was no reason she couldn't enjoy herself while she was here.

But there was something about this man that promised

more than just a good time, and she had enough on her *figuring out my life* plate without adding a potential relationship on top.

"Just passing through," she said again, adding a dash of finality to her tone.

He stood and gave her one last smile. "Safe travels."

"Thanks." Hannah forced herself to turn her attention back to her book rather than watching him walk out the door with the others.

A few seconds after the door closed, she heard a burst of male laughter and winced. She'd let him down easy, but she'd still turned him down, and it sounded like he was going to take a ribbing over it.

It wasn't often Hannah regretted letting a man walk away from her, but this had been a tough one. She would have liked to be a part of his two-person book club, so it was probably for the best it was unlikely she'd ever see him again.

Chapter Two

Somehow Rob had gotten the short end of the stick again. Actually, it wasn't *somehow*. As the youngest of four boys, he'd learned early that by the time things trickled down to him, they were crap. Whether it was hand-me-down clothes or chores left on the list, he got what his three brothers didn't want.

Today was no different. Joey and Danny were in the store. Joey was greeting people because, according to him, he was the most personable. That was actually Rob, but whatever. And because Joey was also the most organized, he was stocking the shelves in between campers arriving. That part was actually true. Rob would have just stuck the stuff on the shelves wherever and let people hunt for what they needed.

Danny was handling the paperwork because the guy who spent his life sitting at a desk was a logical choice for being behind a desk. In theory, he could sneak some writing in, but Rob didn't think that was happening. He could tell how the writing was going by his brother's temperament, and Danny wasn't a lot of fun right now.

Brian was all over the campground, Stella at his side, helping new campers find their sites. Returning seasonal campers—those who'd been there under the old owners—

had been given first crack at their old sites, and they'd been thrilled to have almost half of them return. Brian also had to mediate husbands and wives trying to maneuver trucks and trailers into small spaces together, but at least he was interacting with people.

Rob had been stuck fighting today's battle in the ongoing war with the pool. Turning a neglected algae swamp into a sparkling pool fit for swimming came with a learning curve, but they'd decided the budget didn't allow for professional intervention. By the time it was warm enough at night to ensure freezing wouldn't be an issue, they'd been busy with electrical and sewer upgrades and left it too late. Then the pump broke on the second day they ran it.

The pool had seriously tested their theory they could learn how to do anything by watching YouTube videos, but Rob was confident they'd have it ready for swimming by Memorial Day weekend. And because he'd said so out loud—and because nobody else wanted to do it—making sure that happened had become his job.

Babying the pump. Chemical tests. Skimming dead bugs and leaves and chasing frogs. Not the most glamorous of jobs. And on the day they officially opened for business, it didn't feel very important. Birch Brook Campground was supposed to be a turning point for him—he was capable and responsible and dammit, he wanted his family to see it—but here he was wielding a skimmer pole.

He glanced up when he heard a vehicle slowing to pull in. Another truck pulling a camper, though this one was coming from the north, which was unusual. And this camper was smaller than the others that had arrived today. Many of the seasonals had big campers with multiple bump-outs and screen rooms. They spent a lot of time in their campers and they wanted to be comfortable. But this was a smaller

Airstream, and he guessed the camper was either single or a couple with no kids or kids who were grown. It also looked very familiar.

The driver stopped the truck in the parking area for checking in, and Rob set the skimming net down as the woman from the restaurant got out. She didn't look in his direction as she walked around the back of her camper to the office door, which was good since she would have caught him staring.

His phone buzzed in his pocket, and he pulled it out to see a text from Joey. Dude, you're never going to believe who just walked in.

Yeah, he would, because he'd watched her do it. He was about to slide the phone back into his pocket without responding when another text came through.

She's one of our seasonals. Her name is Hannah.

Rob didn't even have to try to get an image of her in his mind. Her face was unforgettable. *Hannah.* It was a pretty name, but it was also none of his business.

Well, it actually *was* since she would essentially be their tenant for the summer. But it wasn't his business in the way his brother was implying.

When she told you she was passing through, she left out the fact it's taking her three months to do it.

He was going to keep ignoring Joey's text messages since any response at all would only encourage him.

Only one adult on her site, so no partner in the picture.

Rob rolled his eyes at his brother's text message and then

set his phone down on the closed bucket of pool chemicals by the fence's gate. Anything he said would just keep Joey going, and he had work to do. But he couldn't resist glancing over his shoulder at the store's big window, hoping to catch just a glimpse of her.

And that's when he tripped over the pole of the pool skimmer and hit the water with a splash.

Hannah was waiting for the man behind the desk—Danny, he'd said his name was—to finish filling out her receipt for the balance of her site fee. Rather than stare at him, she turned to look out the window at the pool.

She barely had time to register that the man inside the pool fence was the man from the restaurant when he tripped and fell into the water.

Hannah gasped, but the two men in the office immediately started laughing.

"You've got your phone," Danny told the other man—Joe, she thought he'd said. "Get a picture of that."

"Is he okay?" she asked them, because there was a lot of flailing happening in the water.

"He can swim," Danny said. "He's just mad."

"If his phone was in his pocket, he's going to be *really* mad," Joe said over his shoulder before he went out the door.

"My brothers and I spent a lot of time in that pool as kids," Danny told her. "Our family—the *whole* family, grandparents and all—used to come here when we were growing up. When we found out the campground was for sale, we couldn't let it go, I guess."

Brothers. "So you and your brothers bought it together?"

"Yeah. There's the four of us. Me and Joey, of course. He's the oldest, and then me. Brian is next, and he'll help you find your site and get your camper parked. And that's

Rob in the pool. Considering the state of that water, you hopefully won't meet him until after he takes a shower."

Rob. The name went well with that slightly impish grin.

"Although, I guess you've kind of already met," he continued, and Hannah sighed. She knew Rob would recognize her since he'd been watching her and they'd had a conversation. But, considering they'd already had a laugh at his expense, she'd hoped the others wouldn't place her.

She nodded, but didn't add anything to the conversation. Technically, she *was* just passing through, so it wasn't as if she'd lied. She was just passing through with a three-month layover here—in the campground they owned. Her sister was really going to get a kick out of this situation.

It took longer than it should have to finish the paperwork because Danny kept getting distracted by the goings-on at the pool. It was hard to sign things when you were laughing. Hannah turned and looked out the window again, despite her best efforts not to, just in time to see Rob walk by.

Joey was following him, laughing, and taking pictures with his phone, and she wasn't surprised when Rob laughed, too. He seemed like the kind of guy who'd see the humor in any situation.

The back door opened and another guy with dark hair and blue eyes walked in. Now that she knew there were four brothers, she could see the family resemblance and she assumed this was Brian.

He confirmed it by introducing himself, and then the dog who'd come in with him. "This is Stella. She's pretty well trained, but she's also shameless when it comes to wanting new friends to hang out with."

Hannah rubbed Stella's head. "Dogs make the very best friends."

"If you want to head to your site, I'll help you get your

camper in place. Just take a right at the fork and go around the playground. Then it'll be a left and the road goes into the tree line, but by the time you get there, I'll be there to show you which site."

Rob was nowhere in sight as she drove the truck slowly through the campground. He was probably in the shower, and yeah, that was really not a visual she needed in her head right now. Luckily, his brother appeared on a four-wheeler with Stella running alongside, and she concentrated on following him to her campsite.

This part of the campground was wooded, offering shade and a slight buffer against noise. She didn't have the luxury of appreciating it in that moment, though, because it took all of her concentration to work with Brian on getting the camper into place.

Luckily, there was a minimum amount of backing up. The site was designed for an RV to pull in rather than backing in. And it was tight for her truck, but her camper was small enough so she was able to get it in place without Brian having to go get the tractor to maneuver it.

He didn't stick around after they'd gotten the camper placed the way she wanted it and unhooked her truck. After helping her back out between the camper and the firepit, making sure she hit neither, he pulled a business card out of his pocket and handed it to her.

"You know where to find us if you need anything," he said. "The number for the landline in the office is on there. But our cell phone numbers are on the back, so you can call or text if there's nobody in the store. There are stars next to mine and Rob's because we'll be the two around most of the time. Joey and Danny will come and go."

"Thanks," she said, glancing at the card. "And thanks for the help setting up."

"No problem. Oh, and if Stella makes a nuisance of herself, the words *go home* will send her looking for me."

"Stella's always welcome here." She loved dogs and would have one for company if her apartment building was more pet-friendly. Maybe someday, when she had a yard of her own, she'd rescue a few pups.

For now, it was time to make this spot her temporary home.

Hannah and her sister, Jenn, had been raised by parents who thought camping was the ultimate family adventure. Luckily, their mother had a hard limit when it came to roughing it—learned after their first and last time tent camping—and there had always been campers in their life.

The bugs seemed pretty excited about finally having a human on the site, though, so she took a minute to apply some bug spray before getting to work leveling the camper. After doing the water and sewer hookup, she plugged in the electrical cord and tested to make sure everything was in working order.

It definitely wasn't time for the air conditioner yet, which was a blessing. Hannah hated the constant drone of the fan—like an extreme white noise machine. She liked being able to hear the birds singing and the wind in the leaves.

Once she confirmed everything was on and the fridge was starting to cool, she went back outside to pull the last few things out from under the truck's tonneau cover. There was an outdoor carpet, which she unrolled and spread out under the awning. Then her single camping chair. The site had a picnic table, but she probably wouldn't use it often. They were uncomfortable to sit on, and she'd probably eat inside, out of the bugs.

The last thing was the small, collapsible grill. It was meant for tailgating, but it was the perfect size for her parents' camping trips once their nest was empty. And was a perfect size for Hannah.

The next thing on her list was buying groceries. Distracted by Rob falling in the pool, she'd forgotten to ask them about stores in the area. She wanted directions to the grocery store the locals used, not the local markets that were overpriced and tourist-friendly.

She was about to walk down to the office when a flash of light caught her eye. It was the sun glinting off a camera lens and when she realized it was pointed in her direction, every muscle in Hannah's body tensed.

Somebody was taking her picture, and she was pretty sure it was Rob.

That was a weird invasion of her privacy, making her skin feel hot and prickly. If there was one thing an interest in true crime had taught her, it was that a bad man could have a great smile.

She spun, presenting the camera with her back. Then she walked across her site—not allowing herself to break into a jog—and retreated into her camper.

Chapter Three

Rob didn't intend to take a photo of Hannah. He hadn't even realized she was in the shot until her movement caught his attention, and then he watched her scramble back into her camper.

Dammit, he really hadn't meant to do that. Now that there were campers on some of the sites, he wanted to update the website to show glimpses of the campers and RVs through the trees because semiprivacy and shade were definitely perks for a lot of potential guests, but he hadn't intended to capture any people.

And if she'd seen him and recognized him as the guy who'd hit on her that morning, she might get the wrong idea about him. He'd been interested in her, sure, but she'd made it clear the feeling wasn't mutual. Disappointing, but he'd accepted it graciously. What he definitely would *not* do is become a creeper, trying to get pictures of her without her knowing.

The last thing he wanted was for her to think he'd do something like that and end up feeling unsafe here. And the *next-to-last* thing he wanted was for her to complain about him to his brothers and add this, along with falling in the pool, to the list of ways Rob screwed up on opening day.

He was done with being the class clown of the family,

and with looking like a screwup just because he'd been born last and had three older brothers riding his ass about every little thing all the time.

The responsible thing to do was explain to Hannah what he'd been doing and apologize, so that's what he would do. And he almost managed to convince himself that was the *only* reason, and that he didn't welcome an excuse to see her again.

It wasn't until he saw the California plates on the truck and camper that he realized he hadn't thought about where Hannah was from until now. He wasn't sure it was possible for her to be from farther away from him without involving a boat.

I'm just passing through.

He snorted as he made his way to the camper door. She hadn't been lying, exactly, but she'd certainly been wrong about the likelihood of them crossing paths again.

After taking a deep breath and hoping he wasn't about to make the situation even worse, Rob knocked on the door. "Hannah? It's Rob."

He took a step back, not only because he wanted to give her plenty of space, but because she'd hit him with the door if he didn't. Assuming she opened it, of course. If he'd made her mad, she might. But if he'd scared her, it had been foolish of him to come knock and expect her to answer.

Just when he'd made up his mind to leave her alone and send her an email, the door opened. Hannah didn't come out, but he figured the least he could do was crane his neck to look up at her in the doorway.

"I just wanted to apologize for accidentally taking a picture of you. I was taking pictures of the pond with glimpses of the campers through the trees for the website—trying to make it look good and all that, and I didn't mean to get you in the shot."

"Okay."

"I deleted it."

"Okay." That was all she seemed to want to say, and the silence had grown awkward enough so he was about to turn and walk away when she spoke again. "Thank you for deleting it. It was a little weird, having my picture taken for no reason."

He gave her a sheepish grin. "And I've pushed the boundaries twice, and it's only the first day. I promise I'll do my best to make sure it doesn't happen again."

"Thank you. Have you been crying?" As soon as the words left her mouth, she pressed her lips together and gave a sharp shake of her head. "I'm sorry. That's none of my business."

"No, it was pool chemicals." He chuckled. "I took an unplanned dip in the pool and because we're trying to get it straightened out after some neglect, the chemicals are a little intense."

"Right. I was in the office at the time and it was hard to miss it happening since your brothers were *very* entertained by it."

"I bet they were. And the entire family was sent the photos Joey took, so everybody's entertained." He shrugged because that was just another day for the Kowalski family. "Since you're a guest, I feel it's my duty to let you know that it's still very cold at night here, so the pool is *not* warm right now."

She laughed at his joke, which he appreciated because he wanted to dispel any lingering awkwardness between them. "I'm not much for swimming. Especially when it's still sweatshirt weather and, oh, the chemicals are potent enough to make your eyes look like you've been crying for two hours."

He chuckled. "Oh, one more thing before I go. I don't know if Danny remembered to tell you, but the weekend before Memorial Day—which is when we open to transient campers—we're going to have kind of a get-acquainted cookout next to the playground for all the seasonal campers."

She nodded once. "Thank you for letting me know."

He noticed she didn't tell him she was looking forward to it, or even commit to being there, but he didn't push. Between the restaurant, the pool and the camera, he'd made a bad first, second *and* third impression and the best thing he could do now was walk away before he made it any worse.

"Have a good night," he said. "You know where to find us if you need anything."

As he walked away, he heard her go inside her camper and a moment later, his phone chimed. For a second, he thought maybe Hannah had gone inside and then sent him a text message, but it was from Joey.

Brian said you're at Hannah Shelby's site. Don't forget the rules, bro.

No, he hadn't forgotten the rules they'd agreed upon— one of them being that fraternizing with campground guests was strictly prohibited. But talking to one of the campers wasn't fraternizing. Or he didn't think so, anyway. When they'd made the rule, they'd all presumably meant there would be no *hooking up* with any of the campers. It had been strongly implied that was what it meant.

Regardless, he didn't bother responding to Joey. So far, owning a campground with his brothers wasn't nearly as fun as he'd hoped it would be.

* * *

Hannah smiled as she moved around the camper, making it feel like home. Most things had to be secured or put away during the towing process, but now she could have her Keurig out. The salt and pepper shakers from a family trip to the Grand Canyon over twenty years ago were unwrapped and set on the counter. She arranged her toiletries in the bathroom.

The nineteen-and-a-half-foot Airstream had a compact layout that offered all the space she needed and was an easy tow behind her dad's truck. The construction was solid, and when the door was closed, it was like being in an expensive, well-appointed cocoon.

Once she was finished, she wanted to relax for a few minutes before moving on to the next thing. Rather than sitting at the dinette—and dammit, she still hadn't asked about grocery stores—she went to the back of the camper and flopped into her "nest." With a ton of pillows and a luxurious throw in addition to a regular blanket, the bed was a lot more appealing to her than the rigid dinette bench. The pillows often ended up tossed aside when she was sleeping, but they supported her back nicely when she was reading one of the few paperbacks she had stowed in a box under one of the dinette's bench seats.

She usually read ebooks on her phone almost exclusively, but she hadn't wanted to get stranded without something to read if the cell signal wasn't great at the campground—and it wasn't. At least not back in the trees. But she'd noticed when she was checking in that her signal was strong enough so she could hot-spot if she wanted to tote her laptop to the pool area.

Now, though, she settled against her pillows and closed

her eyes. Then she opened them again when an image of Rob Kowalski filled her mind.

The man's smile was as potent as his blue eyes.

His poor eyes. They'd looked awful after his unplanned dip in the pool. It was good they had almost a month before the pool was scheduled to open because, based on the current chemical situation, they were going to need it.

When her phone chimed, she realized she'd left it on the counter. Sighing, she crawled out of her nest and retrieved it. It was for the best, she told herself. There was still stuff on her to-do list for the day, and she wouldn't check anything off while snuggled in a mountain of pillows.

The text message was from Jenn, and it had come right after a missed FaceTime notification. Her sister must have tried it first, though Hannah hadn't heard the ring.

Your dot stopped moving and it says Birch Brook Campground, so you're parked? Call wouldn't go through.

The guilt for not telling Jenn she'd arrived as soon as she pulled in had her tempted to walk down into the stronger signal to call her back, but she settled for typing in a response.

I'm parked and all hooked up. Gorgeous spot. Will send pics soon. But in this part of the campground, signal's not great. Will have to schedule video calls in advance. Texts go through, though.

I'll tell Mom & Dad but you should call them later. Also, call Erika. She's messaged me three times today.

Hannah winced. She'd silenced all notifications from Erika—her best friend *and* business partner—on the morning of her second day on the road because the woman didn't seem to understand Hannah was driving and couldn't read or respond, so she just kept piling them on. And then she'd realized how nice it was to have a short break from Erika's energy and the stress of making a decision about the future of *Improbable Causes*—their podcast about historical true crimes.

I'll text Erika now, and I'll call the parents later. Kiss my nieces for me.

Since she had her phone open, she went in and skimmed all of the increasingly strident text messages from Erika, and then listened to the voicemails. If she moved to a spot with a stronger signal, she'd probably find Instagram DMs and Facebook messages, too. Her friend was high-maintenance— she had boundless energy and a capacity for drama that was exhausting—but they'd been close for years and Hannah regretted having silenced her. She should have at least touched base with her each evening.

Now she had to text her, but her thumb hovered over the phone's keyboard without actually touching it. Once she made contact, Hannah was also going to have to reiterate that one of the reasons she'd gone camping was to give herself the space and time to figure out if she was comfortable with Erika's plans for revamping their podcast. And if Erika wouldn't give her that time and space, they were going to have a problem.

Sorry about the silence. I arrived at the campground this morning. All's well and I'm looking forward to some time off.

She wasn't sure if the message was pointed enough to

remind Erika about the boundaries she'd tried to set before leaving, but she hoped so. She'd hate to have to silence her again. Plus, it didn't do much good if it led to Erika trying to reach her through Jenn. Her sister would only put up with that so long.

You scared me! I'm glad you're safe! You know how many women get murdered while traveling? It's a LOT! So no pressure, but there are a few emails for you with some thoughts I've had. I know you want time off, but since they're emails, they can just sit until you want to read them. Have fun! And be safe!

Hannah sent back a heart emoji and considered the conversation over. She'd known even when she set the boundaries that Erika would struggle with them, so emails sitting in her inbox were more than she'd hoped for. When she was in the mood, she could skim them, but she already knew her friend's thoughts.

When they'd started the *Improbable Causes* podcast, it had been a passion project. Their focus had always been crimes throughout history, with Hannah bringing the research and facts, and Erika bringing the entertaining color commentary. A few years ago, a sustained level of moderate success allowed them to become full-time podcasters.

Then, by fan request, they'd done a deep dive on an unsolved murder from the 1970s. Hannah had balked at first, not wanting to focus on a crime that left loved ones for whom the victim was a living memory. But Erika had been excited to test the waters with a more current story. Hannah knew the victim had no siblings or children, and her parents had passed, so she caved.

The episode had gone viral, spreading beyond their corner of the true crime community and landing them in the national spotlight, thanks to Hannah's research into one of the lesser-studied theories. There had even been television interviews after talk of reopening the case surfaced.

Their subscriber numbers had skyrocketed. Sponsors had lined up to throw money at them. They had the opportunity to grow their joint business venture into a joint empire.

Then came the first of many emails and social media comments from the victim's best friend. She'd called them vultures and accused them of profiting from her friend's tragic murder, and others had piled on. It reached the point of having to hire a social media manager because Hannah couldn't stomach it and Erika had a hard time not engaging. Then the victim's uncle had broken down during an interview with a prime-time news program because the renewed interest in his niece's case had reopened old wounds, and people wouldn't leave him alone.

Erika wanted to keep pushing into general crime—telling the stories was important, even if it was painful. Negativity and pushback were an unavoidable result of visibility, but they could continue to outsource the social media management, so Hannah wouldn't have to see it.

It felt wrong to Hannah, even though she knew it would be good for their business, because Erika wasn't wrong about the potential to grow the audience for *Improbable Causes*. She didn't know what to do because there was a good chance that choosing not to move in that direction meant ending her business relationship with Erika. And that would almost certainly affect their personal relationship.

So she was here at the Birch Brook Campground for three months to figure out her future steps. And her choice of this place hadn't been random. A crime over one hundred and fifty years in the past had brought her here—the crime that had set her on a path to a satisfying and potentially lucrative career—and it was here that she was going to figure out the rest of her life before going home to California.

Chapter Four

Rob met his brothers in the house for a late lunch. The meal was thrown together sandwiches and some chips of questionable freshness, but they'd take the quick break when they could. They had several more campers arriving over the course of the afternoon, and they wanted to get everybody in place and settled before dark.

Plus Joey and Danny would be heading home in the morning, so Brian and Rob wanted to get as much work out of them as possible before they left.

"Why would a woman pull a camper all the way across the country alone?" Rob mused aloud because the question had been on his mind since he left Hannah's site. "And then spend three months at a campground, also alone?"

"Maybe she's on the run from the law," Joey said, and Rob snorted.

Danny chuckled, but then he paused for a moment before frowning. "Wait. Should we be doing background checks on people? Are we even allowed to do that?"

"It's a campground. I'm pretty sure asking for people's fingerprints before they can pitch a tent will be bad for business," Rob said. "Also, it's really unlikely she's running from the law."

"Why?" Joey held up his hands. "How do you know?

Have you ever scrolled through the true crime category on the streaming apps? Based on how many documentaries there are, if this campground was full, probably like five of the campers would have committed murder."

"Okay, maybe not fingerprinting people who are just here for the weekend," Danny said, obviously still stuck on background checks. "But for the seasonals? I mean, serial killers can buy campers. They do stuff like fishing and hiking and riding four-wheelers, right?"

"Sure. Four-wheelers would be a great way to scope out places to bury bodies."

Danny nodded. "I'm going to do some research."

"On burying bodies? If you could *not* do that on the shared computer in the office, that would be great."

"No, dumbass. On doing background checks. Maybe we ask the local police."

"There *are* no local police." The town really was that small.

"The state police, then."

"We're not running background checks on campers," Brian said. "And we're off topic. We were talking about twenty-nine."

"Her name is Hannah," Rob snapped.

When all three of his brothers stopped what they were doing and turned to look at him, he realized he probably should have kept his mouth shut. He knew from spending so much time at this campground growing up, and from visiting others, that it wasn't unusual for the owners to refer to site numbers rather than trying to remember names when those names usually changed every weekend.

But Hannah Shelby was a seasonal camper. She'd be here for half the summer, and when it came to long-term guests, he didn't think using their names was unreasonable.

"Do we need to actually write the rule about fraternization with the campers in Sharpie on the wall?" Danny asked, giving Rob that big-brother look he'd gotten so many times it didn't even faze him anymore.

Joey snorted. "I thought it would be Brian who broke it first."

Brian shook his head. "Then you haven't been paying attention. I'm not a big fan of relationships."

"The divorce was a couple of years ago," Joey pointed out. "What are you waiting for?"

Rob kicked his brother's leg under the table, hoping he'd take the hint and back off of Brian. Maybe the divorce had been final for a couple of years, but their brother wasn't over Kelly, or the way she'd told him there was somebody else and divorced him out of the blue. The fact some paperwork had severed their marriage didn't help heal the anger and lack of trust that had been Brian's vibe since then.

Joey kicked him back and Rob almost choked on his coffee. That was going to leave a mark.

"You need to get over her," Joey insisted. "You can't be alone because Kelly—"

"Enough," Brian said in a low voice that made Stella get up and put her head on his knee to make sure he was okay. He put down his mug to rub her head. "Stay out of my business."

"Back to the running-from-the-law thing, I'd like to go on the record now," Rob said to distract them, and it worked. They all looked at him. "Danny, if you do decide to write a book about a serial killer hiding out in a campground, you better use a pseudonym."

"I should ask my accountant if I could write off my investment in this place as research." Danny pulled out his phone, presumably to make a note. "You know, if I did write a book like that."

"I mean it about using a pen name," Rob insisted. "I don't think one of the owners of a campground writing about murders in said campground is good for business."

"Or maybe it's great cross-promo," Brian said. "You know, as long as the part about it being a work of fiction and not based on real people is written in a really big, bold font."

"Maybe it'll be about a guy who buys the campground with his brothers and then murders them one by one because they're annoying," Rob said, resisting the urge to reach down and rub the sore spot where Joey had kicked him. "And then he gets to own the campground all by himself."

Brian nodded. "Make it about Bobby here and it can be a comedy. The guy tries to off his brothers but keeps falling in the pool and tripping over firewood and screws it all up."

"But he still wins in the end because their mom rushes in to help him," Danny added.

Rob snorted. "Or maybe it's based on Danny and he plots out how to kill off his brothers, but never gets around to actually killing them."

"Ouch," Joey said, and they all laughed. Danny's was a little forced, but at least the tension was broken. For now.

Before anybody could speak again, the sound of a truck slowing as it went past the house caught their attention. Sure enough, it turned into the campground. Another seasonal had arrived.

"Rob's turn," Danny said.

Of course he got a turn in the office now because they were eating and didn't want to get up. He downed the last of his coffee and pushed back his chair.

"Tell them you want to search the camper for axes and dead bodies," Joey said.

"Half of them probably have axes," Brian said. "For fire-wood, dumbass."

They were still arguing about the difference between axes and hatchets when Rob walked out.

As afternoon started tipping toward *late* afternoon, Hannah thought about the lack of food in the camper—other than the granola bars, of course—and the fact she still hadn't scoped out grocery store options.

Option one was to walk down to the store and ask whoever was in there for recommendations. But as she'd been in and out of her camper, putting the finishing touches on her home for the summer, she'd seen several campers pull in and everybody seemed busy.

Option two was a second restaurant meal in one day. It wasn't so much the money—she had a comfortable savings if she kept to burgers and not fillets—as it was the camping experience. Her dad always thought restaurant meals were cheating, but her mother loved a night out. Somewhere along the way, Jenn had taken her mother's side and Hannah was a daddy's girl, and even in adulthood, doing it Dad's way had stuck.

If she went to the restaurant, though, she could sit in the parking lot and have a quick video chat with her parents before having supper. And after, she could run to the overpriced gas station convenience store that wasn't too far past the restaurant to get milk for her coffee in the morning. And ice cream, too, if they had it. A good book and some chocolate ice cream would be a good way to end her first day at Birch Brook Campground.

But when she walked around her truck to put her cooler in the space where the passenger-side back seat was folded up, she found two boys on the ground next to it. They were twins from the look of it, and the one in a red T-shirt was stretched out on his stomach in the dirt.

"Hi," she said.

"Our ball went under your truck," the one in the blue T-shirt said. "Sorry."

"Boys!" A woman appeared at the end of the site slightly up the hill, and Hannah realized they were her neighbors. "Are they bothering you? I'm so sorry."

"Not at all. My truck ate their ball, I guess."

The woman sighed and crossed the distance between them. "I'm Melissa Scott."

"Hannah Shelby," she said, shaking the hand the woman offered.

"That's my husband, Scottie, over there," she said, and a man waved from the site. "His name's actually Jim, but everybody calls him Scottie because…well, Scott, obviously. And these guys are Jackson, in the red, and Jayden, in the blue. They're ten and they can be rambunctious, but if you snap your fingers at them, they'll take it down a notch."

"You can call us Red and Blue, if you want," Jackson said. "Everybody does. Our nicknames match our shirts."

Melissa gave her a chagrined look. "It's a long story that involves us bringing them home from the hospital, cutting their ID bracelets off, and then within three days, me having a total emotional breakdown because I'd lost track of which was which."

"I can imagine," Hannah said. "They're very identical."

"I have a freckle on my—"

"Jayden!" Melissa shook her head. "My mom remembered Jayden has a tiny birthmark freckle, so we got them sorted, but we knew they'd reach an age where having to drop their drawers to know which kid was which would get awkward, so Jackson always wore red and Jayden got blue. It stuck and they like it, so…"

"And you have a purple shirt," Hannah pointed out. "Red and blue."

"Mom always wears purple," Red told her.

"Oh." The woman looked down at her shirt. "That's funny, but yeah. I wear a lot of purple."

"Got it," Blue declared, crawling out from under the truck with an orange Nerf ball. Being ten, he didn't bother to dust himself off.

"Okay, off we go. I just wanted to introduce us and let you know to boot them back to me if they get out of hand."

"It's nice to meet you," Hannah said, and she thought about how it wasn't really a lie as she put the cooler in the truck. They seemed like a nice family, and she knew from years of camping with her parents that wasn't always the case. You didn't get to pick your neighbors in campgrounds.

She waved to Brian on her way out, but she didn't see Rob anywhere. Not that she was looking for him—okay, maybe she was.

There were only two vehicles in the parking lot of Corinne's Kitchen, so after a quick video chat with her parents, Hannah took a seat at one of the small tables without feeling guilty. She was tired and sitting on a stool didn't appeal to her. If they started filling up, she could always move to the counter.

When Kenzie brought her a menu, she was surprised because it seemed like an awfully long shift. "You were working this morning."

"And I'll be here working tomorrow morning." Kenzie sighed. "I have a high schooler who works part-time, but it's a busy time of year for seniors. What can I get you?"

"I'll have a water, please. And a small garden salad with

ranch." Hannah hesitated, glancing at the menu. "With a side of cheeseburger, medium-well, with mayo and pickles, please."

Kenzie laughed and wrote out the order before taking the menu. "Good call. My dad makes a pretty good burger."

When she walked away, Hannah pulled out her book, but she didn't open it. There were a bunch of ads for local businesses printed on the paper place mat, and she looked it over. She didn't really need excavation work or an alarm system, but there was an ad for a camper repair company she hoped she wouldn't have to call. It was nice to know there was somebody local, though.

"Are you just in town for the weekend?" Kenzie asked when she brought her a tall glass of ice water.

"No. I'm staying at the campground for the season. Birch Brook. They opened for seasonal campers today."

"I'm glad they bought that place and reopened it. It's not only good for my business, but it was sad to see it closed. And the guys—the Kowalski brothers—they come in here a lot, and they're good guys."

There was something about the way she said it that made Hannah wonder if she'd witnessed Rob trying to talk to her that morning. "They do seem nice."

"Do you have anybody else with you?"

"Nope. Just me."

"Wow." Kenzie tilted her head. "You just travel around alone?"

"Yeah."

"That's awesome. I wish I could do that. Just pick a place on a map, park a camper and see what's there to be seen." Kenzie sighed wistfully, and then shrugged. "Maybe someday."

"Sometimes you have to just decide it's someday or it never comes."

"True. I was going to leave once. I had a plan to start with Boston and then figure it out. But my mom passed away and there's this place. It's her legacy, I guess. And without it, my dad would have nothing, really. So here I am…until someday."

"I'm sorry about your mom." Hannah couldn't even imagine not having hers. Even now, while she was clear across the country, she could hear her voice on the other end of the phone whenever she needed to.

"Thanks." The door opened and an older couple walked in. "Guess I'll get back to it."

With other people coming in, Hannah opened her book and read until her burger arrived. It started getting busy around the time Hannah finished eating, so she didn't get another chance to talk with Kenzie, other than when she paid her bill.

After running to the store to grab the necessities— which always included ice cream—Hannah drove back to the campground. It was nice to not be hauling the camper behind her, and it definitely made pulling into the campground's driveway easier. As she slowly made her way toward her site, she spotted Rob.

All four of the Kowalski brothers were standing with another man, and all five of them had their arms crossed as they looked at a camper that had ended up wedged between a couple of trees and a large rock.

Rob glanced over as she drove by, and she lifted her fingers off the steering wheel in a wave that felt like an acknowledgment without being too awkwardly enthusiastic.

And good lord, she could see that smile from here. He

lifted his hand in greeting, and then she saw Joey point to something, which took his attention away from her.

But just before she took the turn that would take her into the tree line, Hannah glanced in her rearview mirror, and Rob was definitely watching her.

Chapter Five

Rob wasn't sad to see Danny pull out of the campground, headed south. Joey had left an hour earlier, as soon as the breakfast dishes were washed, and now it was just him and Brian.

Splitting the work between two instead of four didn't seem great on the surface, but the workload changed now that they were semi-open. It was less about the physical work of getting the campground ready after a harsh winter and years of owners who let the upkeep slide, and more about the day-to-day running of the place. And the energy between him and Brian was different when the older two weren't around. Calmer, somewhat, with less fighting for attention. Maybe it was their personalities or maybe it was being the youngest two of four boys, but they'd always gotten along better when it was just the two of them.

"How's the pool doing?" Brian asked as he unlocked the store for the day.

"I'm almost afraid to say it out loud, but I think it might be good. The chemical cocktail will dilute and I should have the feel for that line between no slime but safe for the little humans by Memorial Day." Rob watched Stella walk past the dog bed that had her name on it and hop onto one of the leather chairs they'd put in the store for rainy days.

"It's supposed to be a nice day, so I'm hoping to get some good photos for the website and social media. It looks a lot better now that the cement's painted and the water's clear."

"You did a good job on it, for sure."

Rob paused, surprised by the praise. "Thanks."

"What's on the agenda for today?" Brian flipped open the notebook Danny had provided for them to write notes and tasks in so there was a central place for everything.

They'd started with sticky notes, but that had gotten out of hand pretty quickly. There were sticky notes everywhere, even some in the house, and there was no organizational structure. They'd fall off, and then Stella ate one and nobody called the propane company.

"I'm going to set up the camping shelves, I think." There was a section of shelves in the back of the store that would stock a variety of things people might have forgotten or need to replace—especially tenters. Things like generic tent pegs, tarps, parts for Coleman lanterns and stoves. They'd even decided to stock a couple of sleeping bags, though the markup on those would probably encourage folks to make the drive into town.

They also had a section with commonly needed things for RVs—light bulbs and hose fittings and the like—and some stuff for ATVs. That was harder because every brand was different, but they stocked several common weights of oil, gloves and some miscellaneous parts. And plenty of duct tape and zip ties.

They'd already done the shelves of snacks and canned goods, along with staples and condiments. There had been a lot of debate about being a campground store versus being something of a general store that served the community. The latter meant a lot more in the way of juggling groceries and expiration dates, and they'd decided to start small and see how it went. And the priority up to now had been the food and the RV stuff, but even though they weren't open to tenters yet, there were a lot passing through the area.

"I'm going to set up this laminator thing and get some signs made," Brian said. They'd decided rather than paying a professional to make signs, they'd print and laminate their own for things like showering trail grime off before getting in the pool because it wasn't a bathtub, and not flushing anything down the toilets that wasn't supposed to be. They'd assumed those things were obvious, but the previous owners had informed them that was definitely not the case.

An hour later, Rob was on his hands and knees, half in the shelving unit as he tried to reach the dust in the back corners of the bottom shelf. It had been there so long, he wasn't sure it even qualified as dust anymore. It was more like a grimy cement film that defied anything but extreme scouring.

The bell over the door rang, but he ignored it. Brian was still behind the counter, having a long, obscenity-laden argument with the laminator after winning an intense fight with the printer, and he'd probably welcome the opportunity to deal with a human. Technology was kicking his ass.

"Good morning," he heard Brian say. "What can I do for you?"

"I was hoping you could point me in the direction of a decent grocery store."

Hannah. Rob's head jerked toward the sound of her voice. Unfortunately, he didn't remember the shelves until his skull hit the one above him with a solid thunk.

Biting back a curse, he eased away from the shelves. Once he was clear of them, he pushed himself to his feet, rubbing the back of his head with one hand.

"You okay over there, Bobby?"

Rob clenched his jaw. He had no doubt Brian had used his childhood nickname deliberately.

"Bobby?"

"Oh, my brother Rob. Old habit, I guess." Even though Brian wasn't in his sight line, Rob could imagine the smirk on his brother's face. "I don't know if you've met him yet. He was in the pool when you checked in."

Yeah, he was definitely doing it on purpose.

"I've met Rob," he heard Hannah say, and he held his breath as he waited to see if she'd tell Brian about his photography faux pas yesterday. "We ran into each other while he was taking pictures for the website, but I didn't think to ask him about grocery stores."

With a sigh of relief, Rob stepped out of the aisle so she could see him. "Hi, Hannah."

She didn't smile, but her expression softened slightly. "Hello again."

"There's a market not too far down the road," Brian said. "You would have passed it on your way in."

"I did, but I'm looking more for an actual grocery store. Like the one where the locals shop, not places to grab a few things. I'm out of pretty much everything and I want to stock up so I'm not running to the market a few times a week."

"Sounds like a Grocery Shopping Trip of Doom," Rob said with a chuckle.

Hannah, on the other hand, didn't look amused at all. She frowned. "I'm really hoping there's no doom in my shopping."

"Oh, sorry. Not *actual* doom." He wasn't sure how to explain it, and he looked to Brian for help. "It's an expression my family's always used. It means..."

His brother shrugged. "Epic, I guess?"

"That's a good word for it." Rob looked back to Hannah.

"When we were kids and something was epic, it was always like the Camping Trip of Doom or the Volleyball Tournament of Doom. We used to play a game in the pool called Water Ball of Doom."

"Everything was doom," Brian muttered. "Why did we do that? Who started it?"

"I don't remember."

Hannah shrugged. "It sounds like your childhoods were pretty epic, so there's that."

"True. We had some good times—especially here." He pulled out his phone. "I can send you the location of the store we like. It's about a half hour from here and the prices are higher than they are down at home, but they have a decent selection and it's the cheapest in the area."

A moment *after* he sent it and her phone chimed, he realized it might appear strange that he had her contact info saved in his phone. But maybe she'd just assume he had all of the campers' information in there in case there was a problem.

He should probably do that.

"Thanks," she said, after checking the text. "Oh, and one more thing while I'm here. Is it okay if I walk out back in the woods? I don't have an ATV, obviously, so I'm not very interested in the trail system, but I like to walk."

Rob looked to Brian, who only shrugged. They hadn't talked about it since most of their campers were there for the ATV trail systems. "I guess that's okay. The cell phone reception is pretty sketchy, from what I remember when we walked the land, so you have to be careful."

Her smile twisted him up inside, but he did his best not to show it. "I'll be careful. I promise."

He didn't even realize he'd watched her leave and then stared at the door until the pen Brian threw hit him in the back of the head.

* * *

Hannah almost made it back to her site without any more interaction, but then she ran into a couple walking a small dog that started yapping hysterically as soon as it spotted her.

"Sorry," the woman said, picking up the dog, which immediately bared its teeth and gave Hannah a look that promised as soon as it could figure out how he'd manage it, he was going to tear her apart. "He's not very friendly."

"No problem."

"I'm Tony," the man said, holding out his hand, which Hannah shook. "My wife is Barb, and the little guy's Oscar."

As in *The Grouch*? Hannah didn't ask the question out loud, and she was thankful Barb didn't extend her hand because she was pretty sure if she reached out, she was going to lose a finger or two to the dog in her arms. "It's nice to meet you."

"We're on site eleven."

"Twenty-nine." Hannah pictured the campground map in her head, and site eleven seemed far enough away so she wouldn't hear Oscar threatening everybody who walked by once the campground fully opened.

"Where are you from?" Barb asked. "We drive up from Rhode Island."

"I'm from Northern California," she said, and the couple looked surprised. "A little north of San Francisco."

"I guess you won't be doing the weekend thing, then," Tony said, and they all laughed.

"I'll be here until the end of July, and then I'll head home and get back to work." *Probably*. She wasn't sure exactly what that work would entail, but she'd have to do something. The podcast had given them nice savings accounts—hers a little nicer than Erika's thanks to her lack of interest in shoes—but she'd burn through a big chunk of it this summer.

"What do you do?" Barb asked, and Hannah winced because she'd opened that door herself.

"I'm in education," she hedged, and then quickly pivoted the conversation back to them. "What do you do?"

"I'm a plumber," Tony said. "Self-employed, and Barb handles the office."

His wife rolled her eyes. "He likes to call me his intern because it sounds better than 'free office help.'"

They parted ways, and as she walked back to her camper, Hannah scolded herself for not being totally honest about her job. She was going to be here for three months and people who stayed at campgrounds tended to be chatty. There would be a lot of conversations in her future, and she didn't necessarily want to spend half the summer trying to dance around what *in education* meant.

She just hated telling people she was a true crime podcaster—especially a podcaster who earned enough to call it her day job. Everybody either had a great idea for a podcast and wanted to pick her brain, or they had a true crime story they wanted to share in length because it would be great for her show. Sometimes both. When she met somebody in passing, it was easier to claim she did something that wasn't a lie, but wasn't the entire truth.

Back in her camper, Hannah pulled up the shopping app she used and looked over the list she'd been compiling. She had to scroll several times to see it all. *Grocery Shopping Trip of Doom indeed*, she thought with a smile.

After making sure she had everything she needed, she locked the door behind her and once again, walked around the truck to put the cooler in the back seat.

And once again, there were kids there.

"Where are you going?" Red asked.

"Grocery shopping."

Blue groaned. "Boring."

"I know, but it's more fun than running out of food."

They both nodded and then ran off in the direction of the playground. Hannah watched them for a few seconds, and then she glanced up at the site they'd come from. Melissa was outside and she waved. She looked like she was going to move toward Hannah, so she waved back and then turned away. Without looking hurried, she got the cooler in the back seat and herself in the driver's seat without any more conversation being required of her. If she didn't get this grocery shopping done today, it was granola bars for dinner. And breakfast.

She very deliberately didn't look in the office windows as she passed by on her way to the exit and turned north onto the main road. If it seemed as if she was looking for Rob, not only would his brother probably make fun of him some more, but it might encourage him, and she didn't want to do that.

Well, she *did* want to, but it wasn't a good idea.

The scenery was gorgeous. Everything was green and lush from the spring rains, and the road followed the Connecticut River. She spotted a few places she'd return to once she was settled and ready to spend her summer exploring.

The grocery store was busy, and she resigned herself to being there awhile. Not only because of the number of shoppers, but because her list was ordered by aisle, but by the aisles in her store at home. And she didn't know the layout of this store, which meant she'd probably be backtracking a lot. Multiple laps of the store was good exercise, she told herself. And the piped-in music wasn't bad.

She was about halfway through the store when a man

standing with the cart while the woman with him looked at the jarred sauces glanced at her and then did a double take. "Wait. I know you."

Hannah had been recognized a few times over the last several years, but it was usually her voice that gave her away. She would expect fewer people to look at the makeup-free woman with her hair in a ponytail in a northern New Hampshire grocery store and connect her with the glammed-up promotional photos they used on social media.

"You're on site twenty-nine, right? The Airstream?" he continued. She nodded, realizing they must be seasonal campers, too. "I thought so. I'm Dave and this is my wife, Sheila. We're on site four. Have been for almost thirty years."

"What brings you here?" Sheila asked, and then she laughed and waved her hand. "Not the grocery store, of course. But here to the campground."

"I was in New England for a few years at UNH, but I've always wanted to come back and see this part of the area. And as for the campground, they were the only ones who didn't have a waiting list." That wasn't quite true, but she didn't want to get into it.

Dave's laugh was loud and slightly abrasive. "That'll do it. We were sad it closed down and clearing our stuff out was no fun. But then those kids bought it and gave us the opportunity to come back. We talked it over and I'm not sure they'll make a go of it, but there aren't many places you can access the ATV trails right from the campground, so we're back."

Kids. The word amused Hannah. "After so long, it must feel like home."

Instead of looking happy to be back, Dave scowled. "Well, that's the problem with campgrounds. It feels like home, but we're just renters, really, and at the whim of who-

ever owns it. Those kids are already making changes and
we liked it just the way it was."

"They took down the tree that was Bert and Connie's
only shade, over there on site seventeen," Sheila said, shaking her head and folding her arms over her chest. "Didn't
even ask them. They got here yesterday and their shade
was just gone."

Hannah didn't know who Bert and Connie were, but
since she knew showing off the amount of shade in the
campground was something Rob had been trying to capture in pictures, she assumed the tree needed to be taken
down or it was going to *fall* down. But she had refrigerated
stuff in her cart, and also a feeling it wouldn't matter what
she said. Dave and Sheila liked complaining.

"That's sad about the tree, but it was nice to meet you
and I'm sure I'll see you around. I have an appointment and
I'm running behind on my shopping." And she smiled and
started walking before they could really respond, or ask
what she could possibly have an appointment for on a Saturday when she'd just arrived.

Of course, she'd have to circle back to this aisle because
there were several items on her list she'd find here, but it
could wait. From now on, she was Pac-Man and Dave and
Sheila were the ghosts to be avoided at all costs. And there
were no power-ups in grocery shopping, so she'd have to
be quick and keep her eyes open.

Grocery Shopping Trip of Doom, she thought again, and
she giggled right in the middle of the coffee aisle.

Chapter Six

"If there *is* a serial killer in this campground, I hope he takes out Dave first," Rob said as he walked through the back door of the store, going straight to the cooler and grabbing a soda. "I'll even lend him a shovel."

"Hey, Rob?" Brian called.

He turned to face the front desk and then froze in the act of twisting off the cap when he saw his brother wasn't alone. And, of course, it had to be Hannah. He hadn't seen her in two days, and naturally she was seeing him in a bad moment. *Again.*

They really needed to stop meeting like this.

"Sorry," he said, because she was looking at him funny. "There isn't really a serial killer in the campground."

"That we know of," Brian said, and Rob gave him a look that should have set the paper he was holding on fire. "It's a statistical probability."

"Really," she said. "A statistical probability?"

"Okay, a statistical possibility, at least."

"But even if there was," Rob said, "I definitely wouldn't aid and abet him in taking out *any* of our campers."

She blinked, and after a few seconds, her body relaxed. "If we do have to sacrifice somebody, Dave would get my vote. If he's the killer, though, I wouldn't bet money on him having acted alone."

"Ah, you've met Dave and Sheila?"

"They were the doom in my Grocery Shopping Trip of Doom. I don't remember seeing any bleach or duct tape in their cart, if that helps narrow your suspect list."

He was about to explain why this was something of an inside joke when he remembered that the talk about a murderer in the campground had started with Hannah traveling alone. Somehow he didn't think confessing that the four of them were talking about whether or not she was a criminal would make this situation any less uncomfortable.

"Okay," Brian said, startling Rob because he'd forgotten his brother was there for a moment. "I guess we can add 'make sure there are no campers in the store before complaining about the campers' to our list of lessons learned since buying the place."

"Yeah, but…it's Dave." Rob shrugged. "I think even Sheila would understand."

"Anyway, you want both tanks filled?" Brian asked Hannah.

"Yes, please. I didn't fill them for the road. I just kept enough in one to run what I need, but it's almost out."

"We can do that. And from now on, you don't have to walk all the way down here. You can just text me or Rob and we'll take care of it for you. You can also call, but we always welcome visitors to the store because it gets boring in here."

"Except Dave," she said.

He grimaced, making her lips twitch. "No, even Dave."

"I'll go grab my propane tanks and bring them down."

"We can come get them," Rob said.

Hannah crossed her arms and he recognized the body language of a woman about to get stubborn. "Do you do that for all your campers or just for me because I'm a woman?"

Brian snorted. "To be perfectly honest, I feel like our

father has some kind of dad radar that would ping if we sat on our asses and let a woman wrestle a propane tank and we'd hear about it. But to answer *your* question, it's a service for all of our campers. The utility side-by-side has a holder built into it for just that purpose."

Rob was relieved when she dropped her arms. "Okay, thanks. And to be perfectly honest, as you said, I would have let you do it anyway. I was just curious whether you thought I couldn't do it myself."

"Mom's radar is even stronger than Dad's," Rob said. "There's zero chance we tell any woman there's something she can't do."

"I think I'd like your mom."

"You'll get to meet her next weekend—the weekend before we fully open. Along with almost everybody in our family," Brian said, and Rob groaned. He couldn't remember who had come up with the idea of the cookout— probably his mother—but he wasn't looking forward to it.

"I'm not sure what my plans are," Hannah said. "But maybe."

After the door closed and they were alone again, Rob took a long swig of soda. His mouth always felt dry when he talked to her.

"Maybe it's her," Brian said with a chuckle. "For all we know that camper's full of bodies of hitchhikers and she wants to go out in the woods to find a good place to bury them."

Rob barked out a laugh that made Stella lift her head. "She's not a serial killer."

"That's what everybody who's known a serial killer has said about that serial killer before the bodies were found in the freezer." Brian grabbed a set of keys from a hook under the counter. "I'll go get her propane tanks. If I'm not back in an hour, call the FBI."

"I'll go."

Brian looked at him for a long moment and then shook his head. "I don't think so. Since meeting her, you've fallen in the pool and you've hit your head. With your luck, you'll wreck the UTV or blow up the propane station."

Rob didn't bother to protest. If he fought to fill Hannah's propane tank, he'd just take more crap about how she'd turned him down flat at the restaurant.

He'd come into this endeavor with the intention of earning the respect of his family, and so far it wasn't going well.

Hannah woke feeling more rested than she had in a long time. The camper was comfortable and her nest was cozy. Plus, the campground had been almost silent, other than the faint sound of traffic on the main road and the low rumble of the nightly train.

Because they were all in New England and had mostly shown up just to set up their campers for the summer, the other seasonals had left for the week. She knew when it warmed up and they were open to the general public, that would change, but for now she looked forward to quiet weekdays.

Today felt like a good day for a walk. She'd come here to clear her head, and nothing accomplished that for her like spending time outdoors. Before going to bed, she'd checked the weather forecast and it was going to be on the cool and breezy side—which would help with the bugs—but the sun would be shining.

But first, coffee. After setting the Keurig to brew, she went into the tiny bathroom. Then she looked at her phone, still plugged into the charging cord. Usually she'd scroll through social media while she drank her coffee, but the signal wasn't strong enough for that. And it was probably for the best because scrolling social media would funnel her straight into her email inbox, and she wasn't awake enough for Erika yet.

She also didn't want her partner's thoughts and projections and business plans in her head before she set off on her walk. Instead, she took her coffee and the pocket notebook she usually had within arm's reach and sat at the dinette.

Flipping the pages, she skimmed the bullet points she'd transferred from the very extensive binder she kept about Elizabeth Cook Whaley. The woman had disappeared in 1872 and considering how diligently her family had maintained records and how extensively they'd journaled, the fact nobody knew what had happened to her was remarkable. Also remarkable was the fact she had lived here, on the campground's land, and it was the last place she'd been seen.

Several hours later, Hannah had to admit defeat. She was soaked to the knees, had tangled with some pucker brush, and she hadn't found a single stone she thought might have been the remains of the Whaley house's foundation.

Not that she expected to find much, of course. But finding old foundations in the woods wasn't uncommon in New England, and she'd known from historical documents where Elizabeth's husband had built their house. So when she'd set out for what was going to be a leisurely walk and had become quite the trek, she'd been hoping to find the homesite of the young woman who'd captured Hannah's interest when she was in college and sent her into the rabbit hole of historical true crime.

She was picking some kind of burrs out of her ponytail when her phone rang. It was in silent mode and she'd interacted with enough insects already so she jumped when it buzzed in her back pocket.

Then, laughing at herself and thankful nobody else was around to hear the high-pitched squeaking noise she'd made, Hannah pulled out the phone. For whatever reason, she had almost full bars in this spot, and Erika was calling her. This time, she decided to answer it.

"Hey, Erika."

"Hannah! You actually answered!"

"I'm out in the woods, so you can keep me company while I walk. Unless I lose cell signal because it's kind of spotty here."

"You're in the woods alone?"

Even over the phone, Hannah could hear her friend's concern. "It's not the wilderness. It's just some woods in the back of the campground."

"Have you had a chance to read my emails yet? I mean, I'm not trying to be pushy but—"

"And yet you're being pushy." There was affection in her tone, and she knew Erika wouldn't be offended. She was a full-steam-ahead kind of person, and as soon as an idea popped into her head, she wanted to act on it. Hannah served as a good counterpoint to her, but it meant being firm about her boundaries sometimes. "I'm here to think things over, and I can't think and talk to you at the same time."

"But you'll think better if you have all the data," Erika pointed out. "You can't make an informed decision without the information."

"Good point." She let her friend have the win, even though it wasn't actually a good point. No amount of data or information was going to help Hannah with this decision because it was about her own sense of right and wrong, and it had nothing to do with money or numbers. "I'll read the emails when I get back to the camper and shower off the mud and bug spray."

"Mud?" Hannah knew her friend wrinkled her nose after she said it. Erika was an inside cat, and preferred city streets to country roads.

"I'll send you a pic, but it's not for the socials."

"Unless it's cute?"

"Trust me, it won't be cute, but even if you think it is, it's just for you."

"Fine. Not for socials even though it's hard to be interesting across all the platforms when we're in between seasons."

The last few words Erika said were broken up, so Hannah took a couple of steps backward and then stopped moving. "I'm going to lose you if I keep walking and I have to pee, so I'm not going to stand here long."

Erika laughed. "You're the outdoorsy type. Can't you just pee on a log or something?"

"I'm not hanging my naked butt over a log. You wouldn't believe the mosquitoes here, and I'm doused in enough bug spray to strip the paint off a car, but none of it is inside the underwear zone."

"Okay, fine. I'll let you go so you don't get a bunch of bug bites on your butt because scratching them would be *so* awkward. Maybe we can talk next week, when you're not walking around in the woods covered in chemicals and mud."

"I'll read your emails today," Hannah promised, and after they disconnected, she continued her walk back.

The closer she got to the top of the campground, the faster she walked. She was itchy all over and she wasn't sure if it was bug bites or the bug spray. Luckily, her mother had taught them all the various plants and leaves to avoid contact with when they were kids—even the ones that weren't indigenous to where they were camping—so she wasn't worried about poison ivy and the like.

But maybe she should have gotten a stronger bug spray because she was pretty sure she did, indeed, have a bug bite on her butt.

Chapter Seven

Rob was sitting in a chair in the store, reading a book, when Brian walked in with Stella on his heels. After moving his bookmark to his current page, he watched his brother grab a water from the fridge and plop in the other chair. Stella got a drink from her bowl in the corner before stretching out on the floor and closing her eyes.

"You didn't write down that water," Rob pointed out. They were supposed to be keeping track because grabbing water bottles from the soda case was grabbing money out of the business. They all had tumblers to refill in the house, but this still felt like a losing battle.

"I will when I go over there." Brian downed a third of it, and then sighed as if it had been days since he'd hydrated. "Twenty-nine's back from her walk."

"Hannah," Rob muttered under his breath.

"I'm kind of curious about what she was up to."

"She took a walk." They'd known she planned to, but when he glanced over and saw Brian's scowl as he stared out the window at nothing, his interest was piqued—even more than usual when Hannah was involved. "What are you stuck on?"

"I don't know. I mean, I get wanting to go for a walk in the woods, especially since she doesn't have an ATV. And you've been out there. There aren't really walking trails, but it's not tough terrain."

"No, it's not. As long as you keep track of where you're at, they're easy woods to explore."

Brian nodded. "But I was changing the outside light at the bathhouse up the hill and saw her come back in. Mud up to her knees. Leaves and a twig or two in her ponytail. I think she even had a scratch on her face, which was a little red like she'd been exerting herself."

That didn't make sense to Rob. "She went *way* out back, then. The only spot still that muddy right now is a strip of low wetlands, and there are plenty of woods to roam around in on this side of it."

"Exactly. Why would a woman on a casual stroll in the woods fight through that just to get to more woods on the other side?"

"Maybe there was a bird or something she wanted a closer look at?"

"Not that badly."

"Okay, but if it was deliberate, what could the reason be?"

"That's what I'm trying to figure out." Brian gave him a questioning look, and Rob shrugged. "Do people still do that geocaching thing?"

"You think she pulled a camper all the way across the country and paid for three months in our campground to find a little fake treasure somebody buried?"

Brian snorted. "I was thinking maybe once she was here, she looked up any that might be in the area."

"Maybe? I don't know much about it, so I can't say for sure if that makes sense."

"Stella and I could probably retrace her steps."

The dog, who was sprawled on the floor, opened her eyes

but didn't move, and Rob laughed. "I think you're mistaking your dog for one with actual skills."

"Do *not* insult my dog."

"I love your dog, and you know it. You're sensitive about it because Stella loves me more than she loves you."

"Stella doesn't love you. She just has a thing for guys who wipe bacon grease on their pants." Brian chuckled. "And you're just trying to distract me from what *Hannah* was up to in the woods."

The way he stressed her name made it clear his brother had caught how referring to her by her site number had irritated Rob. "You could have just asked her. 'Hey, what happened to you? Did you fall in?' Or something casual and totally a typical thing to ask *in the moment*."

"I was on a ladder. And by the time I registered just how rough she looked, she'd passed by, so it wouldn't have been as casual as you think." He smirked. "But I guess it'll be another good reason for *you* to talk to her."

"Hell no. I'm not going to go and demand to know what she was doing in our woods after we told her she could walk around in them if she wanted."

"But you could bring it up, casually. Feel her out."

Rob shook his head. "Oh, *now* you want me to talk to her."

"I don't care if you *talk* to her. You just can't hook up with her."

"That's a dumb rule."

"But it's one we all agreed to." Brian shrugged. "It makes sense, and you know it. If we start messing around with campers, there's going to be drama, and I feel like there's enough of that without adding sex into the mix."

Rob knew his brother was speaking the truth. When they'd had the discussion before the closing, he hadn't balked at all. Hands off the campers. But that was before he'd met Hannah.

There was no way he could have anticipated meeting a woman on day one who he definitely wanted to put his hands on.

"I mean it," Brian said, using his slightly-older-brother voice.

"I know." Rob nodded slowly and closed his book. "You know I won't let you down."

Hannah's days fell into the familiar, low-key rhythm that she'd come to appreciate since arriving in New Hampshire almost a week before.

Wrapped in a thin flannel throw blanket to help ward off bugs and because it was a comfort fabric for her, she drank her first coffee sitting in her camp chair under her awning. Though she usually slept past sunrise, it was quiet and still early in the morning. Peaceful.

Of course, the Kowalski brothers were around. Just Brian and Rob during the week, and Stella of course. The dog visited her daily, sometimes just jogging over for a belly rub before moving on. Other times, though, she'd stretch out on the camping rug under the awning and keep Hannah company while she read.

She was alone today, and after reading a few pages, she leaned her head back against the chair and closed her eyes, listening to the birds chirping.

As was often the case since she'd arrived in town, her thoughts wandered from a peaceful contemplation of the beauty of nature to a not-so-peaceful contemplation of her attraction to Rob Kowalski.

Sure, he was good-looking. And funny and kind. Rob was definitely her type. She hadn't seen him to speak to in several days, but she often saw him from a distance and he always waved if he spotted her. He hadn't stopped by her site at all, though, and she hadn't been able to come up with a good reason to visit the store without being obvious.

"Hannah?"

Her eyes flew open and she jerked straight up in her chair, almost dropping her book. Rob was standing at the end of her camper, his hands in his pockets, and sure enough—*zap*—there it was. And her face was probably flushed because she'd been thinking about being attracted to him and now here he was, as if she'd summoned him somehow.

"Hey," she said, pushing herself to her feet. She took a second to open the screen door and toss the book inside because she had a bad tendency of forgetting them outside and then finding them swollen from rain or dew. "What's up?"

"My dad called this morning to let us know that even though we're super busy and two hours north and everybody knows that, my mom's dropped some pretty strong hints she still expects us to be at her Mother's Day brunch Sunday. We'll put a sign in the store, but since you'll probably end up alone in the campground, I wanted to make sure you knew."

"Yeah, my sister sent me a text to remind me to call our mother Sunday because she knows it's easy to lose track of the days when you're camping."

"I wish my mom would accept a phone call." He shifted, leaning against her camper. She only had one chair, or she would have invited him to sit down. "Are your parents in California?"

"Yes, they are. My parents still live in the small town where I was born. My whole family does, including my uncles and *their* families. My sister's the elementary school's librarian and she's married to a construction foreman. They have two kids and they bought a duplex so our parents could live next door. There's a white fence around the property and they have a cocker spaniel."

"That all sounds very...stable. What do they think of you roaming the country alone with a camper?"

"I didn't roam. I stuck faithfully to the route my dad mapped out for me, both on my phone and on an actual paper map. They don't love the idea, though, and I heard more safety lectures than one person could ever remember." She grinned. "But you know how us youngest kids can be."

His laughter echoed through the trees. "Yeah, I sure do."

"Thanks for letting me know you'll be closed."

He must have taken that as a sign to leave because he stood up straight. "No problem. I don't mind the walk."

When he hesitated, started to turn and then hesitated again, Hannah frowned. "Is there a problem?"

"A problem? No." He smiled, but it wasn't his usual high-wattage grin. And somehow, even as the corners of his lips turned up, his brow furrowed. "It's just that...no. Nothing."

"What?" she pushed. She *definitely* wanted to know what he was trying to say.

"Since you'll be alone here Sunday, maybe you shouldn't go walking out in the woods until we get back."

Because she'd been hoping that awkwardness was a lead-up to maybe asking her a more personal question—like an invitation out for ice cream or something—she couldn't quite hide the dismay, because he immediately looked embarrassed.

"We won't be long," he said. "I mean, we'll actually be gone all day because it's four hours of driving to eat pastries with my mother, but only the one day."

He'd misunderstood her disappointment, and she let him. "I understand. I won't go out back while you're gone."

"Thanks." He exhaled slowly. "It sounds like you get pretty adventurous on your walks. Brian saw you after your last walk and he said you looked like it was a rough one."

She laughed. "Yeah, I got a little muddy. Also got very well acquainted with the local insect population."

He nodded slowly, and she could tell there was more on his mind. "We were surprised you went that far—like past the wetlands and all that."

"By the time I realized it was probably a bad idea, I was already in it, so I kept going."

"But...why? We can't figure out why you'd work so hard at taking a walk in the woods."

Understanding dawned and her hand failed to cover the bark of disbelieving laughter that burst from her. "You think *I'm* your statistical probability serial killer!"

"No!" He shook his head emphatically. "No, I don't."

"Yes, you do. You think...what? That I was muddy because I was dragging a body through the woods to dispose of it?"

"No." He paused. "Okay, Brian's not so sure, but I don't believe it for a second."

Hannah knew she shouldn't laugh. She should be absolutely horrified, but she couldn't help it. The irony of having built a career around murders and serial killers, only to end up on vacation in a place where they were speculating about *her* was too much.

"It's not me," she said, her stomach already aching from laughing. This was the most ridiculous conversation she'd ever had.

He held his hands up, palms facing her. "I believe you."

"It's probably Dave," she said, mostly joking. Sure, she

could just tell him what she'd been looking for out there, but what fun would that be?

"It could be Sheila. I'd want to murder people if I lived with him for decades."

She shook her head. "Since you're all so obsessed with statistics, you should know your resident killer is more likely to be a man."

"Really?"

"Sure. Female serial killers are a very small subset. Then you narrow that subset to New England, then New Hampshire and then this campground... I mean, it's unlikely you even have a serial killer at all, but a female one is highly improbable. Plus, if it was Sheila, she probably would have killed Dave years ago."

"Good point." He nodded. "Okay, I have to get back because we've got deliveries coming in. Sorry we talked about you maybe being a killer and all."

"I'm tempted to leave a shovel leaning against my truck and some rope on the ground just to freak Brian out."

He laughed. "Please do."

Hannah watched him walk away, which was why when he spun suddenly, he caught her looking. His eyes sparkled as her cheeks heated, and she lifted an eyebrow. "Something else?"

"Yeah. I still want to know what you think of the plot twist at the end of that book."

Then he walked away and kept going, leaving Hannah with a silly smile on her face and an urge to grab her book and read straight through to the end.

Chapter Eight

On Monday morning, Rob declared the pool saved from the neglect *and* their attempts to rescue it. They weren't going to open it to campers until Memorial Day weekend, but at least it was just a daily to-do now and not a nightmare.

"What are we going to do about Joe?" Brian asked out of the blue. He was sitting on the stool behind the counter, his chin propped on his hand.

"What do you mean?"

"You know what I mean."

Rob did know what he meant. They'd both done some grumbling about Joey not being around to put some sweat equity into the business, but it was probably on Brian's mind because they'd seen him yesterday at their parents' house for brunch.

"He has a wife and a kid, though, so he has to consider them," Rob pointed out.

"I know, but he's also left us holding the bag."

"I've been sitting here reading and you're over there doodling on a sticky notepad. It sucks that Joey's not here to count the ceiling tiles." Brian called him a string of names that made Rob laugh. "I get where you're coming from, but I don't think there's much sense in riding his ass about it until Nora's school lets out for summer break."

"They're not taking a cabin unless they pay full price for it," Brian muttered. "And it's not like he's going to bring them with him all the time, because he's supposed to work, not be on vacation."

"No, but schedules probably get more flexible when school's not an issue." He wasn't sure if that was true or not, but Brian was in a mood and Rob didn't really want a minor annoyance with their brother to blow up into a whole thing.

The entire family would get involved, choosing sides. And since a good chunk of the family would be there on Saturday for their first cookout, it wasn't a good time to throw that grenade.

He and Stella both looked up when the door opened and Hannah walked in. Rob's pulse kicked up a notch, though he did his best not to show it. But Stella had no reservations about showing Hannah how glad she was to see her. Once she'd gotten her fill of scratching and rubbing, Stella went back to her bed.

Rob expected Hannah to ask about something campground related, but he was pleasantly surprised when she sank into the other chair and smiled at him.

"I'm bored," she said. "How was your trip home?"

"Good. It was nice to see everybody, though I had some trouble sleeping because I was so thrilled to be back in the land of drive-through coffee shops, I might have done too many laps. How was your call home?"

"Good. I guess it worked out that I was the only one here because I was able to sit in an empty site down here, where the signal's stronger, and video chat with my mom. But I was careful not to pick a site too close to the store so you couldn't spy on me." When both men looked surprised— and maybe a little affronted—she laughed. "Oh, Dave and

Sheila told me all about how you *kids* put in one of those fancy doorbells with the camera, and how it tapes audio, too, so you can listen to our conversations even though they say it's illegal."

Brian and Rob both laughed, and Brian shook his head. "Does it do audio?"

Rob shrugged. "I don't remember. We should probably check, though, especially if it *is* illegal."

"Why does he think we want to record his conversations? I don't even want to hear them live, the first time."

Rob grinned at Hannah. "We put in the doorbell and hooked it in so it rings in the house and we can say 'Hey, be right there' and not have to stay in the store all the time."

"I assumed it was something like that," Hannah said. "They weren't interested in a logical explanation that didn't cast you *kids* as the villains, so I gave up and pretended I had a headache."

"I'm surprised you had to pretend after talking to them," Brian said.

"I should have told them you installed surveillance equipment to catch me scoping out places to bury my victims. That would have gotten them going."

Rob groaned. "You're not going to let me off the hook for that, are you?"

Brian held up his hands. "Dude, did you tell her you thought she was a serial killer?"

"We," Rob shot back, pointing an accusatory finger at his brother. "*We* talked about her being a serial killer."

"No, we talked about her being on the run from the law," Brian said, and then he winced. "No offense, Hannah. We were just speculating on the reasons a woman might drive across the country to stay at a campground alone and it went sideways. I don't remember who brought up serial killing."

"And you think if a woman travels alone, she must be on the run?" Both men froze, the silence broken only by a questioning whine from Stella. "Women travel alone. We wear pants now. We even get to vote."

Rob chuckled. "In our defense, we weren't serious."

"I was looking for an old foundation," Hannah said. "On my walk, I mean."

Rob leaned back in his chair, turning her words over in his mind. He didn't remember coming across a foundation—either literally on the property *or* in the paperwork. "You think there's a foundation out in the woods?"

"There should be, yes. It's on the far edge of your property, but within your boundaries, I believe."

Before Rob could respond, Brian jumped in. "How would you know what's on our property?"

"Research."

"Why are you even researching our land in the first place?" Brian demanded, with just enough of an edge in his voice so Rob shot him a look that told him he needed to take it down a notch. "I'm sorry. I'm just really confused."

"I'm not researching your land. Not specifically, anyway. I'm low-key looking into a missing person. Possibly a murder."

"A murder?" Rob and Brian repeated at the same time, and Stella sat up, cocking her head.

"You're investigating a possible murder in our campground? What does low-key even mean?" Brian continued. "Are you a detective? Why would you get a seasonal site? Don't you need a warrant? Wouldn't the real estate agent have to disclose that? Or do you think it happened since we bought it, because—"

"It was in 1872," Hannah interrupted, holding up her hands.

"Oh." Rob sagged back against his chair and reached out to scratch Stella's ears so she'd relax, too.

Brian shook his head. "I'm still not sure how a murder and this campground are related, but if it happened over a hundred and fifty years ago, I guess it's not something we need to add to the never-ending list of things we lose sleep over."

"To be fair, it might not be a murder," Hannah said. "She was a missing person. The research that's been done on the case over the last century and a half included the location and description of the home, and as of about sixty years ago, the remnants of the stone foundation were still there."

"And you want to find it…why?" Brian asked.

She shrugged. "Why not? I have an interest in historical true crime, and Elizabeth Whaley's story was one of the first to capture my attention. I guess spending three months in New Hampshire is like going back to my roots."

"This state can't be *that* interesting for historical true crime," Rob mused.

"The only famous murderer I can think of off the top of my head is Lizzie Borden," Brian agreed. "But that was in Massachusetts."

Hannah laughed. "The man many consider to be the first known serial killer in the country was born in New Hampshire, you know. Then you have the Isle of Shoals murders in 1873. And a New Hampshire man who might actually be more awful than Jack the Ripper was executed in 1874 for crimes I don't even like to think about."

"So if Elizabeth was killed in 1872, do you think that guy did it?" Brian asked.

"No, I don't. I've never seen anything to substantiate he was this far north, and I think if she'd been one of his victims, they would have found evidence. His MO was pretty brutal."

"I'm still confused," Rob said. "You drove all the way across the country to spend three months here—alone—to find a few old stones? You could have emailed and asked us to send you a photo."

Hannah was amused by the bizarre conversation that had ended with the guys still being confused. What were the chances she'd end up in a campground owned by people who wouldn't stop talking about serial killers? As fun as it was to wind them up and watch them go in circles, though, she also knew they were tired and under some stress, so she shouldn't toy with them too much.

"I'm from California, but I've been in the area before," she said. "I was obsessed with Boston but didn't want to actually live there, so I got my degree in history from UNH. It was a nice central location for trips not only to Boston, but into Maine and the rest of New Hampshire. That's when I first read about Elizabeth Whaley as well as some of the other women who've just disappeared from history."

"Okay, so you chose this campground on purpose," Rob said.

"Yes and no. I had a list of campgrounds that my dad had vetted as good enough for his daughter to be alone in."

"We're flattered," Brian said.

"Oh, you weren't on it," she said, and they all laughed. "All the Dad-approved ones had waiting lists, so I started casting a wider net. And when I pulled Birch Brook Campground up and saw the location—especially the satellite view—it pinged in my memory and yes, from that moment on, I chose this place on purpose."

"I think this calls for ice cream," Brian said. "You want one?"

"I never turn down ice cream," Hannah said, and when Brian tossed her a chocolate-and-vanilla ice cream cup, she caught it easily, and then the small wooden spoon in plastic wrap.

Rob caught his and then scowled at his brother. "Write them down."

"I am right now. Get off my back."

Rob looked at Hannah before opening his ice cream. "We're supposed to write down anything we use or consume from the store."

"It's one of the reasons we got the superspy doorbell," Brian added. "If we can spend more time in the house, we can eat more of the food we bought for us and less of the food we bought to resell to you guys for a profit."

"A *small* profit," Rob said after giving his brother a look, and Hannah chuckled.

She didn't bother pointing out that they had the doorbell now but she'd found them both sitting in the store. It worked for her because she got company *and* free ice cream.

"I've always wanted to come back to New England when I didn't have classes and finals and everything hanging over my head. I have some big decisions to make in the near future and I wanted some time away to think. Coming back to New Hampshire, where a lot of things started for me, felt right, so I borrowed my parents' truck and camper, and here I am."

Rob wanted to know more. She could practically see the questions swirling around behind his eyes, but he only nodded and took a bite of ice cream. Clearly he was smart enough to realize if a woman said she had big decisions to make and needed time away to think, it was personal, and possibly a touchy subject.

"So you didn't find it?" he asked after a few minutes of ice cream eating. "The foundation, I mean."

"No, but it's not exact, you know? An old, tattered rough sketch and some notations in a diary don't match up that great with current maps. Obviously you try to use some common sense and look at it the way they would have as far as terrain and drainage and whatnot, but it's pretty over-grown."

Brian made a low humming sound of concern. "If there's an old foundation, there could also be an old well."

"Absolutely, which slows down the walking pace con-siderably. There's a lot of woods left to walk back there." When Rob and Brian exchanged a look, Hannah caught the meaning behind it. "I'd be happy to sign some kind of waiver or whatever."

"Yeah." Rob scrubbed his hand over his face. "But it's not just the liability. The cell signal's really spotty, and it's probably not great from the bottom of a well in the middle of the woods."

Hannah didn't want to lose access to the woods. Even if she didn't find the actual foundation, knowing she might be walking in Elizabeth's footsteps grounded her somehow— it connected her with the sense of purpose that had driven her since her time at college. It hadn't been social engage-ment and income, but the need to remember the past and the people who had disappeared from it.

"If the foundation is still there, it would make for great photographs," she said, and she saw the spark in Rob's eyes. "This is your land now, and from what I've been able to glean from old records, the Whaley house was the first per-manent structure built on it. It's quite a history."

Brian snorted. "A little over a week and you already know Bobby's magic words."

She noticed the slight clench of Rob's jaw at the use of the old nickname and smiled. "And I can make sure you don't fall in a well."

Rob laughed. "Okay. We've got our hands full with this cookout coming up and then the campground opening to the weekenders, but I could probably find a day when we could go out and look around. And the previous owners told us that strip of marshy stuff does dry up, so a little time wouldn't hurt."

"Sounds like a plan," she said, relieved she'd still be able to walk the woods.

As far as Rob accompanying her, she had mixed feelings. Obviously, it would be safer. The back of their property was overgrown, and she'd already considered the possibility of old wells or caved-in root cellars. But having somebody with her would mean less quiet time to sort through her thoughts and reflect on what she wanted from her future.

Exploring the woods with Rob added an entire new column to the pros and cons list, though, because she wasn't sure if it was a good idea or a bad idea, but *alone time with Rob* was definitely starred, underlined and highlighted in her mind.

And there was something in the smile he gave her that made her wonder if taking pictures of old stones while keeping her from falling in an abandoned well wasn't *his* only motivation. "Definitely a plan."

Chapter Nine

"Today's going to feel three days long," Brian mumbled while poking the yolks of the eggs sizzling in the pan with a fork.

Rob didn't bother pointing out he liked his yolks runny. The last time he'd reminded his brother of that fact, there'd been a lot of grumbling about being a short-order cook and slamming of pans.

"What time is everybody getting here?" he asked instead.

"Last time I opened the group chat, they were still arguing about what time to leave and how many vehicles to bring, and I'm not looking again. We'll know they're here when they pull in, I guess."

"Do we at least have a head count?" Rob asked, splitting the last of the coffee in the carafe between their two mugs.

"Nope. Still not sure if the grandparents are coming. They haven't un-winterized their RV yet, and a four-hour round trip with a cookout in the middle is a lot for them."

Rob didn't roll his eyes because his mom had cured him of that habit during his middle school years, but he wanted to. "I offered them a cabin, but Gram let me know in no uncertain terms she has no interest in walking to the bathhouse every time she has to pee, and she's convinced Danny made us cheap out on the mattresses."

Brian snorted. "She's not wrong."

Leo and Mary Kowalski called themselves campers, but the extravagantly luxurious RV they so-called camped in barely met the definition of the word. It was nicer than the house he'd grown up in.

"What time are Danny and Joey planning to show up?" Rob asked when the overcooked eggs were ready to eat and they were seated at the table.

"Don't know."

Rob bit back a frustrated growl. Brian's ability to just go with the flow was something he had always envied, but at the same time, it was a source of never-ending frustration. They were also both beat after the work they'd done yesterday. Not only had they put up a big canopy tent alone to offer shade, but they'd gone around and borrowed a bunch of picnic tables from the sites that weren't occupied yet and brought them to the grassy area next to the playground. Two grills and three folding tables for food. And each of the tasks had been punctuated by one of them grumbling about how nice it must be for Joey and Danny, who got to reap any profits they might sow without doing the labor. Danny had coughed up a lot of money and was *supposed* to be silent, though, so mostly they'd complained about Joey.

Instead of pushing at Brian now, which probably wouldn't get Rob anywhere but even more frustrated, he ate his breakfast in silence. After cleaning up, Brian went to take Stella on her daily walk around the campground, and Rob went into the store just to check on everything. There were already signs on the front and side doors letting people know they'd be closed today due to the cookout. It shouldn't be a problem because most of the seasonal campers were planning to attend—though he still didn't know what Hannah would

do—and if there was an urgent need, one of them could always leave the cookout for a few minutes.

Once Brian and Stella were back, they started carrying
stuff outside. Not anything that needed to be on ice yet,
but there was a lot they could bring out in advance, like
the king's ransom's worth of paper products they'd bought
for the occasion.

Joey was the first to arrive. He pulled in at the end of
the vacant transient sites they'd marked off for parking, and
Rob wasn't sure the vehicle was even at a full stop before
Nora burst out through the back door.

The seven-year-old had only been his niece for less than
a year, but Rob adored her with his whole heart. The entire Kowalski family did, and they were just as fond of her
mother, Ellie.

"Uncle Rob! Uncle Brian!" She ran toward them, but
then suddenly veered off to the left. "Stella!"

They laughed as they watched her collapse on the grass
and wrap her arms around the dog's neck. Rob didn't take
it personally. Who *wouldn't* want to hug a dog before doing
anything else?

After greeting Joey and Ellie, Rob looked around, but
he didn't see Hannah anywhere. There was still an hour
before the posted start time, though, and if she did come,
it probably wouldn't be early. He could see some of the
other seasonal campers gathering on their sites, watching
and probably deciding when it would be a good time to
head over.

"You guys got a lot done," Joey said, looking around.
"I'd hoped to get here earlier and help out more, but we ran
late and then I got stuck behind the only person in the state
doing the actual posted speed limit."

Rob wanted to make a snarky remark about how they'd

gotten used to doing most of the work without him, but he didn't want to start this cookout off on that note. Especially with Ellie standing next to him. She fit in well with the family, but she was still newish and he didn't want to make her uncomfortable. If he made a comment that set Brian off, things could go from snarky to ugly pretty quickly.

"It's probably time to bring more coolers out, since people are starting to wander over," he said. "You can give me a hand with those."

Nora ran back to the adults, Stella loping after her. "Uncle Rob, look at my shoes."

He did as he was told and looked down at her sparkly pink sneakers. "They're very shiny and pink. I like them."

"Grammy Lisa bought them for me and I love them."

Rob smiled. His mother, after raising four boys, had been waiting not so patiently for grandchildren in hopes she'd have a little girl to shower in girlie stuff. "I can see why. I have to go bring more drinks out now, though."

"I can help!"

"I think they're kind of heavy for a little girl," he said, and he realized his mistake when she scowled and crossed her arms.

"The only thing a boy can do that a girl can't is pee in his own face," she told him sternly.

He had no idea what to say to that, and he looked to his brother for help. Joey shrugged, trying pretty unsuccessfully to keep from grinning. "She's got you there."

Ellie held up her hands. "I didn't teach her that. I mean, I might have if I'd thought of it, but I'm not sure where she got it from."

"Not me, either. Oh shi—" Joey cut off and glanced at Nora. "Oh damn, incoming."

Rob didn't even have to look to know Dave and Sheila

were making their way to the grass. He could tell by his brother's expression who it was. And of course *they'd* be early. They literally did nothing but seek out people they could complain to.

But he fixed a smile on his face and turned to greet them. "Dave! Sheila! Glad you could make it."

"It was a bit of a walk, since we always had group gatherings over there," Sheila said, pointing to a different grassy area that didn't offer enough space to host the cookout.

"This is more central and gives people a little more room to spread out."

Dave crossed his arms. "We always had plenty of room."

Rob forced a chuckle. "We invited our family and they take up a lot of space, but we'll keep it in mind for future campground events."

That seemed to mollify them for the moment, and he was saved from having to come up with something else to talk about when a vehicle turned into the driveway, followed by two more.

"Speaking of our family, more's arriving, so you'll have to excuse us. Feel free to rummage through the coolers for a drink or pop open one of the chip bags."

He walked away before they could tell him they bought the wrong chips or that their coolers were wrong. One thing he knew for sure was that when the time came to decide who was grilling the meat, he'd be in the bathroom. He wasn't going to flip burgers and dogs with Dave critiquing the way he used a spatula.

By the time he reached the parking area, there were Kowalskis climbing out of four vehicles, since his grandparents had ridden with his parents. He hugged them each, giving his grandparents extra squeezes.

Next up were his uncle Kevin, aunt Beth and their fifteen-year-old son, Gage.

"Lily said she'd try to come," Beth said after hugging him, "but then she started talking about cramming for finals and had a bit of a breakdown, so we told her you'd all understand. Her plate's pretty full right now."

His cousin was a freshman at a university in Vermont and he definitely understood. "Of course. And she's welcome anytime she needs to get away, you know. We can always find a space for her."

"She was talking about making a day trip with Gage once they're both out of school," Kevin said.

Rob nodded at his young cousin. "If you want to take the weekend, or even just one night, let me know and I'll hold a cabin for you."

"Cool. I don't know if we can swing it with our jobs and stuff, but I'll let her know."

Then it was time to hug his uncle Joe, who slapped him on the back. "Hell of a job you guys are doing. Terry and Evan are on a cruise, but I'll send her pictures she'll pay an obscene amount to download on the ship."

Rob laughed. His aunt Terry was Uncle Joe's twin sister, and nobody messed with anybody in the family the way they messed with each other. "Well, Uncle Evan's with her, so if they didn't buy the fancy Wi-Fi package, he'll make her wait until they can find free internet during an excursion."

Steph, who was Danny's age, was Terry and Evan's daughter, and she'd ridden with Joe and Keri. She kissed his cheek before moving on to his brothers.

Then it was time to embrace Joe's wife, Keri, and their daughter, Brianna, who was graduating from high school this year. As he hugged her and thanked her for coming, he made a mental note to find out the exact date and add it to the calendar. It was going to be tough navigating the big family events he and his brothers would all want to attend. It was one thing to be closed when you were still on the property or nearby, but all four of them being two hours away didn't seem like a great idea.

Something to worry about later, he thought as he stepped forward to greet Sean and Emma. Sean felt like an uncle to him, but he was actually his dad's cousin. There were a bunch of Kowalski cousins in Maine, and ironically, they owned a lodge and campground, but Sean had settled in New Hampshire when he married Emma. Their kids—sixteen-year-old Johnny and twelve-year-old Cat—gave him a cursory greeting before heading off to hang with Gage and Brianna. Nora tagged along, skipping in her pink sneakers and smiling happily at her new cousins, before veering off toward the snacks.

"You sure did a good job on that pool," his dad said, dropping an arm around his shoulder. "I remember those first pictures you sent of it, and it looked like a science experiment."

"It basically *was* a science experiment. It took a lot of YouTube videos, reading, and trial and error, but I got it ready for the big weekend."

"Joey told us how hard you worked on it, and it paid off."

Rob glanced at the food table where his brother was helping Nora get a watermelon slice, surprised he'd been talking him up. "Thanks, Dad."

"You've *all* done a great job. I had some concerns. It's a lot of work and responsibility, and owning the campground is a lot different than playing here. Plus, you boys don't always get along. But the place looks great, you're booking up, and you're all still speaking to each other. We're proud of the whole bunch of you."

Rob cleared his throat and nodded. "That means a lot."

"And don't listen to Dave."

Rob laughed. "So you've met him?"

"We've crossed paths with Dave and Sheila a few times over the years, even though they eventually tried not to be here when we came for our camping trips."

"Of doom," his mom said, appearing at her husband's side.

As she launched into one of her favorite memories from those years, Rob listened, but he couldn't help looking around. Hannah wasn't here. And maybe that meant she wasn't here *yet*—it was still early—or maybe it meant she wasn't coming at all.

Not a surprise because she hadn't seemed really excited about it, but still disappointing.

"Are you looking for somebody in particular?" his mom asked, and Rob realized he'd zoned out.

"No. Just looking around, making sure nobody needs anything," he lied.

"It's not like you to not laugh at the part where Danny's trunks fell off and he couldn't get out of the water."

Rob chuckled because that *had* been a good day for everybody but Danny, but his mom was right—he hadn't been paying attention. There was zero chance he was going to tell his mother, but he was looking for Hannah and he still didn't see her.

Hannah was tormenting herself and she knew it. She'd made up her mind she wasn't going to attend the cookout because the only other campers she'd met that she'd really like to spend time with were the Scotts and they were right next door. If she went to the cookout, she had no doubt she'd end up cornered by Dave and Sheila and probably not even get to talk to Melissa.

And the last thing her runaway imagination needed was to see Rob with extended family. She was having enough trouble keeping her attraction to that man in check. Seeing him relaxed and happy, laughing and enjoying time with people he loved, wouldn't help.

But none of that explained why she'd made a special trip to the grocery store and then spent hours cutting up fruit and mixing the creamy whip to make the fruit salad her family had devoured at every summer barbecue they'd ever had.

Hannah was going because it was an excuse to spend an afternoon with Rob, and she knew it. And that was before her phone chimed with a text message from him.

There's too much food here. You should come eat some of it.

She smiled at the screen and typed a response before she could overthink it. I'm on my way.

Hannah faltered when she broke from the tree line and saw all the people milling around, though. It was a *lot* of people, and she might have changed her mind and fled back to the peace and quiet of her camper if she hadn't already told Rob she was on her way.

Her gaze sought him out and she finally spotted him talking to Tony and Barb. Luckily, they seemed to have left their exceptionally cranky dog in their camper, but they were on the other side of the gathering, and Rob had his back to her.

She walked straight to the food tables so she could set

the fruit salad down. She wasn't sure if she'd mingle or flee once it was out of her hands, but it could go either way.

"Hi, I'm Mary Kowalski," an older woman said, taking the bowl and spoon from her and shifting dishes to make room for it. "I'm the boys' grandmother. The matriarch of the family, they all like to call me. It's such a stuffy word and makes me sound old, but it also means I don't have to lift a finger to do anything. They can call me whatever they want as long as I don't have to wash any dishes."

Hannah laughed, already feeling more at ease. "I'm Hannah. I'm a seasonal camper."

"Hannah. What a lovely name." Mary smiled and put her hand on her arm. "Let me introduce you to everybody."

Her opportunity to run was lost, and what followed was a dizzying round of introductions that included all of the family present as well as a few campers she hadn't met yet. There was no way she was going to remember all the names—even though Mary had jokingly told her there would be a quiz later—but she had a general impression of dark hair, blue eyes, warm smiles and a family vibe that made her heart ache to be with her own.

Once Mary decided it was time for her to start hounding the guys about the grill, Hannah spoke to Bert and Connie for a few minutes—they were still mourning the loss of their shade tree, though Connie confessed she'd rather lose the shade than have the tree fall and crush her camper, just as Hannah had suspected—before circling around to Scottie and Melissa. Red and Blue had discovered Nora was close enough to their age to play with, and they'd commandeered the cornhole boards.

Then Hannah finally managed to speak to Rob. She wasn't sure she would ever have gotten through everybody, but he spotted her and made a beeline straight to her.

"You came," he said, his grin lighting up his face.

"I did. I've been here for a while, actually, but your grandmother wanted me to meet everybody." She chuckled. "You have a *lot* of family."

"You have no idea. When we came up here when I was growing up, we took up, like, half of the campsites and one of the cabins."

"That's pretty amazing."

He chuckled. "That's one word for it."

"No, I mean it. All of you being so close and having all those shared memories is definitely amazing."

"Yeah." His face softened and her heart skipped a beat. "It is pretty wonderful."

"Uncle Rob!" It was Gage, who was approaching at a fast walk. "One of the cornhole bags landed on a camper and Uncle Brian said you have to deal with it because he's at the grill."

"Okay, *mostly* wonderful," he muttered. "How did a bag end up on top of a camper? The cornhole boards aren't anywhere near them."

He shuffled his feet. "The little kids decided to play Frisbee so we were going to play cornhole, but then it became a game of cornhole dodgeball, and then cornhole keep-away and…you know how it is."

Hannah put her hand over her mouth, trying to hide her amusement. Based on the stories, Rob and his brothers *did* in fact know how it was.

Rob turned to her, giving her an apologetic look. "I have to deal with this because Brian's cooking and apparently Danny and Joey are *guests* today? But don't leave, okay?"

"I won't," she promised, and she meant it, even if it meant artfully dodging Dave and Sheila until he was done.

Chapter Ten

Once he'd retrieved the cornhole bag from the camper roof, which involved getting the ladder, his uncle Kevin footing it, and all the men in the family who weren't running the grill watching and offering unhelpful tips, Rob wanted to grab a drink and go relax in the shade. Preferably with Hannah.

Unfortunately, she was talking to Melissa and he'd have to run a gauntlet of his family to get to her. He wasn't surprised at all when his mom managed to corner him before he got far. It seemed as though she'd deliberately intercepted him in a spot where they were alone, and he braced himself for a maternal interrogation. Or maybe a lecture. He couldn't really judge *why* she'd singled him out, but he knew she'd done it on purpose.

"Hannah seems nice."

His head whipped around to face her, and his eyes narrowed when he saw that fake-innocent look she never actually managed to pull off. "What did you just say?"

"Hannah," she repeated with not even a hint of chagrin. "She seems nice."

"What have you heard and who did you hear it from?" Not that it really mattered which of his brothers was talking, but Brian liked to push his buttons a little more than the other two when it came to their mother being involved. Rob's money was on him. Luckily, Hannah was far enough away—talking to the kids and Stella—that she wouldn't overhear this conversation.

"Oh, you know. A mother hears things." She smiled and rested her hand on his arm. "Listen, honey. I know it's hard to own a business with family and it requires setting boundaries, but if she's the one, don't let a rule about fraternizing with campers stand in your way."

"The *one*? I've known her for two weeks, Mom."

"When you know, you know."

"I know she's pretty and smart. I know we share a similar taste in books and that she loves history. And I know she's going back to California at the end of July. That's what I know."

"She just needs to get to know *you*."

"Mom."

"I could tell you were looking for her earlier. You said you were just making sure nobody needed anything, but as you've learned, moms know things."

Mothers heard things. They knew things. Basically, they didn't mind their own business. "Fine. I like her. But if you make it awkward, she'll go back to her camper, so leave it alone."

"You must really like her to be taking that tone with me."

"I'm sorry." He sighed. "It's just that when it comes to this family being up in her business, she'd probably rather be left alone."

"From what I've heard, she doesn't want *you* to leave her alone."

"We're getting to know each other and that's all I'll say. But please keep in mind everything you're hearing is filtered through my brothers."

"Oh, trust me. I *never* forget that."

When he saw Danny making his way over, Rob was relieved. He could hand Mom off to his brother and then make his way back to Hannah.

But his grandmother called his mom's name, and it turned out Danny was actually looking for him. "Hey, are there any cabins open next weekend?"

"Memorial Day weekend? Nope. We'll be totally full, which is both awesome and terrifying."

"What about the weekend after?"

"Pretty sure the small one's open, but I can't guarantee it'll stay that way. We get more calls every day."

Danny snorted. "Of course it's the small cabin. That's the same one Uncle Joe used to stay in so he could write in between family activities."

"You thinking about coming up? You can just stay in the house. I know it's not great, but you don't have to go outside to get to the bathroom."

"I need to lock myself away and figure out how to push through this writer's block."

"I thought you didn't believe in writer's block."

"Yeah, I didn't—until I got writer's block."

"If you really need to lock yourself away, it makes more sense to come up during the week when it's quiet. I have a feeling weekends won't be quiet."

"And we won't lose the weekend income on the cabin, I guess," Danny said.

"Oh, you weren't going to pay?" Rob asked, and they both laughed. He'd only been half joking, but he'd let it go. Without Danny, they couldn't have gotten the financing to buy the campground, so they'd all be cutting him slack for a long time.

"Later, let's get together and figure out which week I

can come up for several days. I just need space and quiet to get out of my head. Or deeper into my head. I don't even know what I need anymore."

"We'll get you set up." Over Danny's shoulder, Rob could see Hannah looking around, and judging by her expression, she was thinking about leaving. "Right now, though, I've gotta talk to somebody about something."

Danny snorted. "Tell her everybody loves the fruit salad."

Hannah was about to head back to her camper when she saw Rob heading her way. He looked determined about it, too, brushing off several people who tried to talk to him. He even dodged his grandparents, which was flattering, she thought. He *really* wanted to talk to her.

"Hey," he said when he finally reached her. "Sorry about that. It only took a few minutes to rescue the cornhole bag, but my family loves to talk and, as you said, there are a lot of them."

"*Everybody* here loves to talk. If the goal was people getting to know each other, you succeeded, because life stories were shared." When he gave her a questioning look, she smiled. "Except mine, of course. But I did learn a lot about everybody else. Want to hear about Connie's colonoscopy?"

"No. No, I don't." He frowned. "That's fun cookout conversation."

"I think she was trying to explain the mountain of potato salad on her plate." She shrugged. "As if potato salad that good needs justification."

"The meat should be coming off the grill soon," he said, his hand on his stomach.

She mimicked the gesture, but for an entirely different reason. "I've already eaten so much, I can't imagine having a burger now."

Rob laughed. "We've told Mom I don't know how many times over the years that they should hold the salads and chips and all that until the grill's fired because people eat it because it's there, and then the meat gets done and everybody's full of pasta and veggies and dip. Oh, and fruit salad. I'm told it's excellent and I really hope it's not gone."

"If it's gone, I'll make you another batch sometime. And you can leave it in my camper's fridge so you don't have to share it with your brothers."

"And so they can't eat it all at two in the morning while I'm asleep."

"Well, they can try, but if they're rummaging around in my camper in the middle of the night, they might get clocked with a frying pan."

Even his laughter couldn't distract her from her phone buzzing in her pocket. Her family knew she was busy today since she'd made a call home to ensure she was remembering the fruit salad recipe correctly, which meant it was probably Erika trying to reach her. She felt a pang over ignoring the call, because her friend's career plans were in limbo while Hannah decided what she wanted to do going forward. But the pang wasn't strong enough to make her leave Rob's side and take the call.

"Okay, I see movement over by the grill and the chicken goes fast," he said. "What do you want me to grab for you?"

She really wasn't hungry, but—unless she was mistaken— the way he'd phrased the question was a gambit to keep her here. And as long as she was with him, she didn't really want to leave.

"If you just put an extra piece of chicken on your plate, I'll nibble on that. I wasn't kidding about being full."

"I won't be long. Why don't you go claim those two camp chairs over in the shade."

She looked at the chairs, which were tucked away under a tree. "Don't they belong to somebody?"

"They're my uncle's, but they're sitting at a picnic table with my grandparents already."

As she went and sat in one of the chairs, it occurred to her that her and Rob sitting off by themselves was going to attract attention—especially if she was eating off his plate. She'd overheard some comments today that led her to believe none of the Kowalski brothers were allowed to dally with the campers, and this would definitely give the impression they might be dallying.

She didn't want to cause any problems between Rob and his brothers, but he was an adult and he knew what he was doing. If he wanted to spend the time with her, she wasn't going to be able to summon enough willpower to walk away from him.

When he returned, Hannah laughed at the mound of food on his plate. "How many people are eating from that plate?"

"Just the two of us, but I wasn't sure what you'd want with the chicken, so I got a little of everything." He handed her one of the two forks he'd stuck in the pile of potato salad.

"I don't see any fruit salad."

"It was gone," he said with exaggerated sadness.

"Was it *really* gone, or do you just want an entire bowl of your own?"

He grinned. "It was *mostly* gone. And it will definitely be gone by the time there's enough room on this plate for it."

While they ate—or he ate and she picked at the chicken and a little bit of the coleslaw and pasta salad—he told stories from his family's trips to the campground and how they used to have picnic lunches up on one of the scenic overlooks, complete with hot dogs grilled on a hibachi grill strapped to one of the machines. He explained the rules of Water Ball of Doom to her—essentially there were no rules other than nobody was allowed to actually drown. It sounded like a combination of volleyball, keep-away and football, but played in the pool, and it was a good thing Hannah wasn't very hungry because she spent more time laughing than eating.

When the plate was empty, Rob set it on the grass next to his chair, but he didn't make any move to get up. "Your parents' camper is nice, and obviously you've been camping before. Did you ever tent camp?"

"We went tent camping once. It was our very first camping trip and it wasn't in a campground like this. We had two tents—one for my parents and one for me and Jenn—and we were just out in the woods. For some reason, my dad thought taking his wife and two daughters to a spot where they'd have to dig little holes to go to the bathroom in the woods would be super fun."

"Oh, he went super rustic, then." He laughed. "Yeah, we don't camp that way."

"We never did that again. We also went home early because my mom had assumed there would be bathrooms nearby and didn't pack enough toilet paper. Even though we got our first camper the next summer, that was the last time my dad got to plan a family vacation without running it in detail past my mom."

"That was us the first and last time we went to Six Flags and my dad just gave us money and told us to have fun and try to stay in groups of two, at least."

"How old were you?"

"I was probably eleven or twelve, and the others went up in age from there." He chuckled. "That night was the first time I saw my mom pay restaurant prices for wine, and she kept saying she thought she was never going to see all four of us together at the same time again."

"She must have been exhausted."

"Yeah, and I think that wine was the only reason my dad's still with us." He looked over to where his family was mingling with the other seasonal campers. "She wasn't very happy with him."

Hannah followed his gaze and saw some of the women taking plastic wrap off of trays. "Rob, is that actually *more food*?"

"Desserts." When she groaned, he laughed and put his hand on her leg. It was only for a moment, but his touch triggered a heat that spread through her entire body. "We told them not to bother but they always bother when it comes to food."

"I don't know if I can eat another bite," she said after clearing her throat to make sure her voice wouldn't be husky from the lingering effects of his touch. "And I mean it this time."

"Gram made her blond brownies. They're amazing."

She groaned. "Okay, maybe *one* more bite."

Chapter Eleven

Rob wasn't surprised when Hannah returned to her camper after sampling some of the desserts. Well, she sampled *most* of the desserts. The blond brownies, though? She devoured two of those before declaring she wasn't going to eat again for at least two days.

He wasn't sure why it made him so happy that she'd enjoyed one of his grandmother's signature baked goods, but he couldn't deny it pleased him when she'd asked Gram for the recipe. Of course, she'd offered to text it to Hannah, and there was a moment of awkwardness when he realized Gram texting Hannah would give all the women in his family access to her number. He'd panicked and tried to intervene, promising to get the recipe later and pass it on. They overruled him, of course, and the message was sent.

Once Hannah had thanked them both again and headed back to her camper, his grandmother shook her head.

"You're gone for that girl."

"Do *not* give her number to Mom," he said, not bothering to deny her words. "Please, Gram? Don't even tell her you have it. Actually, if you give me your phone, I can delete it so you won't even be tempted."

"Don't you worry about my phone," she said, giving him a look that let him know she might not have her wooden spoon with her, but if he tried to take her phone, she'd grab one of the plastic serving spoons and give his knuckles a good whack.

"Sorry. It's just that Mom's got ideas in her head, but when we bought this place, we made a pact not to have *ideas* where the campers are involved, so it's a bit of a mess and I don't want Mom to…help."

"If there's one thing I know about Kowalski men, it's that you can all use a little help when it comes to figuring out relationships."

"Oh no," he said, and then realized he probably shouldn't have said that out loud. "Hey, Joey got you a great-granddaughter."

"Yeah, with some help."

"And Danny, Brian and I are just focused on the campground right now."

"Mmm-hmm." She looked as if she had more to say, but Danny walked up behind her at that moment and wrapped his arms around her shoulders.

"Delicious desserts as always, Gram," he said, and then he dipped his head to kiss her cheek.

"Thank you." She sighed. "I should start rounding people up. It's been a long day and we've got a long drive back, but from the time I say it's time to go to the time we actually leave is at least an hour."

"You need an air horn," Rob said.

She laughed. "Don't think I haven't considered it."

Once she'd gone to start nudging people, Danny looked around. "I'll stay and give you guys a hand putting all those picnic tables back, and whatever else you need."

"Appreciate it." He looked around, thankful his family was starting to deal with the leftover food. There was a solid several hours of stuff to take care of before he could relax for the night. "Oh, what now?"

Steph was coming their way, and she looked annoyed. "It's impossible to catch all four of you together, you know."

"You've got the best two here anyway," Danny told Steph, and she rolled her eyes. "But why do you want all four of us together?"

"Because I want to talk to you guys about Kyle and me getting married here, even though he had to work today so it's only me doing the talking."

Married? Rob knew they'd been engaged for months— there had been a family party to celebrate it, of course— but considering how much time she spent on Instagram and Pinterest, he'd assumed Steph would be going all out for her wedding. If somebody had suggested she get married at the campground, he would have laughed and he would have bet *she* would have laughed, too.

"Why would you want to get married *here*?" Danny asked. "I get that we had a lot of fun here growing up, but you want it for your wedding?"

Steph blew out a breath. "You don't remember Kyle, do you?"

"Yes, I remember Kyle. He's the guy you've been dating for almost two years and you've brought him to all the family stuff, and—oh yeah, we went to a football game together."

"No, smart-ass. I mean from when we were kids—or teenagers, actually. Kyle and I met here one summer. He was my first kiss."

Rob's mind was blown. "What? You had your first kiss during a Family Camping Trip of Doom?"

"Yeah."

"First Kiss of D—"

"Stop it." Steph held up her hand. "And don't even think about saying *Wedding of Doom*."

Rob was surprised the fact they'd crossed paths with Kyle at the campground in the past hadn't come up before, but maybe it had—just not when he was around. Though Danny didn't seem to know it, either. Also, he didn't think they'd seen Kyle since Christmas, which was before they'd decided to buy the place. Once they had, they'd barely had time to sleep, never mind reminisce with the family.

"Brian told me you've already got a week blocked off for the family in August, so it won't be a big deal," Steph continued, as if it was settled. "We'll just get married then."

"We know you, so we know 'it won't be a big deal' is a big lie," Danny said. "It's going to cost you."

"You can't charge me extra for getting married here when we'll all already be here."

"It's called event hosting and people charge a lot of money for that."

"I'm your cousin."

"We'll give you a family discount," Rob said, and Danny snorted, no doubt because Rob had implied he'd have to pay to stay in the small cabin.

"I'm serious," Steph said. "He only has his brother and sister-in-law, and his grandfather, so we'd probably rent them a big RV and they'd only need one site."

"You really want your wedding to be here?" Danny asked.

"We really do. We've talked about it a *lot* since you told us you were buying the campground and we think being here with our families and having a few chill days with people we love in a place we love and where we met is what we both want."

"Then we'll make it happen," Rob said, and tears filled her eyes. "Though I want to go on record right now about that word *chill*. I might have a small sign that says it so every time you try to go bridezilla on us, I can hold it up."

"I'll even make you the sign."

"And maybe two separate group chats? One for wedding planning that doesn't include us, and one that does but only has details relevant to us." Rob really wanted to get started on that cleanup because there were still campers milling around, helping put stuff away. They absolutely weren't the ones supposed to be doing the work. "I have to get back to it. I do have to talk to other people besides family, you know."

"That's funny considering you spent more time talking to Hannah than anybody else."

"She's a person who's not family, which was the point of the cookout—to get to know the campers."

"I only talked to her for a few minutes, but I feel like I know her from somewhere and I can't place it." Steph tilted her head, thinking. "Do you know where she's from?"

"She's from California," he said. He didn't really know what else to tell her. "She went to UNH, but you were probably finishing up at U Maine while she was there."

"Huh." She shrugged. "Just one of those things, I guess. But she seems wicked familiar. It's totally going to bug me until it comes to me, probably at two o'clock in the morning."

"Don't call me if that happens."

"I totally will," Steph said, and then she held up a hand. "Wait. I wanted to ask you how we can make a solid aisle so I can wear heels with my dress without the heel getting stuck in the grass and pulling my shoe off in the middle of my grand entrance."

Danny groaned, and Rob scrubbed his hand over his face. "There are going to be at least a hundred text messages about this, aren't there?"

Steph grinned. "At least."

* * *

Even though she was so full she could barely move, Hannah walked up to the top of the campground, where the overflow parking was. It was mostly for parking trailers or guests' vehicles, but she'd discovered that the upper part of the lot had great cell reception. It also had a few fallen trees that made for reasonably comfortable seats, so she was able to video chat without being down in the busy part of the campground.

At some point she'd reply to the missed calls from Erika, or at least shoot her a text message, but right now she wanted to talk to her parents. It was probably seeing Rob interacting with his family, but suddenly she was very aware of the distance between herself and home.

Her mother answered on the second ring, her warm smile filling Hannah's screen. "Hannah! How was the barbecue? Did the fruit salad turn out okay?"

"Everybody loved it," she said, blinking twice to clear away the moisture that filled her eyes when she heard her mom's voice. "And I got a recipe from Rob's grandmother I can't wait to try. Blond brownies, but unlike any blond brownie you've ever tried before."

"You'll have to make them for us when you get home. Your father went to help his friend John hang some drywall, and then next weekend, John's going to come over and help your dad fix that leaky spot on the garage roof. You know how they love their beer and power tools but, assuming he comes home instead of to the emergency room, I'll tell him about them."

Hannah laughed, and it eased the ache of missing them. "He does love his power tools. I'm sorry I missed him, though."

"So tell me about the people you met today. Did you make some friends?"

It was such an elementary school question to ask, but it opened the door and that was how Hannah spent the next twenty minutes telling her mother about Rob Kowalski.

"He sounds wonderful, honey," her mom said, but Hannah could hear an undercurrent of concern. "But you don't really know him. Did you tell him who you are? Does he listen to the podcast?"

"I haven't told him about the podcast, and I doubt he listens to it."

"But you don't *know*."

They'd all reacted differently when *Improbable Causes* went viral. Her dad and Jenn were proud and happy, though they didn't totally understand the podcasting business model. Erika had focused on the potential dollar signs. Hannah's guilt over causing the victim's loved ones fresh pain had colored everything.

And her mom had run on pure anxiety. As the harassment increased, so had her fear for Hannah, and the decision to travel to New Hampshire for three months alone hadn't helped.

But it was what Hannah needed—time away from how everybody else had felt so she could focus on her own feelings. She wanted to be away from the pressure of what more money could mean for the people in her life and the chaos of heightened emotions. She needed to figure out what *she* wanted.

"He's not allowed to have personal relationships with the campers anyway, Mom," she said, hoping to put her mother's mind at ease. "I don't want to get him in trouble with his brothers."

"That's for the best, since you live *here*."

"I know." Of course she had to go back to California. She had their truck and camper, for one thing. Her family was there. Erika was there. Her apartment and their office were there.

"Have you talked to Erika lately?" her mom asked in an overly bright voice. Clearly she also wanted to change the subject away from Rob, which was perfectly fine with Hannah.

"I've talked to her a couple of times, but nothing in depth. I haven't decided what I want to do yet, which frustrates her."

"Understandably. What you do affects her."

"I know. But I also know if I get pushed into doing something I'm not comfortable with for her sake, it'll come between us—both professionally *and* personally. I want to be sure before I make a decision."

"That's one of the reasons you're such a good team. Erika would just dive off a cliff, but she has you to check the depth of the water first."

Hannah laughed because that was a pretty good description of their relationship. "But sometimes, after I've checked the depth of the water and know it's safe, I still need Erika to give me a shove off the edge."

"You'll know when the right answer comes to you. You'll feel it."

The certainty in her mom's voice comforted Hannah because she was right. Hannah liked to think things through, but she put a lot of stock in her intuition and when the right course presented itself to her, she'd know.

"Thanks, Mom." She shifted on the log because fallen trees weren't actually that comfortable to sit on for very long. "I should go. I ate so much I'm going to fall asleep on the phone, and this log is probably a worse bed than it is a chair."

Her mom laughed and blew her a kiss. Once they'd disconnected, Hannah stood with a groan and slid her phone back into her pocket. Next time she came up here for a chat, she'd bring a pillow with her. Or just drag her camp chair up the hill.

She'd just arrived back at her site when she heard a vehicle accelerating up the main road and a horn beeping, followed by another. It sounded like Rob's family were starting to head out, and she smiled as she imagined him flopping face-first on his bed, utterly exhausted.

Imagining Rob on his bed wasn't going to lead her to anything but more sexual frustration, so she went inside and grabbed her book. After settling into her nest, she tried to convince her brain the story was more interesting than imagining things she really shouldn't allow herself to think about.

But the book wasn't *that* good.

Chapter Twelve

Rob had just finished skimming the pool when he saw the twins from site twenty-eight headed toward the store. Their mom said they could come in once per weekend for ice cream, but they'd had ice cream during the cookout yesterday with all the other kids. And he was sure Melissa once mentioned them not having sugar before the long drive home on Sundays.

Also, they weren't running, but were doing that weird fast walk-skip thing kids did when they were in a hurry, but an adult had told them not to run. After hanging the skimmer on the hooks looped on the fence, he left the pool area and took the second to reset the lock. Then he met them by the door of the store.

"Do you have a ladder?" Red asked before Rob could even say hello.

"What kind of ladder? How tall?" It seemed weird Scottie would send the boys down rather than coming himself.

The boys looked at each other and then Blue shrugged. "Tall like to get up on a roof, I guess."

"Okay." Maybe Scottie needed to get on the roof of his camper to seal a leak or something. "I can bring one up and give your dad a hand."

"Dad's not here."

He was confused. "Your mom needs a ladder?"

Red shook his head. "She's not here, either."

Okay, that wasn't great. They weren't old enough to be here alone, and he definitely wasn't going to give them a ladder so they could go on a roof to retrieve a ball or Frisbee or whatever got stuck up there. "Back up. What's stuck on the roof?"

"Hannah," they said in unison.

His heart skipped a beat. "Hannah's on a roof?"

"Yep." Blue nodded. "She climbed up a tree and hopped across and got the boomerang, but she said jumping onto a tree branch is scarier than jumping onto a roof and then she said…what did she say?"

"She said, 'I didn't really think that through,'" Red replied, doing a decent imitation of an exasperated woman. It was a tone he probably heard a lot from their mother, actually. "We're supposed to ask Brian and not you, though."

"Brian's not here." He went to talk to a guy about the price of having cordwood delivered already split to bundle for resale to campers versus splitting it themselves. They were both hoping to make the former work, but the two brothers who *weren't* on-site or doing the work were only looking at the dollar signs. "Where are your parents?"

"Mom got stung and she has an allergy pen, but Dad said she still had to go to the doctor. It's super boring there, so Hannah said she would keep an eye on us. And we told her we're allowed to come to the store, but she made us promise not to run and to look before we cross the road even though it's dirt and nobody drives through the campground fast, and we had to come straight here and not talk to strangers and we had to find Brian."

Rob smothered a chuckle. She'd really covered the nervous babysitter bases there. As far as he could tell, the Scott rules for the twins were stay off other people's sites and don't go out on Route 3. "Since Brian's not here, I'll get the ladder and be right there. Wait, which roof?"

"The bathhouse on the hill," Red said, and then they headed back, doing the same not-running half trot.

It took him a couple of minutes to get the key to the UTV and write a "be right back" note for the door, which he locked. Then he had to go into the walk-out basement under the house and get the ladder to strap to the rack on the UTV.

When he got to the small bathhouse on the hill that served the cabins on that side of the campground—new since they were kids and Uncle Joe and Aunt Keri had to walk all the way to the big one in the middle of the campground—the boys were trying to throw something up to Hannah. Red would throw it up and Blue would catch it. They'd switch and try again.

"We're trying to give her a snack," Red told him when he turned off the UTV.

"Huh." He looked up at Hannah, who was sitting on the eave of the roof with the flats of her sneakers braced against the shingles. "How long have you been up there?"

"Long enough to want a snack," she said. "Plus, if they're standing here trying to throw me a snack, I know where they are."

"True." He put his hand out. "Let me try."

"Just get me down and I can eat it on the ground."

"I don't know." He tilted his head up to grin at her. "The boys said you only wanted Brian."

She groaned. "I thought you'd be busy and I didn't want to interrupt you."

That was such a lie. "Really? That's the reason?"

"Okay, fine. I didn't really think this through, which wasn't very smart, and since Brian already thinks I'm a——" She stopped, glancing at the boys. "I figured this wouldn't make much of a difference in Brian's opinion of me. Happy?"

Yes, Rob *was* happy because that meant she cared about *his* opinion of her. He unstrapped the ladder and found a solid place to foot it. "Do you want me to come up and help you?"

"I can do it," she said, moving sideways across the roof. "And if you come up and the ladder falls over, then we're both on the roof and the boys are in charge of the campground."

The twins seemed excited by that possibility, but Hannah had no problem swinging around and climbing down the ladder on her own. And he didn't mind the view from the ground, though he didn't comment on that.

As soon as her feet hit the ground, Melissa's SUV turned up the road and Scottie braked when he saw them all farther up the hill with the UTV and the ladder. The boys took off running, probably to fill them in on Hannah's adventures on the bathhouse roof.

"I guess I won't be asked to babysit the twins again," she said, brushing old pine needles off her backside.

"On the plus side, you won't have to babysit the twins again."

She laughed and helped him lift the ladder onto the rack, then she crossed the road to sit on the stone bench set into the trees between the two cabins while he tied it down. Then, because she was still sitting there when he finished, he crossed and sat next to her.

"Thank you for the rescue," she said. "Climbing the tree and hopping onto the roof wasn't a big deal, but on the return trip, the branches didn't look quite as solid and the gap seemed a little bigger."

"I would have gotten the boomerang for them."

"I told them a ball would have just rolled down, but they're practicing with the boomerang because they saw it in a movie."

He snorted. "I didn't think you threw them up in the air like that."

"Well, I don't think they've really mastered it yet." She sighed. "So yesterday seemed like a success for you guys."

"Yeah, it went better than I expected. I guess the next hurdle will be Memorial Day weekend. The trails will be open so we'll have to police the machines going through the campground. And weekenders will be another learning curve for us."

"Don't worry. Dave and Sheila will tell you if you're doing it wrong."

Rob laughed. "You know, I think Dave yelled at me once when I was here as a kid."

"Only once?"

"Well...probably more than once. We got yelled at as a group sometimes. Brian had an attitude even when he was a kid, so adults tended to focus on him. But I think Dave yelled at me once for taking pictures because he thought I was trying to take one of him."

"So that's a pattern for you, then?" she asked in a teasing voice.

"You'd think I'd have learned to pay more attention to the background by now."

"Speaking of when you were a kid, I heard you being called Bobby a lot," she said, and he groaned.

"Yeah." He shrugged. "I get that a lot when the family's all together because I was Bobby from the time I was born until around middle school. I guess I went through a phase where I thought Rob sounded more adult, and by being Rob,

I could make my family see me as a responsible grown man and not the *baby*. But sometimes they either regress or do it deliberately to get under my skin."

"I've noticed your brothers do it to annoy you sometimes. But your parents and grandparents just seem to forget."

"Yeah, old habits and all that. They do try, though."

She smiled. "Just look at it this way—the people who really love you call you Bobby sometimes, and Bobby's very loved."

"I like that." He returned the smile. "I've never thought of it that way, but you're right. The people who call me Bobby love me. Even my brothers, who often do it to push my buttons."

"I don't have three older brothers, but I have an older sister, and pushing our buttons is part of their jobs, I think."

"You said she's married with kids and lives next door to your parents. What about you? Ever been married?" He just wanted to learn more about Hannah, of course. He couldn't help himself.

"Nope. No husbands, ex or otherwise. No kids. It's just me and my parents and my sister and her family. That's it. Other than that, what you see is what you get." She gestured in the direction of her site when she said it. "What about you? Ever been married?"

"No. Never found the one, I guess. I thought I had once, but then I brought her home to meet the family. She didn't really fit in."

"Ouch."

He tried not to think about Hannah and Gram, heads together over the recipe. "Well, it started with her launching into a lecture about how doom is actually a bad thing, and it went downhill from there."

"It's not as though you use the word literally. Nobody's lining up to go on an *actual* Camping Trip of Doom."

"Exactly. But I guess she needed to be right more than she cared if they liked her, and maybe it was wrong of me, but she knew how important my family is to me, so I took her lack of caring about them as a sign she cared less about me than I thought."

"I'm sorry, but you're probably right. I can't imagine wanting a future with somebody who didn't get along with my family."

Right. Her family that was in California, all the way across the country. If she didn't want to be involved with somebody who didn't get along with them, she certainly wouldn't get involved with somebody who lived so far away, she'd rarely get to see them.

But still, when he heard Brian's truck turning into the campground, he looked over at her and grinned. "You want to go for a ride?"

Hannah should say no. It was only yesterday she'd had an entire conversation with her mother about how messing around with Rob wasn't a good idea. Not that he'd invited her to mess around, exactly, but the more time they spent alone, the more inevitable it felt.

And the way he was looking at her now, with mischief and hope shining in his eyes? There was no way she could resist him in this moment. "A ride?"

"Yeah, in the truck, I mean. Not out on the ATV trails. Unless you want to, of course. They're not open yet, but we can be a maintenance crew. But we can't get to the spot I want to show you from the trails."

She arched an eyebrow. "You and your brothers are convinced the campground must have a serial killer in it, but you want to take me on a ride to a secret spot somewhere?"

He chuckled, but then his forehead creased. "Wait. Are you implying I should be afraid to take you there, or that you're afraid of going there with me? Which one of us is the murderer?"

"Well, I know it's not me."

"It's not me, either." He held up his hands. "I promise."

"Oh. Okay, then." When he laughed, she laughed with him.

"Meet me at my truck in ten minutes?" he asked.

"Okay." She started to stand. "Do I need to bring anything?"

"Got trash bags, duct tape and a shovel?"

She laughed. "No, but I'll bring water and some snacks."

He grimaced and reached into his pocket to pull out a crumpled package of Oreos. "I forgot, I put your snack in my pocket and...they're crushed."

She took the package anyway. "That just makes them perfect for topping off a scoop of chocolate ice cream."

After he drove off in the UTV, Hannah walked down to her camper. The Scotts were all inside, but Melissa saw her through the window and poked her head out of the door. "Thank you for watching the boys. Sorry about the boomerang."

"No problem. Are you doing okay?"

"I'm fine, but I'm supposed to go to the ER anyway, as a precaution. We're packing up to leave now, but we'll see you next weekend?"

"I'll be here," Hannah said, and then she gave a little wave and kept walking.

By the time she put a couple of water bottles and some snacks in a small insulated bag and brushed her teeth—

annoying herself in the process because she knew exactly why she wanted minty-fresh breath—Rob had his truck parked next to the store. She caught him in the act of trying to clean out the passenger side.

She picked up a hardware store receipt that had gotten away from him and was being blown in her direction by the breeze.

"Thanks," he said when she handed it to him, and then he gave her a sheepish grin. "Got a little lazy, I guess, but it's mostly coffee cups and receipts."

"You should have seen my dad's truck after a few days on the road. Around Illinois, it reached the point I told myself I couldn't buy any more coffee until I'd cleaned it out."

After shoving the receipt into the pile of papers stuffed in the glove box, he brushed a few crumbs off the seat and stood back so she could climb in. She set the bag and cross-body purse on the floor by her feet and was going to reach for the door, but Rob was still standing there.

"You in?" he asked, and when she nodded, he closed her door for her.

Hannah smiled as she watched Rob walk around the front of the truck. It was kind of sweet, the way he'd closed her door, especially since she couldn't remember the last time she sat on the right side of a vehicle. Whenever she and Erika went somewhere, she drove because her friend was the target market for those distracted driver PSAs.

Once Rob had climbed into the driver's seat and they'd buckled up, he pulled onto the main road, heading north. The radio was playing the same station she'd chosen, and the volume was perfect—loud enough to fill an awkward silence, but not so loud as to discourage conversation.

It was strange, though, watching their surroundings go by without having to do the actual driving. She'd never been a nervous passenger in the past, but she was definitely out of practice and her right foot actually twitched as if going for the brake when he went faster into a corner than she would have. Not that he was speeding, but they had different driving styles, for sure.

"You okay over there?"

"What?" She looked at him and he gestured toward her hands, which were balled into fists on her lap. She laughed and flattened her palms against her thighs. "Yeah. It's been a while since I was in the passenger seat."

"Do you want to drive?"

It took her a few seconds to realize he was serious. If it made her more comfortable, he'd actually let her drive him around in his own truck. "No, I'm fine. And I'm enjoying the scenery."

She'd driven this road already, since this was the way to the grocery store, but since she wasn't driving, she was able to appreciate the views more. Then they reached town and he took a right turn, diverging from the route she'd taken.

"It's not much farther," he told her.

"It's so pretty here. And very green."

She was taking in the pops of spring color when they drove by a sign at the edge of a lawn. She didn't get a chance to read it, but she got the impression it had more than one curse word on it. *Probably protesting something*, she thought.

"What did that sign say?"

Rob chuckled. "I don't remember what that particular sign says and I didn't see it, but people are pretty opinionated around here."

When he flipped on his turn signal to indicate a right turn, Hannah was confused. They were in the middle of nowhere, and for a few seconds, her imagination—fueled by thousands of hours spent obsessing about true crime—ran away on her. Then she saw the waterfall.

It was just a pull-off on the side of the road, with a gravel parking lot and a grassy area that sloped down to the edge of a brook fed by a cascade of water over an almost hundred-foot drop.

By the time Hannah unbuckled her seat belt and tucked her bag under the seat, out of sight since she wouldn't need it here, Rob had gotten out and was walking around the truck. Sure enough, he opened her door and offered his hand to steady her as she stepped down.

It was funny—she got in and out of her own truck all the time without a guy's assistance—but she didn't reject the gesture. He'd probably been raised to do it, and she didn't want to hurt his feelings. Mostly, she didn't want to miss out on a chance to hold his hand, even if only for a moment.

His fingers grasped hers for a few seconds after her feet hit the ground, and then his hand fell away.

Hannah was disappointed, and she wondered what she would have done if he hadn't let her go. Or if she'd threaded her fingers through his instead of letting his touch slip away. Maybe they would have walked hand in hand, and she wouldn't have minded that at all.

"My mom took so many pictures of us here over the years," he said, heading toward the waterfall. "We even came up here in the winter once because she thought it would be a good Christmas card photo, with all the ice."

"What happened?"

He laughed, looking sideways at her. "I'd ask how you know something happened, but you've met all four of us, so not hard to figure out, I guess."

"Well, you said your mom *thought* it would make a good

Christmas card picture." She chuckled. "And yes, I've met all four of you and heard some stories. There *is* that."

They reached a small wooden bridge that crossed the water and led to a path that followed the brook to the bottom of the waterfall. He stood aside and gestured for her to go first.

"We were all dressed in red sweaters and jeans," he told her. "Dad didn't like it when she made us dress up in matching outfits, but she insisted it was festive and the red would really pop against the snow and ice."

"Especially with the dark hair." She could almost picture it—four handsome boys with dark hair, blue eyes and red sweaters, all lined up with the frozen falls as the backdrop.

"So the first thing that went wrong was my mom watching the weather at home, but forgetting it can be a lot colder two and a half hours *north* of home. We were all bundled up because it was maybe twenty degrees and that didn't count the wind chill factor. Mom decided we'd all get into position, and then we'd take our coats and hats off just long enough to take the picture."

"And somebody's coat went in the water?" she guessed. Even with heavy ice, brooks like this one rarely froze over completely.

He chuckled, shaking his head, and Hannah realized they'd both fallen into a walking pace so slow it could barely be considered walking. And while it would be even better if they were holding hands, she didn't mind at all.

"Somebody's coat *did* go in the water. Or rather, my dad fell in while holding *all* of the coats."

"No!" She covered her mouth with her hand. "It's not deep, though. Was he okay?"

"It's not deep, but it was damned cold at the time, and while slipping and sliding on the ice and floundering in the open parts, he managed to soak all four coats. Plus his own clothes."

"Did your mom at least get the picture?"

"Oh, it's not over yet," he said, giving her a grin that made her pulse quicken. "Danny grabbed for Dad, but he missed. He was off balance, though, so with his other hand, he grabbed Joey. Joey stopped Danny from going in, but it was icy and in keeping their balance, they knocked Brian into the brook with Dad."

Hannah was laughing too hard to say anything, and he laughed with her. They were almost to the base of the waterfall, and she wished it was possible for them to walk even slower. She loved listening to him talk about his family, and she didn't want the story to end.

"I should ask Mom to send me a copy of that Christmas card."

She put her hand on his arm, sure she'd heard him wrong. "Wait. She actually got the picture taken? In that cold?"

"Oh, she took the picture that day…more or less. She took a picture of us all grouped together in the back seat of the minivan—from the waist up because Brian wasn't wearing pants—and we're all sweaty because we're wearing those red sweaters and she'd jacked the heat up to about ninety, but we were all laughing because Dad had just grumbled about having to do the speed limit all the way home because if he got pulled over, the cop would see *he* wasn't wearing any pants, either."

"I would *love* to see that card," she said, and then she focused on the water rushing over the rocks, close enough so she could feel the mist on her face.

Rob made his way across some rocks in the brook until he was standing on an outcropping of granite right in front of the waterfall. He held out his hand and helped her across.

It wasn't a big slab of granite, so they had to stand close together.

And again, she didn't mind at all.

"I can see why she wanted to take the picture here," she told him. "It's a gorgeous spot."

"It is. A black-and-white photo I took at this spot was used for the cover of one of my uncle Joe's books, actually."

"Really? That's amazing!"

He shrugged, but the pink that tinted his cheeks gave away how pleased he was. "He writes horror, of course, so they made it grainy and added some atmospheric mist, along with a super creepy shadow figure in the trees."

"Do you have a copy on your phone? I'd love to see it."

After sliding his phone out of his pocket and tapping a couple of times, he handed her his phone. "I printed a copy of the photo for him to hang by his desk while he was writing, for inspiration, I guess. He brought it to his publisher when it was time to do the cover."

"It's a great picture, even with the bonus creepiness."

Could he hear the way her breath caught when his hand brushed hers as he took the phone back? Or the shakiness of her slow exhale? Hopefully not, with the rushing of water over the falls acting like a natural white noise machine.

As he slid the phone into his back pocket, his arm brushed hers. She didn't pull away, and a few seconds later, the back of his hand rested against her hand. Hannah shifted hers slightly, and his fingers threaded through hers.

They looked at the water falling in front of them and despite the chill in the air and in the mist from the falls, so much heat was coursing through Hannah, she was surprised steam wasn't rolling off of her.

"This feels like a great place for a first kiss, doesn't it?"

he asked quietly, and Hannah looked up at his profile, her pulse racing.

Her body trembled, and she knew Rob could feel the shaking in her hand, because his fingers squeezed hers. But she ignored the voices in her head urging her to think about what she *should* do, and instead let her heart—or her body, at least—take the lead for once. "It's a perfect place for a first kiss."

When he turned to face her, resting his free hand at her waist, every thought in her head that wasn't about desperately wanting his mouth on hers was silenced.

Rob's hand slid halfway up her back. "For *our* first kiss."

"Yes." It came out as a whisper, and then his lips were on hers.

There was no hesitation or gentle exploration. Rob claimed her mouth as though he'd been wanting to so badly that he couldn't take the anticipation another second. It was the same way she felt, and Hannah parted her lips, letting his tongue sweep over hers.

He let go of her hand and cupped the side of her jaw, while his other hand pressed against her back to hold her close. Not that she wanted to go anywhere. Her entire world was the warmth of his hands and the hunger in his kiss.

A breeze kicked up suddenly, and the amount of mist it brought their way was like a cold shower from Mother Nature. They broke apart, and Rob chuckled as he wiped the wetness from her cheeks.

"It's still a little chilly to get wet," he said, and when she nodded, he made his way back across the rocks.

This time, when he took her hand to help her across, he didn't let it go. They retraced their steps down the path, at a little less leisurely of a pace this time because the wind was cold.

And they were both quiet. Hannah thought it was an easy silence, but she couldn't help but wonder if he was thinking the same thing she was. *What does this mean? What comes next?*

She told herself to relax and enjoy the moment. She'd shared a first kiss with the first guy she'd liked in a very long time in what had to be one of the most romantic spots in the state. Tomorrow would be a good day to worry about tomorrow.

They were almost back to the truck when his phone chimed, and it was in the pocket he could reach with his free hand, so he pulled it out. Hannah didn't get more than a glimpse of the text message—and that was an accident, since she tried not to be nosy like that—but she saw that it was from Brian.

And she also saw her name.

Rob made a low growling sound and shoved the phone back in his pocket without replying. "Work stuff."

"Involving me?" she asked, and he sighed. "I wasn't trying to look, but I did catch my name on the screen."

"He wants me to come back and help him with something. Where your name came in was the added not-so-subtle reminder that I'm not supposed to *fraternize* with the campers," he said, complete with half a set of air quotes, since he still hadn't let go of her hand.

"Then we should probably keep this little field trip to ourselves," she said.

"Pretty sure that ship sailed when I drove out of the campground with you in the passenger seat." He squeezed her hand. "But they don't need to know everything."

Yet, she thought. They didn't need to know everything *yet*. She suspected it wasn't easy to keep secrets in the Kowalski family.

Chapter Thirteen

Rob hadn't brought his camera when he and Hannah visited the waterfall almost a week ago. He kept a small, cheap digital camera in the truck's console storage compartment, but he hadn't wanted to focus on anything but her in that moment.

But not having photographs didn't stop a slideshow of memories from playing through his mind. When he was working. When he should have been sleeping. And *definitely* when he was showering. No matter what he was doing, the memory of kissing her played on repeat in his head.

Brian and Stella had been outside when they'd pulled back into the campground, so all he could do was tell Hannah he hoped she'd enjoyed visiting the waterfall, and she'd smiled and thanked him.

"We're giving tours to the campers now?" Brian had asked with an edge in his voice.

"It's a cool spot. I thought she'd like it. And she did."

"Maybe some of the other campers new to the area would also like to see it."

"Then I'll take them, too," Rob snapped, and that had been the end of the discussion—for the time being.

But now it was Friday and he hadn't really had a moment alone with her since they got back. And to make it worse, he wasn't sure how to make that happen. There was very little privacy in the campground, and every time he turned around, it seemed as if Brian was watching him. And Joey had shown up yesterday to spend a few days helping out as they welcomed transient campers for the long weekend that kicked off the summer season. Rob welcomed another set of hands, but now he had to share the bedroom *and* he had two brothers watching him like he was a teenager about to sneak out his window in the middle of the night.

"You look pissed," Brian said, breaking into his thoughts.

They were in the living room, taking a breather before the campers who'd had to work a full day or got stuck in city traffic straggled in. The day had been chaotic and they probably would have been too tired to eat if they hadn't been smart and thrown chili makings in the Crock-Pot first thing that morning.

"It's been a long day and it's not over yet," Rob said, not wanting to get into how annoyed he was with them.

"Definitely been a long day."

The seasonal campers, once they were set up for the summer, were pretty low-maintenance. They occasionally needed propane or firewood or conversation, but for the most part, they kept to themselves.

Having weekenders coming in was an entirely different ball game. They all had to be checked in and told the rules of not only the campground, but also the ATV trail system. Because the dirt roads through the campground were barely more than a lane wide and turning around could be a problem, Brian guided many of them to their sites. And then came requests for ice and firewood, and they'd already sold a set of tent pegs to a guy who'd told his wife four times that yes, he'd remembered to pack the tent pegs.

"But you don't look tired," Brian insisted. "You look pissed."

"Fine. I'm pissed. I took Hannah to the waterfall and we had a nice time, but I haven't had a chance to spend any time with her since because you've decided you're some kind of campground chaperone."

"One, we had an agreement about not messing around with campers. And two, I think we've been running our asses off getting ready for today, so I don't think it's all me."

"The whole don't-fraternize-with-campers thing is getting out of hand," he said. "It's not like I'm making my way around the campground, hitting on every woman who checks in."

"That would almost be better, I think."

"How do you figure that?"

Brian shrugged. "Because you're a single guy and hitting on single women doesn't really mean anything. But this thing with Hannah? I'm telling you, Bobby, I don't think you should get in over your head with her."

He laughed, but it was a mirthless sound. "Tell me you're not back to the serial killer crap."

"No, of course not. But she lives all the way across the country, and I worry about you getting hurt, dumbass."

Instead of snapping back at his brother, Rob forced himself to take a beat. He didn't want to hear it, but he also knew Brian was coming from a good place.

Before he could decide how to respond, a loud boom made Stella sit up, her head swiveling toward the back wall, which faced the campground. She didn't bark, though, and they all sat in silence for a moment, waiting to see if it happened again.

It didn't, but Rob didn't think he'd relax if he didn't identify the source of the sound.

"Tell me that wasn't a gunshot," Brian said.

"That wasn't a gunshot. I think. I sure as hell hope not." Rob pushed himself to his feet. Usually Stella would have been interested in where he was going, but she was shaking a little, and she shifted closer to Brian. The dog did *not* like thunderstorms and she was probably confused by what could have been a single clap of thunder. "I'm going to take a look around."

"What the hell was that?" Joey asked, coming out of the small bedroom in nothing but sleep pants. He'd gone to bed early because—thanks to the fact he'd gotten out of most of the work thus far—he was the one getting up at five in the morning to clean the bathhouses before the campers stirred.

"I'm going to check on things, but probably nothing," Rob said, and he grabbed a lightweight hoodie off the pegs and a flashlight on his way out.

The campground wasn't exactly quiet. Some campers were still setting up their sites. A lot of them were sitting around campfires, telling stories and laughing a little too loud. For many of them, this was the first outing after a long winter, and Rob and his brothers had decided as long as the vibe stayed positive and quiet hours were respected, they'd only interfere if somebody else complained.

But he could see quite a few of the transient camper sites from the back of the house and nobody seemed particularly alarmed by the sound. Or if they had been, they'd shaken it off already. He'd walk around, though, and make sure nobody looked like they'd been up to no good.

It was dark, and once he entered a section in the trees, it got *really* dark and he managed to trip over a rock. Luckily, he didn't fall, but he did curse under his breath and pull the flashlight out of his pocket. He didn't really want to use it since he'd attract a lot more attention, but he also didn't want to break an ankle.

Movement in his peripheral vision made him pause, and he saw Hannah. She was standing at the end of her camper—out of sight of her neighbors—and when he looked in her direction, she gestured for him to join her. Then she put a finger over her lips to signify he should be quiet.

"Did you hear the boom?" she whispered when he reached her.

He wasn't sure why Hannah was whispering, but he went along because it gave him an excuse to stand close to her. "That's why I'm creeping around the campground in the dark."

"Creeping?" She snorted. "Not so much. But anyway, the boom was courtesy of Red and Blue, and I don't think they'll do it again anytime soon."

He gave her an exaggerated look of alarm. "What did you do to them?"

"I'll never tell," she whispered, laying her finger over her lips again. But then she had to cover her mouth with her entire hand to smother a giggle. "Sorry, I shouldn't joke about that since your brothers think I'm a serial killer."

"It's not that they think *you* are. It's more like they realized that, statistically speaking, somebody in this campground *could* be." She rolled her eyes, but in a cute way. "So anyway, did they blow something up? They didn't damage your truck or camper, did they?"

She shook her head before nodding toward the chairs and heading that way. That's when he realized there were two of them.

"Hey, you have two chairs now."

Even in the dim, yellow glow from her camper's outside light, he saw a pink flush across her cheeks. "When I was shopping, I grabbed another one in case, you know, I had a guest who wanted to sit down."

He nodded and sat, but it seemed a little odd that she'd been doing the campground thing for almost a month and only now thought it might be nice to have guest seating. Maybe it was foolish, but he wondered if she'd been hoping *he* would sit and visit.

Hannah pulled her chair closer to his before sitting down, which he liked. "Basically they poured bug spray into some kind of bottle, put the cap on it and put it in the fire. I'm not sure why."

Rob chuckled. "Probably for the same reason we did it back in the day—to see what would happen. We never did find the cap."

"I don't think they will, either. Not that they'll have a chance to look for it, because, by the sound of it, they're grounded until they're twenty-five."

"If they continue to follow in our campground footsteps, she'll get so tired of listening to them be bored, they'll be ungrounded by lunch tomorrow."

"I guess since you've done the same thing, you won't be too hard on them?"

"Somehow harmless pranks don't land the same when you're the one responsible for the safety and property of everybody in the campground." He smiled. "I'll try to keep a straight face while I lecture them, at least. And it can wait until tomorrow."

"I didn't want to rat them out, but I know what it sounded like, and I didn't want you walking around worried about it."

"I appreciate that." He pulled his phone out of his pocket and sent a thumbs-up emoji to Brian. "Just letting my brother know all is well."

"It must have startled Stella."

"Yeah, it did. And she's not a fan of thunderstorms, so she got anxious, but she's probably snoring again already."

"I hate thunderstorms, too," Hannah said, leaning her head back against her chair. "Mostly because I'm terrified of them. I have been since I was a kid and a tree crashed through our neighbor's roof. Nobody was hurt, but I could hear her screaming in my room."

Because they were keeping their voices low and it was dark, there was an intimacy to the conversation he didn't want to get up and walk away from. He wanted to keep talking. "That must be hard to deal with in a camper."

"It is. I usually turn all the lights on so I can't see the lightning as much, and play loud music through my headphones. But it's impossible to totally block it out, of course."

"You're always welcome to ride out storms in the store. Or in the house, if we're closed."

She smiled. "I probably won't cross the open space to get there, but thank you for the invitation."

His phone chimed and he read the text message from Brian. What was it?

Bug spray in a capped bottle in the fire. Site 28.

That was a lot funnier when we were kids and didn't own the place.

Rob smiled and locked the screen, but he caught Hannah frowning at the phone. "Sorry. Brian wanted to know what it was."

"I don't blame him. I'd want to know what that sound was, too." She shrugged. "I was trying to decide if I should walk over to my truck or something and maybe scare them out of doing it, since Scottie's off at another campfire and

Melissa went inside to clean up, but I didn't make my mind up quickly enough, I guess."

"It sounds like they're kind of loud if you could hear them scheming. Are they bothering you at all?"

"No, they're fine. I don't think it's so much that they're loud, but that I'm pretty quiet. And sound carrying is part of being in a campground."

"Are you sure?"

She waved a hand at him. "I'm sure. And what are you going to do? Throw them out because they talk to each other and laugh a lot? I like hearing the boys play, actually. They're good kids, and Melissa's friendly without being… you know, *that* neighbor."

"I know what you mean." He cleared his throat, not sure how to bring up their trip to the waterfall and the distance between them since.

"You guys have been busy this week," she said, and he was relieved to have the opening.

"It's been hectic. It seems like every time we get comfortable, a new challenge is coming up that we have to prepare for." He paused and cleared his throat again. "I've wanted to stop by and…say hi, I guess. But Brian keeps coming up with a million things I should be doing instead."

She chuckled softly. "Operation No Fraternization is going well for them."

I'm telling you, Bobby, I don't think you should get in over your head with her.

Rob thought about what his brother had said and though he wanted to ignore the advice, he knew Brian wasn't totally wrong.

"You should know I have a long history of not letting my brothers boss me around," he said, hoping his grin hid the uncertainty he was feeling at the moment.

She laughed softly and it looked as if she was about to say something, but the sound of a truck slowing out on the main road made him turn. Sure enough, it was dark enough so he could see the red glow of brake lights, and he sighed.

"More campers coming in. I should go help because we *definitely* don't want people trying to find their sites in the dark."

"It's getting late."

"Yeah. The previous owners told us that Friday nights can be long, especially on long weekends when the traffic down south is particularly bad. Sometimes it can be as late as midnight, and we still have a few more to come in."

"It's a big weekend for you," she said, and his phone chimed at the same time.

Rob pulled out his phone to read the text message from Brian. Dude.

It was only one word, but he had a lifetime of knowing his brother and knew he was seriously annoyed that he hadn't come back from checking on the sound, and that he knew he was at Hannah's site.

"I have to go. Thanks for the tip," he said, nodding toward the Scotts' site.

"No problem. And good luck this weekend."

As he stood, he was tempted to lean over and give her a quick kiss good-night, but two things stopped him. One, they hadn't spoken since the last kiss, so he couldn't be sure she actually wanted to do it again. Maybe she'd gotten a taste and didn't like it.

But mostly it was the fact he didn't want to give her a quick kiss. He wanted to give her a long, slow and very thorough kiss, and doing so would require actually getting to spend time with her.

Alone.

Brothers really were a pain in the ass, he thought.

* * *

Hannah didn't leave her site for the entirety of the long weekend. The place was packed and almost everybody but her was there for the four-wheeling. Some of them rode ATVs and some of them drove side-by-sides, but they were all loud and kicked up dust. She wasn't opposed to them, but since she'd already done her grocery shopping and had everything she needed, she wasn't tempted to venture out.

And Rob was busy. Without the temptation of getting to talk to him, there was no real incentive for her to leave her comfortable, reasonably private site. She'd heard him once, from a distance, yelling to a guy who was exceeding the five-miles-per-hour speed limit on his four-wheeler. And she'd been leaning against the front of her truck, talking with Melissa Scott, when he'd driven by in the UTV pulling a small trailer filled with bundled firewood to sell to the campers.

He'd waved and though he didn't stop, his gaze had definitely lingered on Hannah before he gave her a smile that made her feel like she wasn't the only one who'd rather he was sitting under her awning with her at that moment.

She sat under the awning now, even though it was getting dark and she usually would have blown out the citronella candles and gone inside at dusk in favor of burrowing into her nest with a good book.

There was no denying—especially to herself—that she was hoping if she sat outside long enough, Rob would be able to squeeze out a few minutes to stop and chat.

And she'd *really* like to kiss him again.

Sometimes Hannah wondered if he regretted kissing her and didn't want to do it again. But that didn't seem likely because as far as she could tell, he hadn't been disappointed at all by the kiss at the waterfall.

It was more likely his brothers were more of an issue than he'd led her to believe. He *was* the youngest, and she'd gotten the impression he felt as though he had something to prove to them, so if they were adamant about him not spending time with her, he might have to give in.

In the few times they'd managed eye contact since the kiss, though, the look in his eyes made her think that if he was really forced into choosing between pleasing his brothers and kissing her, she had a chance.

A flash of movement in the brush caught her eye, and Hannah smiled when she spotted the skunk.

It was adorable, snuffling around as it looked for an evening snack. While she gave them a wide berth for obvious reasons, Hannah had always thought skunks were one of the cutest of the campground critters. Raccoons were chaotic and they could be destructive. And as gorgeous as bears were, their visits weren't a good thing.

But skunks were cute little creatures, with precious faces and fluffy tails. She especially liked the way they stomped their tiny front feet as a first warning that things were about to get smelly. Of course, she'd never been sprayed herself. Being doused might have changed her opinion of them slightly. But she enjoyed watching them from a distance, hoping a dog or a human didn't startle them or harass them.

She'd probably see a lot of little critters while she was here, since the smart ones would avoid the other side of the campground. Oscar might not be a big dog, but that honey badger mouth and attitude would have the skunks and raccoons—and any bears who wandered in—finding quieter spots to go foraging.

In her peripheral vision, she saw a camera lens, but she didn't run into her camper this time. One, she didn't want to startle the skunk. But also, she could make out enough of the photographer's face to recognize Rob, even though he was crouched in the shadows.

Hannah watched the skunk, humming softly to let it know she was there without being threatening, until it decided to forage farther up the hill. The Scott family was outside—making s'mores, judging by the sounds—so Hannah figured the skunk would cut their site a wide berth and check out the quieter side of the hill. But with kids, graham crackers and sugar in the mix, it would probably circle back later.

Once it had moved on, Rob crossed the road to join her under the awning. He sat in the other chair, which she'd left out and open for just this purpose. "Here I am taking pictures in your general direction again. You might change your mind about whether or not I'm actually trying to take them of you."

She laughed softly, so happy to see him she didn't care about the camera. "I'm not quite as exciting a subject as wildlife."

"I wouldn't say that." He hit a few buttons on the back of his camera and then showed her the display screen. "But it was a cute one."

He'd captured the skunk in the act of pawing at a spot on the ground, with the legs of Hannah's picnic table in the backdrop. Even in the dim light, his camera had picked up on a lot of detail, especially in its face.

"That's adorable," she said.

"I'll put it up on our social media with a reminder we share the space with furry little woodland creatures, and maybe a few tips about food storage and trash disposal."

"They're lucky to have you to take pictures for your accounts," she said. "It gives you a bit of an edge over using stock photos. Cheaper, too."

After setting the camera carefully on the ground at his feet, Rob pulled out his phone. He unlocked the screen and tapped on it a few times before holding it out to her.

It was open to the campground's Instagram feed, and she noticed he had a decent cell signal. *Probably a different provider*, she thought as she scrolled through it, noting the photos and captions, along with the number of likes and comments, and his generic hashtags. He should be getting more likes, especially if she assumed quite a few of them were probably from his large family. And there were probably some Birch Brook campers following it, as well.

"The photos are fabulous," she said, handing him back the phone. Then she had to bite her lip to keep from laughing when he actually preened a little, like a peacock. "But then your captions are just…the locations."

"Captions should tell people what they're looking at, right?"

"Yes, but you want them to do more than that. You're showing people these gorgeous places and telling them what those places are."

"Right."

"But you want to show them these gorgeous places and let them know they can actually *come* here and see it for themselves. And you want to sell them on why this is the place to stay if they want to do that. Think of the words less as a caption and more as marketing copy."

"I think I get what you're saying."

"You're displaying your art, but for this account, you're supposed to be making commercials, so to speak, for Birch Brook Campground."

"Okay. Yeah." He nodded and then looked at her. "Will you help me?"

Hannah was torn. Taking a break from social media was

a big part of why she'd told Erika she wanted three months off. Even though they'd hired somebody to take over their accounts, Hannah had seen the shift from a typical amount of criticism and negativity to what had come after the viral episode—anger, hate and harassment. The internet was so baked into her regular day-to-day life that this trip not only gave her the time and space to think, but it encouraged her to stay offline.

Ways to tweak and improve his captions were already popping into her head, though. Maybe it wouldn't hurt to coach him a little.

"I can do that," she said, and the smile he gave her felt like a reward.

"That would be amazing," he said. "Most of the campers will be leaving tomorrow, so maybe we can get together this week. My brother's coming up to stay in the small cabin to get some writing done, but other than that, it should be quiet. I hope."

She hoped so, too. Even if it meant doing some marketing work, she welcomed an excuse to spend more time with him. "I'll give it some thought in the meantime."

"Me, too," he said. He looked like he was going to say more, but then a dog barked and a woman made a sound that wasn't quite a scream, but was definitely distress. "I think our furry friend wandered into the wrong site."

"That's going to put a damper on their weekend."

He pushed himself to his feet and then picked up his camera. "I'll go see what's up and then probably grab some Dawn and white vinegar from the store, since I doubt they brought any with them. But we'll figure out a time to get together, right?"

"Absolutely," she said. "I'm looking forward to it."

Just not for the reasons he thought.

Chapter Fourteen

"You should go see if Danny's planning to leave today."

Rob laughed, shaking his head. "Nope. All my life, you've been dumping the stuff you don't want to do onto me, but I'm not going to be the one who breaks Danny's concentration if the writing's going well."

When their older brother arrived Monday morning with his laptop and a bulk-size box of K-Cups, he'd said he only needed a couple of nights to clear his head and he'd be gone Wednesday. And while he wasn't expected to honor the 11:00 a.m. checkout time exactly, it was midafternoon and as far as they knew, he'd yet to emerge from the cabin.

"I cleaned the bathhouses this morning," Brian pointed out.

"And I did them yesterday, and Joey did it the whole weekend. What's your point?"

"What's it going to take? An extra turn scrubbing toilets? Cooking for a week? I get stuck on lifeguard duty?"

Rob snorted. "Looking out the window a few times to make sure nobody's breaking the rules is hardly lifeguard duty."

"I've got it," Brian said as he slapped a hand down on the counter, waking Stella, who wasn't at all impressed by having her nap interrupted. "I won't tell our two business partners that you're violating the business agreement."

"Seriously? First, I haven't violated anything."

"*Yet.* But you've been at site twenty-nine a lot, for no good reason, and I know she was in here for, like, an hour yesterday."

"A lot of the campers come in and start talking, sometimes for an hour. Sometimes for two."

"I guess it's all in how you frame the story."

"Are you blackmailing me?" When Brian shrugged, Rob threw his empty water bottle at him. Stella sighed, but didn't get up. "You know, there's nothing in any of the business documents we *signed* about me not being allowed to spend time with Hannah."

"We all agreed not to fraternize with the campers."

Rob grinned. "Prove it."

Brian held up his hands. "Okay, how about I'll keep my mouth shut about Hannah…within reason."

"What does that even mean?"

"You're my younger brother, so I'm going to have big-brother-type thoughts about what you're doing. But I'll lay off the fraternizing nonsense."

"Done." He was probably going to be the one who went to the cabin anyway, but at least he'd gotten a concession from his brother. And a concession that might enable him to visit Hannah in peace was a big one.

Now to deal with the other brother.

When he got close to the cabin, he was able to see Hannah's truck was gone, and he felt a pang of disappointment that he couldn't swing by her site after. He hadn't seen her leave, but he'd spent part of the morning in the back part of the campground, trying to fix a muddy spot on the trail that connected to the main ATV trail system. Mud was fun until a bunch of machines tore it up and then it dried into ruts.

When he reached the cabin, he peeked into the windows of Danny's car. It didn't look like he was ready to hit the road anytime soon, so Rob walked onto the porch and knocked on the door.

"What?"

It was definitely more of a roar than an invitation to enter, but Rob opened the door and stepped inside anyway. Danny was at the small table, tapping away on his keyboard. He didn't even look up when Rob closed the door.

Empty gallon-size water bottles were lined up by the door, and the small trash can was full of used K-Cups. At least there were also empty snack wrappers in there and they'd seen his vehicle leave a few times, so he knew Danny had been eating something and wasn't running on caffeine alone.

His brother's hair was sticking up in several directions, and Rob wouldn't have bet against those being the same clothes Danny had been wearing yesterday.

"I guess you pushed through the writer's block."

Danny's fingers paused, hovering over the keys. "Yeah. Kenzie helped me figure out where I'd taken a wrong turn."

"Kenzie from the restaurant?"

"Yeah, I went in there to have some food before the coffee ate a hole through my stomach lining and I sat at the counter with my notebook. There was nobody else there and we started talking and next thing you know, I'm talking through some plot issues and she's really good at being a sounding board."

"I'll leave you to it, I guess."

"I might not leave today."

"I figured that out. But Friday afternoon, a nice couple from Connecticut plans to sleep in here, so things will get awkward real fast if you're still here."

"I'll be out by then."

Rob was going to say more, but Danny started typing again and he probably wouldn't hear him anyway. He backed out of the cabin and, after noting Hannah hadn't pulled in while he was inside, he went back to the store.

"Is he leaving today?" Brian asked when he walked in.

"Doubtful. I told him that the cabin's already reserved for the weekend, though."

"Is he writing or is he lying on the bed, staring at the ceiling fan to keep from throwing his laptop out the window?"

"He's writing. Pretty intensely, too. I guess Kenzie helped him brainstorm some stuff when he went down to the restaurant to eat."

Brian frowned. "He brainstormed story stuff with Kenzie? He usually refuses to talk about his books at all while he's writing them. He won't even tell us what the plot is, never mind let us help with it."

Rob snorted. "To be fair, we don't have a history of being all that helpful."

"I thought his protagonist showing up for Thanksgiving and finding everybody dead would be a hell of a plot twist."

"Uncle Joe writes the horror, not Danny."

A vehicle turned into the campground, and when he saw that it was Hannah's truck, only knowing Brian would never let him live it down kept him from running out the door to greet her. Instead, they exchanged a wave through the windows and she kept going.

When he turned back, he caught Brian staring at him and raised an eyebrow. His brother just held up his hands in silence before going back to the spreadsheet he was working on.

After a few days of making short trips around the area—to the grocery store and the library as well as visiting a few spots of interest—Hannah stayed close to her site on Friday. And her site was close enough to the small cabin so she overheard the heated debate about who was going to clean it.

Rob thought Danny should clean the cabin since he hadn't paid to stay in it and they had people checking in soon. Danny thought Rob should clean it because he had a call with his agent scheduled for the afternoon and he didn't want to talk business while driving, which meant getting home before the call.

It sounded as if Rob actually made Danny show him the appointment in his phone before they compromised and cleaned the cabin together. It didn't take long. They probably argued over who would clean it longer than they actually cleaned, and then she heard Danny's car driving away.

A few minutes later Rob appeared around the end of her camper, as she'd hoped he would.

"Writers are a pain in the butt," he said, dropping into the empty chair. "A writer who's also your brother? I could use a drink right now. I didn't think he was ever going to leave."

"He was a quiet neighbor," she said.

"All he did was type and drink coffee. I was afraid we'd need another dumpster just for his K-Cups."

"Still, having a famous brother must be neat," she said. "I've seen his books. I don't think I've read any, though."

"They're good. Like, literary, I guess. Mainstream? A lot of themes and allegories and all that stuff we had to learn about in high school. They're not as fun to read as Uncle Joe's books, but I like them."

"Your uncle Joe writes, too?"

He chuckled. "I think you knowing Danny's books but

not Uncle Joe's might be a first for the family. Joe Kowalski? The horror writer?"

Her eyes widened. She might live in the true crime space, but she liked her fiction on the nonterrifying side. "Horror? I *definitely* haven't read his books."

"They're both big deals, which is cool."

"You're *all* very cool. You have a great family." She belatedly realized that might be too much and waved a hand. "I mean, from the little time I've spent with them, they seem cool."

"They are. I'm pretty blessed." He sighed. "I have to confess I wish I'd gotten some of those bestselling-author genes, though."

Hannah laughed. "I saw Danny around the campground a couple of times this week, and it didn't look like being a writer's as easy as most people probably think it is."

"Oh, nobody in my family thinks it's easy, that's for sure. But Danny doesn't usually look *this* rough. He's been stuck for a while and finally had a breakthrough, so he was in the zone. The zone is not pretty and can smell sketchy, but it's well caffeinated, at least."

"Did you run those captions and hashtags I sent by your brother?"

He shook his head. "He doesn't care, but I tried some and we're already getting more interaction on our social media. Especially on Instagram. Look."

"You're definitely hitting higher numbers," she said, looking up from the screen a few minutes later. "Are you tracking how much traffic is clicking through to your website from Instagram?"

"I am now. You know, you've never really talked about what you did for work," he said, and she could hear the effort he was putting in to try to sound casual. "It seems like you must have a strong marketing background, and I was thinking maybe you work remotely, but then I remembered you said you were taking this time off. Plus, you know a lot about social media, but you have a history degree."

"I *am* taking this time off." She shrugged. "I'm a podcaster, though it's not something I tell a lot of people."

"Why would you—" He broke off and chuckled. "I guess everybody has a great idea for a podcast, right? Like, sometimes when we're around people we don't really know, Danny will tell people he works at a bookstore."

"At least it's close to the truth."

"Yeah, for a while he was telling people he was an accountant because he thought it was boring and nobody would want to talk about it, but then people would ask him tax questions and he was afraid he'd get them sent to prison."

Hannah laughed, shaking her head. "Never take tax advice from people who get paid to write lies."

"What is your podcast about? History?"

"History, but with a focus on historical true crime events." She smiled wryly. "Which is why it's so amusing to me that I ended up in a campground run by people who think one of the campers is a serial killer."

"Not *is*," he protested. "*Could be.* There's a difference."

"True. So *Improbable Causes* is a podcast like every other true crime podcast, except in our case, all of the crimes happened before 1918." Except for the one that had changed everything—or had the potential to, anyway.

"Why 1918?"

She shrugged. "Because we—my friend Erika and I—started the podcast in 2018 and one hundred years sounded like a good cutoff. I do most of the research and the heavy factual lifting and she does the color commentary and brings the entertainment vibe."

"I'll have to give it a listen."

Hannah imagined Rob falling asleep to the sound of her voice in his ears and cleared her throat. "But what about you? You've never told me what you did before you decided to buy a campground with your brothers."

He sighed. "I had jobs, not a career, I guess. In my heart, photography's my career, but I don't know if you can call it that if it doesn't pay the bills, you know? But all of us did our time with the various family businesses, so I've done landscaping and building. Some bartending. I took a few photography classes at the community college, and I've sold some of my pictures over the years, but I was actually working for Brian—plowing snow, mostly—when we made the decision to buy this place."

"Do you still have a place there or is this your year-round home now?"

"I shared an apartment with a friend of mine, but right around the time we closed on the campground, he and his girlfriend were talking about living together. Since we'd already talked about me and Brian being up here pretty much full-time, it made more sense to put my stuff in Danny's basement and let my buddy and his girlfriend have the apartment."

"You'll live here all winter, then?"

"That's the plan, I guess." He shrugged. "We've talked about maybe leaving the cabins open year-round for snow-mobiling, but we have to shut the water off to the bath-houses and we only have the one heated bathroom in the store, so if we do, it won't be for a couple of years. But if I stay, I can keep an eye on things."

"Brian won't stay here?"

"I doubt it. He's got a lot of contracts for snow removal, and he also owns his house. It's not far from my parents and he loves the place, so selling it didn't make sense for him. During the summer he did some commercial mowing, but he gave up those jobs for this so he'll probably spend winters at home, hoping for a lot of snow, and summers up here."

"The first year or two, I guess it's best to be fluid," she said. "It takes a while to learn a business, but it's got to be easier when there are four of you."

He laughed. "In some ways, yes. In other ways, it can be a challenge. But it feels good to be able to contribute with my photographs, and to be growing the online presence. Thank you for that."

"I think you've done a lot more for this place than grow the social media presence," she said. "But I can see how bringing a skill that's uniquely yours—that none of your brothers can do as well—is important. I'm glad I'm able to help."

"We need to take that walk soon," he said. "To find that foundation. Or to look for it, at least. I'll have to check the forecast because we're supposed to get some rain, I guess. And probably a weekday, but not one when deliveries are scheduled. And Brian will have to be around."

She laughed as he tried to figure it out, scowling the entire time. He was gorgeous when he smiled, but he was also gorgeous when he was serious—when his eyes got intense and his brow furrowed slightly.

"Why don't we play it by ear," she suggested. "When the time presents itself, I'll probably be available since I'm not exactly juggling a heavy schedule over here."

"Okay. I just didn't want you thinking I forgot or anything, or that I don't want to do it."

"I won't let you forget." She held up the book in her lap. "And speaking of forgetting, I finished the book and amnesia? Really?"

"Oh!" Rob leaned forward in his chair. "But do you think the amnesia was real?"

"You think she was faking it?"

"No, like…" He thought about it for a few seconds. "After I read it, I was talking to my mom about it and she has a theory that the author couldn't make the plot work and added the amnesia, like an afterthought."

"Interesting. When I was thinking about the story, there were a lot of things that seemed inconsistent with amnesia, so I thought maybe the character was faking." She growled in frustration. "It was such a good book, but I hate that in the domestic suspense genre, ambiguous endings are okay. Sometimes I guess they want us to draw our own conclusions, but other times I think the author wrote themselves into a corner and the ambiguity is meant to disguise a lack of ending."

Two hours later, when Stella wandered into Hannah's site, the two-person book club was in full swing. They'd even moved their chairs closer together until their legs were touching so they could flip through the book and find passages to back up their arguments.

When Stella nudged Rob's thigh, he looked at his watch and realized how much time had passed. "I think this dog is trying to tell me Brian's cursing my name right now. But let me know if you read the other one, okay?"

"Oh, I will," Hannah said as she gave Stella a good all-over scratch.

In fact, Rob and the dog weren't even out of sight before she had the app open, checking to see if she had a strong enough signal to download the book he'd recommended without walking up to the overflow lot.

If not, she'd make the walk because this was definitely her kind of book club.

Chapter Fifteen

By the following Tuesday, Rob still hadn't managed to carve out time to go for a walk with Hannah. He had some free hours here and there, of course, but he didn't want their time together to be rushed. And he wanted to make sure they had enough time so they could locate the spot she was looking for.

If that foundation was out there, he wanted to find it with her. For whatever reason, it seemed important to her, and that was enough for him.

He and Brian were in the house, relaxing after an unseasonably hot and humid day. It had felt more like August than early June, and since they'd been clearing some woods on the western side of the campground where they were hoping to add two more sites, they were beat.

"It's not supposed to be this hot in June," Brian said, giving the ancient and slightly inadequate window AC unit a sour look. "They said there's supposed to be a bad, slow-moving storm, but that it was going to stay south of us."

The words had barely left his mouth when a flash of lightning lit everything up for a few seconds. Stella bolted from her bed and launched herself onto Brian's lap. She wasn't exactly a lap-size dog, but Brian slid down the chair a little, making his lap as large as possible. The dog curled up in a ball while also managing to get her head under the hem of Brian's T-shirt.

The thunder came in a long, low rumble.

"Way to summon the thunder," Rob said. "Maybe you could manifest us a winning lottery ticket."

"It wasn't a gunshot, at least," Brian said, his arms wrapped around Stella.

"Nope." Rob sighed, going to look out the window. He couldn't see Hannah's camper from here. "Maybe we should assign somebody to pay more attention to the weather."

"Again, they said it was going to miss us. They were wrong, obviously, but it's not like we can change it."

"No, but we could…" He let the words trail off because it was true. He couldn't change the weather, even for Hannah.

The lights dimmed and then flickered, but the power didn't go off. With a curse, Rob leaned closer to the window, but it didn't matter. He still couldn't see her site.

"Hannah's terrified of thunderstorms." He shoved a hand through his hair, remembering that she coped by turning on all the lights in the camper to minimize the lightning. If the power went out, the camper could run off the battery, but those lights weren't as bright. And he was just worried about her. "I'm going over there."

"The storm's here. The sky's going to open up any second and it's going to rain like hell."

"I don't care."

"You know the rules, Bobby."

Rob clenched his jaw for a moment, stopping the harsh words that wanted to spew out. Then he took a deep breath before speaking. "I thought we weren't doing that crap anymore."

"I told you I wouldn't give you a hard time, but Danny and Joey have both expressed some concerns about it."

"What do they even know about it?"

"You know how they all talk down there. And were you trying to hide it? Because eating alone with her at the cookout and feeding her from your plate probably didn't do you any favors."

"She was eating from my plate. It's not like I was hand-feeding her."

"It attracted attention. You know how it is."

Rob spun to face his brother. "Then fire me. Buy me out. Do a hostile takeover. Whatever the punishment is, do it."

Brian regarded him for a long moment, and then nodded once. "Okay. If you think she needs you, then go. I'll leave the outside lights on, assuming the power holds, but take your cell. If you don't come back, I'm going to assume you're with Hannah, so call if you need me for anything."

As predicted, the storm let loose the rain when he was only halfway to Hannah's camper and Rob was instantly soaked to the skin. Even though he ran most of the way, by the time he got to her site, he knew he was too wet to go inside. But he was still going to check on her.

He knocked loudly in order to be heard, and then stepped back so she could swing the door open.

She had a fleece blanket draped over her shoulders, despite the hot day, and her face was pale. "What are you *doing* running around in this storm?"

"You told me storms terrified you, so I just wanted to make sure you're alright. And not too afraid."

"I'm in a tin can surrounded by trees in the middle of a thunder and lightning storm. What could I possibly be afraid of?"

He would have laughed if she hadn't looked so distressed. "If the power goes out, will you be okay?"

"I'm not okay already, but I have an LED lantern that's pretty bright."

Another clap of thunder cut off her nervous chuckle and she leaped back from the door.

"I'll go so you can close the door," Rob said, turning away.

"Wait. Will you…do you have to go?"

"I don't have to be anywhere," he said, but she didn't move. He tilted his head slightly, a small smile playing with the corners of his mouth. "I can just sit here under the awning and you'll know I'm here."

Then thunder rumbled and she moved away from the door and waved him in. He climbed the steps and pulled the door closed behind him. It wouldn't do much to mute the sound of the storm, especially with the rain pounding the metal camper, but it would help.

"Oh, you're soaked."

"You should have made me stay under the awning." He looked down at the growing dark patch on her floor mat where he was dripping.

"I'll grab you a towel from the bathroom."

He laughed. "I'm pretty sure a towel's not going to help. I'll just hang out here and drip."

Just then, lightning lit up the darkness so intensely, even her blackout curtains didn't help. Hannah gasped and grabbed the front of his hoodie, jerking him away from the door.

"It's okay," he said, cupping his hand around the side of her neck so his thumb could stroke her cheek. Her pulse was racing under his palm, and her skin was pale.

There was no way he could stand her being like this.

"I'll be right back."

"*No.* You can't go out there."

"I'm not. I'm going in the bathroom super quick to get a towel."

He didn't just grab a towel, though. After closing the door of the tiny bathroom, he managed to strip down to his boxer briefs, which were slightly damp around the bottoms, but miraculously dry for the most part. The wet clothes, he dropped in the bottom of her shower.

Putting them back on later was going to suck, but there wasn't much he could do about it. Then, even though boxer briefs were no more revealing than shorts or swim trunks and it seemed unnecessary to him, he wrapped the towel around his waist.

When he left the bathroom, Hannah was standing in the same spot that he'd left her. She had her eyes closed and her hands over her ears, and she was trembling.

He didn't blame her for being scared. Thunderstorms didn't bother him, outside of worrying about property damage, but this was a bad one and being in a tin can definitely didn't help.

When she opened her eyes and she saw him, her eyes widened. "Oh."

"I'm not naked under the towel. I mean, boxer briefs aren't much, but I didn't want to soak your cushions with my wet jeans and—"

"No, it's fine. As distractions go, it's a good one." Until another flash of lightning made her jump. "I'm not usually this bad. But this one seems really close for some reason."

"Because it *is* close." And he didn't want to say anything to her, but it was supposed to last for a while. This wasn't one of those quick storms that hit hard and fast at the end of a hot and humid day. "Do you want to sit down?"

She looked at the dinette, which had the panoramic windows. Even with the heavy curtains, he could see she didn't want to sit there. There was a window next to her bed, too. It was smaller, but it would still light up.

Rob looked around, helplessness starting to set in, but then he saw the thin throw made of dark, plaid flannel. He could work with that.

"It's Blanket Fort of Doom time."

"Blanket Fort of Doom?" Hannah hugged her arms to her chest as Rob started moving around.

"Trust me. You'll love it."

She didn't really have a choice, since she'd practically begged him to come in. What had she been thinking? Not only did he probably have to check on other campsites besides hers, but he'd stripped off those wet clothes. That meant, at some point, he was going to have to put them back on.

But he seemed content, so she stood back and let him do his thing. As she watched, he took the cushions off the dinette benches and carried them to the back of the camper.

"Oh, nice pillow situation," he said, referring to her nest. "That helps."

He stood the dinette cushions on end at the head and foot of the bed. It probably wasn't easy since he had to keep grabbing at the towel. Another lightning strike, which seemed impossibly close, made her freeze with fear. On the plus side, it kept her from telling him he could drop the towel.

Then he took her flannel throw and draped it over the top of the cushions. It took him a couple of tries to get it to stay, and he used a few throw pillows to anchor the dinette cushions, but he succeeded in making a cozy-looking tent out of her bed.

"Okay, crawl in there," he said. "We can probably leave the side facing the cabin up so it doesn't get too hot."

We? Hannah walked by him, trying not to brush against

his naked skin, because if she touched him, she might want to keep touching him. She heard him rummaging around, but by the time she'd climbed into the tent, he was behind her.

"It's a small space, but I promise I'll be a gentleman," he said, crawling in after her.

If she was feeling at all sexy, she might have told him how disappointing that promise was, but she was afraid her voice would be squeaky from fear instead of sultry.

She blinked when he turned on the small LED lantern she kept by the stove. It lit up the small space like a surgical suite. After he hit a couple of buttons on his phone, a country love song filled the silence. And he'd also grabbed two bottles of water from the fridge and two granola bars.

"Welcome to the Blanket Fort of Doom," he said, looking very pleased with himself.

To be honest, she was pretty pleased with him, too. Despite his snack choice. "You even brought granola bars."

"Just in case you want a snack. I'm not a fan, but no blanket fort is complete without snacks."

"I'm not a fan of them, either."

He looked from her face to the granola bars and back, his brow furrowed. "But they're yours."

"They're my emergency granola bars."

"So you'll eat them in an emergency? Why not buy emergency Snickers? Or emergency doughnuts?"

"They're my emergency granola bars because when they're all I have left, I know it's an emergency and I have to go grocery shopping right away or I'll have to eat them."

His laughter drowned out the storm and Hannah laughed with him, snug and safe in his Blanket Fort of Doom.

"Tell me about your very favorite book," he said. "Like, if you could only own one book for the rest of your life, which one would it be?"

Hannah should have been able to answer that, but in that moment, she couldn't remember a single book she'd ever read. The only thoughts in her head were about Rob. The way the heat from all that naked skin was chasing away the chill of her fear. The way he must have showered after working outside all day, because she could smell his shampoo, despite him having gotten soaked in the rain.

His arm was under her, so his biceps were her pillow. His leg was pressed against hers. She wanted to rest her palm on his naked chest and feel the slow rise and fall of his chest.

And then she…just did. Hannah placed her hand on his chest, fingers splayed, and felt the quick intake of his breath. She was still, waiting to see if he'd try to shift away from her or signal discomfort in some other way, but he snuggled deeper into the nest and rested his face against her hair.

"You're trying to distract me so you don't have to tell me your favorite book, aren't you?" His voice was low and a little husky. "It's embarrassing, right?"

"I'm not embarrassed by liking things," she said, slightly offended, but not enough to move her hand. "It's just hard to choose. What's *your* favorite book?"

"Like you said, it's hard to choose, but right now, it's our book club book."

She laughed, almost forgetting the storm raging outside. "That was an exceptionally good book club, even without wine and cheese."

"We don't have wine at the store, but I can bring some slices of American cheese to the next one."

"Hey, cheese is cheese."

An intense clap of thunder made her jerk, but he wrapped his arms around her and her body melted against his.

"If books can't even distract you, we might have to try something else."

"The storm is pretty loud. What do you have in mind?"

Hannah caught just a glimpse of the corner of his mouth tilting into a crooked grin before his lips claimed hers. She sighed into the kiss, and her hands explored his chest and his shoulders. Then, when his tongue danced over hers, she slid her arm under him so she could hold him close.

Rob moaned against her mouth, his hand sliding over her hip. Everything faded away except his kisses and his touch. Hannah wanted more. She wanted to be as almost naked as he was—to feel the warmth of his skin down her entire body.

But when her hand reached the bottom of his back and her fingertips flirted with sliding under the waistband of his boxer briefs, he broke off the kiss and she felt the subtle way his body shifted away from hers.

Their quick, shallow breaths mingled, and her pulse slowed beat by beat as he gazed into her eyes and brushed her hair back from her cheek. Then he lowered his forehead so it rested against hers.

"This is going to be the hardest thing I'll ever say in my life," he said, and her stomach knotted with apprehension. "But we're not going to have sex. I mean, we are—I hope—but not tonight."

She frowned, doing her best not to pout. "If we're going to anyway, why not tonight?"

"Because I came here to check on you because you were scared. And I'm halfway to naked because I got soaked by the rain. And we're in your bed because I was trying to make you comfortable." He ran his thumb over her bottom lip. "There are no strings with the Blanket Fort of Doom."

"No strings necessary, but an Orgasm of Doom sounds awesome, doesn't it?"

He groaned. "Very awesome. But when I make love to

you, Hannah, I want it to be after a good day, when I'm in my underwear because you tore my clothes off. I don't want to lie awake after wondering if I took advantage of you when you weren't feeling your strongest."

"The storm has mostly passed," she pointed out.

"But it's still why I'm here in your bed in the first place."

Hannah wanted to argue the point. She knew better than him what frame of mind she was in. But she could see it mattered to him, and she didn't want him to have any regrets because the moment didn't feel right to him.

"Fine," she said, not even trying to sound gracious about it. "But we can make out a little more."

"Absolutely. A *lot* more, even."

"I should warn you now, I don't make breakfast."

He kissed her forehead. "I'll be gone before you wake up, since it's my turn to clean the bathhouses."

"Are you going to get thrown out of the family business for being here?"

"No. Brian gave up, and we don't really care what Joey and Danny think."

She knew that wasn't true. Rob cared very much what his brothers thought. But he clearly didn't want to think about that right now, so she skimmed her fingertips over his chest.

That got his attention. With a growling sound that made her giggle, he buried his hand in her hair and lowered his mouth to hers.

There was a lot more kissing and a lot more touching—her hands caressing his bare skin, but only from the waist up—and as she drifted off to sleep in Rob's arms, she heard the faintest rumble of thunder and smiled.

Chapter Sixteen

The only thing worse than doing the walk of shame was doing it in cold, sopping wet clothes. Rob gritted his teeth and walked fast, willing to risk the chafing if it meant less of a chance he'd be spotted in the dim light of very early morning.

He'd been tempted to gather up the wet laundry and sprint across the campground in his boxer briefs, and he might have done it if he wasn't one of the owners. After all the work he'd put into the social media accounts, he'd be the laughingstock of the family if the campground went viral because one of the owners was running around in his underwear.

After making sure he hummed as he went into the house—a habit he'd gotten into so Stella would know it was him and not bother barking or getting out of bed—Rob stripped out of the wet clothes and took a fast, hot shower. As much as he'd like to stretch out and go back to sleep, he got dressed and crept out of the house.

Luckily, he only had to worry about the main bathhouse this morning. They locked the one on the hill when nobody was staying in the cabins because people would just ride in from the ATV trails, use that bathhouse rather than the one in the store so they didn't feel obligated to buy something, and then leave. They got tired of the bathhouse on the hill being muddy and devoid of toilet paper, even when there were no campers staying up there, so they'd padlocked it.

Because there were only two transient sites rented during this week, he made quick work of cleaning and restocking, but Brian was up and making breakfast when he got back to the house.

After giving Stella a quick tousle, Rob poured himself a coffee and sat at the table to drink the much-needed caffeine. "Can you not kill my eggs today? Over easy would be great."

Brian snorted. "I gave up on over easy years ago. The yolks always break when I flip them."

"You could practice instead of just giving up."

Brian set the carton of eggs on the counter with enough force to make Rob wince. They might have to eat a *lot* of eggs this morning if he broke them. "You're in a pretty piss-poor mood for somebody who had sex last night."

"I did *not* have sex last night, actually, not that it's any of your business."

"Okay. The mood makes more sense now." Brian cocked his head. "But you were out all night."

"Yeah. We hung out, but it didn't feel like the right time, with the storm and all."

When his brother stared at him for a long moment, Rob just stared back until Brian shrugged and turned back to the stove. He didn't have to justify his decisions to anybody, and he had no regrets about not surrendering to his desire for Hannah.

He refilled his coffee cup just as the toaster popped, and he buttered the toast while Brian finished the eggs.

When they sat, he saw that his brother had made an effort

with the eggs. Sure, one of the yolks had broken, but they were in the ballpark of over easy. "This looks good. Thanks."

"No problem."

They ate in silence for a while, the only sound in the house the rattle and chomp of Stella working her way through her bowl of kibble. The quiet didn't bother Rob, except for the fact he could tell by the sighing and shifting that his brother had something on his mind. And when Brian hesitated to voice his thoughts, they were usually heavy.

"Spit it out," Rob finally said.

"Is it serious?"

Rob sighed and set his fork across his empty plate. There was no sense in pretending he didn't know what Brian was asking. "I mean, I'm falling for her. That's not a secret."

"Definitely not a secret." Brian shrugged. "From us, anyway. Have you told *her* you're falling for her?"

"Of course not."

"Don't you think you should?"

"Nope." Of course he knew he *should*, but he wasn't going to. Hannah had taken off for three months so she could figure her life out with no pressure. He wasn't going to pile an entirely different kind of pressure on top of her.

"It seems like she's pretty into you. Has *she* said anything?"

He shrugged. "I mean, it's pretty obvious we're into each other. I didn't sleep on the folded down dinette, if you know what I mean. But it's not going anywhere, so there's no sense in bringing feelings into the mix."

"Seems like the feelings are already mixed in."

"For me, sure. But as long as I keep those feelings to myself, they're my problem and not hers. And maybe I should put a little more distance between us." He wasn't sure how he'd manage that, but just the fact he was having this conversation with his brother was a sign he was already in too deep.

Brian scoffed, pushing back his chair and picking up his plate. "Why are you so sure she'd see you catching feelings as a problem?"

"She's got plans that don't include New Hampshire and my plans sure as hell don't include California, so catching feelings? A problem."

"Hannah strikes me as the kind of person who'd like to work the problem together." He tossed Stella a toast crust and shrugged. "But what the hell do I know? I thought I was happily married and then—*bam*—Kelly doesn't actually love me, there's somebody else and she's divorcing me. Maybe I'm not great at reading people."

"That was a *her* problem, not a *you* problem," Rob said firmly. It wasn't the first time Brian had been told that, but it didn't always stick. He'd been blindsided and spent a lot of time wondering what he'd missed and what he'd done wrong. To say Rob wasn't a fan of his former sister-in-law would be an understatement.

Once they'd cleaned up and gone to the store to do some paperwork—Wednesday had become the best day for it because there was little activity in the campground to distract them—Rob's thoughts kept wandering back to Hannah. They always did, but waking up that morning in her bed had taken it to a new level.

She still hadn't found that foundation, and he'd promised he'd take her out there. He saved the spreadsheet he was ignoring and pulled up the group calendar that tracked the four brothers and their campground reservations as well as deliveries and accounts payable. It was hectic, visually, but necessary.

When he muttered under his breath, it caught Brian's attention. "What are you looking for?"

Rob scrolled to a likely day and then pulled up the weather forecast on his phone. "A good day for me to be gone for a good chunk of it. Hannah still wants to look for that foundation and even with the rain we've had, it should be drying up out there."

"So you're going to put distance between you by spending the day walking around the woods with her?"

"I told her I would. And putting distance between us is one of those things that sounds like the right thing to do in theory, but might not be so easy to actually do."

"I could go out there with her."

Rob scowled, not liking the idea of his brother spending the day with Hannah. Not that he was worried about Brian trying to make a move—he would never be disloyal like that and Rob knew that—but because that would be time he didn't get to spend with her himself.

"I'm going to help her find the thing she's looking for," he insisted, and it wasn't until he noticed Brian staring at him that he realized that could be taken so many ways. "If that foundation is out there, we'll find it."

"Bobby, do you remember when we were kids and Dad took us sledding and he said to stay on the packed-down sled tracks or we'd hit a tree and get hurt? And you took your sled off to the fresh snow and you hit a tree and broke your arm?" When Brian paused, Rob nodded. "This feels like that."

"You're wearing bug spray, right?"

Hannah snorted at the obvious question, even though she was thoroughly charmed by his concern. "I put on so much bug spray, I think it's soaked into my DNA. It might be my superpower now."

"The bug spray that smells pretty and is good for your skin? Or the bug spray that repels bugs?" She leaned closer and he inhaled deeply. Then he coughed and took a step back. "Yep, you're good."

"So I looked over the maps and I have a rough idea of the area I covered the first time."

"We probably don't want to go that way."

"There's a chance I missed it, but it makes more sense to head a little more east and cover new ground."

"I'm just following you."

"Unless I fall in a well."

He chuckled. "It would suck if you fell in a well and you were totally fine until I fell in on top of you."

"Maybe we'll walk side by side," she suggested.

And they did, which made it a lot easier to hold hands. She had a moment when his fingers first threaded through hers to wonder if she was getting in over her head, but it was a very brief moment. He squeezed her hand and gave her a smile that erased everything but the pleasure being with him brought.

"I have to ask," he said when they'd gone maybe an eighth of a mile into the woods. "Do you really think you're going to find something out there that'll solve the mystery?"

She laughed. "Hey, it's only been a century and a half. It's possible I'll just stumble over a skeleton with the murder weapon still embedded in a bone. Maybe a confession in an old glass bottle sealed with wax?"

When he gave her a look—complete with hesitant smile—that made it clear he wasn't quite sure if she was joking or not, she laughed hard, so hard they had to stop for a minute. He held a branch out of her way when they resumed, which was good since she was wiping tears out of her eyes and might not have seen it.

"Tell me about her."

"Elizabeth?" Hannah sighed. "She was born Elizabeth Anne Cook, which was *not* a unique name in colonial New England by any means. She married Elmer Whaley in 1869 at the age of sixteen. In 1872, there's mention in a congregation member's diary that she seemed to have gone away without a word to anybody. Many people have scoured records and personal documents, but she just disappeared from history."

"What do you think happened to her?"

She shrugged. "Nobody knows, and we're not really supposed to guess. But I know she married Whaley in 1869 and that's the last mention of her in the Whaley family bible. No mentions of babies and no death notation."

"They usually kept track of those things, right?"

"Absolutely. They kept meticulous records and family bibles are a treasure trove of genealogical information. But after Elizabeth's marriage in 1869, she doesn't show up in the family bibles—neither the Cooks' nor the Whaleys'— or census or church records."

"And that's unusual. So I can see why she'd be considered a missing person."

Hannah nodded. "And in 1873, Elmer married Elizabeth's sister, Rebecca, and they had a son who was, according to midwifery and church records, quite premature. And that *premature* would be in air quotes if you weren't holding my hand."

"No!" Rob stopped walking, his eyes wide.

"Yes. The marriage and birth are in the family bible."

"But nowhere does anything say what happened to

Elizabeth?" When she shook her head, he started walking again. "So she didn't give him a child right away, so he killed her and married her sister. Or he fell in love with her sister and since they didn't have any children yet, he killed her and started over before it got more complicated."

"Those are two theories, yes."

"What else could it be? That bastard totally killed her."

Hannah laughed, appreciating his enthusiasm, despite the fact he was jumping to conclusions.

"She might have run away," she said. "Or she could have been kidnapped or fallen in an abandoned well. Maybe Elmer Whaley loved his wife and couldn't bring himself to write her out of the family bible without knowing what happened to her. But a man needed a wife and wanted children, so he married her sister."

"According to the midwife, they were getting busy before the vows were said."

"Or she actually gave birth to a premature infant," she cautioned. "But let's say they *were* getting busy. It could have been two grieving souls finding comfort in each other's arms."

He was frowning again. "So your job is talking about stories that literally have no ending?"

"Some of them do, but a lot of them don't. Maybe that's why I get frustrated when I'm reading fiction and the ending is ambiguous."

"What do you really think happened to Elizabeth?"

"It's a question I've been asking for years, but the answers can only be found in and substantiated by historical records, and she disappeared."

"Okay, but you must have a favorite theory." He nudged her with his elbow. "Just between us."

"Just between us, I think he got angry about the lack of

children, killed her and then married her younger sister." Stones in a line that were maybe a stone wall but might be a foundation caught her attention. "Look."

There wasn't much of it left, but when Hannah pushed through the last of the brush in the way, the stones were clearly the remains of a very old foundation. She stood there for a long time, simply breathing and blinking away the tears that kept welling in her eyes.

She was standing in a place Elizabeth Whaley had stood over a century and a half before her, and she soaked it in. There would be no answers here, of course, but it was important to her that a woman who had simply disappeared wasn't forgotten.

That was why her show had mattered so much to her. No, she couldn't change history. And maybe a crime that happened so long ago wasn't relevant. But she liked to share the stories of those whose stories might otherwise go untold.

When she finally moved, she turned to see Rob leaning against a tree, watching her. His camera still dangled from the neck strap, and the lens cap was still on.

"I thought you'd be taking pictures," she said after clearing the emotion from her throat.

He pushed himself away from the tree and popped the lens cap off. "Oh, I will. It just seemed like you were having a moment and I didn't want to intrude."

Smiling, she gestured toward the foundation, indicating that it was all his. She tried to stay out of his way while she explored the area, looking at the stones that made up the crumbling remains of Elizabeth Whaley's home. Cautiously, of course, because there had been a brook running close by according to maps roughly sketched in her time, but there probably would still have been a well and a root cellar of some kind nearby.

Then Rob caught her eye. He stretched out on his stomach, the camera almost on the ground as he framed a shot that had some sinister-looking dead trees behind the most intact part of the foundation.

Setting the camera down and using the display screen to line up his shot probably would have been adequate, but she liked the way he wanted to see it with his eye before he tried to capture what he was seeing with the lens.

"Another book cover for your uncle?" she asked when he was on his feet again, brushing debris from the ground off his clothes.

He grinned. "Or for your book, if you ever write one about Elizabeth."

"I've thought about it," she admitted, feeling the heat in her cheeks. "But there really isn't enough information available for an entire book. And, as we've agreed, stories with no ending are a letdown."

After ensuring it was solid and bug-free, Hannah sat on a fallen log, and she wasn't surprised when he sat next to her. His camera was still in his hand, and he snapped a few more pictures.

Then he put the lens cap on and turned to her. "How does finding this foundation help you make whatever decision you're trying to make?"

"Maybe it doesn't. I don't know." She sighed. "I told you our podcast does historical true crime. The fans started asking for a modern true crime episode, and Erika got really excited about the idea because it would appeal to a broader audience. A broader audience means more listeners, which means more money."

"Money's nice."

"Yeah, it is."

He leaned close, so their shoulders bumped. "You sound really unenthusiastic about the money."

"I like money." She chuckled. "I like money a lot. But the crimes we cover…yes, the people involved have descendants, but generally the folks who knew them personally have all passed on. But we did a murder from the 1970s and I thought the people who were closest to her were gone. I was wrong. The episode went viral and her best friend and her uncle got dragged through the emotional wringer all over again. But it got so much attention and we have the potential to make a *lot* more money. Like significant enough to change not only our lives, but our families', too."

"I don't really listen to podcasts, other than a few sports ones when I remember, but between people *talking* about podcasts and the documentaries on all the streaming networks, I think true crime is a pretty popular thing. I think having to relive the trauma is just a part of life for the family and friends of the victims these days."

"But does that make it right?" She sighed, leaning forward to rest her elbows on her knees. "I can't answer that question for anybody else, but I have to answer it for myself. And, unfortunately, I have to answer it for Erika, too."

Rob rubbed gentle circles on her back. "Do you think having to drive over three thousand miles and then spending three months with Dave and Sheila so you can walk out in the woods and find some old rocks in order to think about it is a strong hint?"

Hannah laughed softly, shaking her head. "To be fair, I didn't know about Dave and Sheila when I made the reservation."

"Can Erika be on two podcasts? Maybe you can continue *Improbable Causes* and she can also do another one with current events."

"Maybe. I know she's had offers, but she said it would stretch her thin and dilute her name, whatever that means. I think I either have to go along or part ways with her. And without Erika's writing and conversational timing, I'm just a history nerd giving a lecture about an obscure crime or mystery that happened so long ago, only I and, like, ten other people care about it."

"I think you're selling yourself short. But something drove you to come here, and that's important."

"Elizabeth was my first episode," she said.

"Ah. I started with the most recent episode and have been working my way back. Your passion for the story really does come through. I mean, your partner's entertaining, but you're *interesting*."

"You've listened to it?" She hadn't really expected him to, but it pleased her that he had.

"Of course I have." The tips of his ears turned a charming shade of pink. "It started as just a way to hear your voice, but you also have a gift for making your listener *care* about the victim, even though it was so long ago."

Tears blurred her vision, and she blinked them away before he could notice them. "I told Elizabeth's story because she'd been forgotten. Most of our episodes have been tales that would otherwise not get talked about."

"I can see why current true crime wouldn't interest you. It's hard to forget a crime that's been a *Dateline* episode and the subject of multiple podcasts and half a dozen documentaries."

"I wouldn't say it doesn't interest me. But my podcast is where true crime and history intersect, and it was Elizabeth who really brought that together for me—wanting to share her story. And it doesn't hurt anybody, which I recently found out can really suck when it does."

"I know it's a decision only you can make, but can I offer an observation?"

She sat up straight, and the hand that had been rubbing her back settled at her waist. "Of course, and not just because you trekked all the way out here with me."

"When you talk about historical true crime, you're very animated. Your face lights up and I can feel your enthusiasm. When you talk about adding more recent crimes to your show, your shoulders drop. Your face pinches a little. You turn your face away." He gave a little shrug. "For what it's worth."

It was worth more than she could say, and since she didn't have words, she leaned over and pressed her lips to his. It was a soft, sweet kiss and he didn't push for more.

Then she ran her hand over his slightly scruffy jaw. "Thank you for bringing me out here today."

"Thank you for letting me tag along," he said. "It was a good day for a walk."

"Of course, now we have to walk all the way back," she said with a groan.

Rob laughed and stood before taking her hands and pulling her to her feet. "I'd offer to give you a piggyback ride, but I split a lot of wood yesterday and I can't guarantee I won't die and leave you to explain to my brothers that you leaving my body in the woods was *totally* an accident."

Chapter Seventeen

"You can look at the calendar to find time to take a walk with your girlfriend, but not see where I blocked myself off of the schedule?" Brian pointed at the monitor. "It's right there."

"She's not my girlfriend."

"Pretty sure she is." Brian's finger swung to point at him instead of the computer. "You two were even seen holding hands, and Sheila sent us a message that it's inappropriate because there should be no special treatment. *And* she sent it through Facebook, so Joey and Danny both saw it before I could delete it."

"I am *not* going to hold Sheila's hand." Rob did like knowing Brian had his back and would have deleted the message. "What exactly do they think Hannah is getting to do that Sheila isn't?"

"Nothing, but that isn't the point. The point is that Hannah *is* your girlfriend."

"I think the point is that you're going to be gone for two days and didn't bother to tell me."

"Two days but only one night. Do you want me to see if Danny or Joey can come up? We won't be busy so I figured you could handle it, but I can probably strong-arm Joey into coming."

Only one night.

For only one night, Rob would have the entire house to himself. And that meant he could have company.

"Bobby." Brian snapped his fingers. "If I'm going to call Joey, sooner is better than later."

"No, I've got it." He shrugged, trying to sound casual instead of like a man who'd just discovered a way to have a real night in with his not-girlfriend. "I was saying you could have told me instead of just entering it and assuming I'd see it."

"Keep giving me crap about it and maybe I'll just stay down south."

For a brief moment, Rob imagined him and Hannah in the house, running the campground together. It was like a punch in the chest because the only thing in their future was the glow of Hannah's taillights as she headed back to California.

"You're not getting out of working that easy," Rob joked, hoping to lighten the mood. "You and Stella can have a great time in the land of drive-throughs and box stores, but you're taking the bathhouses for the whole weekend."

Brian's scowl slowly transitioned to a shrewd look. "How about *you* clean the bathhouses for the whole weekend, and I'll clean my room and put clean bedding on my bed before Stella and I leave."

Rob tried to resist—he didn't want to admit he'd already planned to do just that.

"And I'll keep it to myself," Brian added.

"Done," Rob snapped, and then he turned and walked out the door. Even after it closed behind him, he could hear Brian laughing.

He'd intended to just walk around and cool off—maybe check the recycling bins and see if the UTV or the lawn mower needed gas. Instead, he kept walking and turned toward Hannah's site.

He wasn't sure exactly how he was going to ask her to spend the night in the house, but he wanted to do it now so he didn't get his hopes up. Even worse than her not being interested now that they were out of the cocoon of the blanket fort would be finding out *after* he'd spent two days imagining the night in great detail.

But when he reached site twenty-nine, Hannah wasn't there. The door was open, but he knocked on the side of the camper and got no response. Through the screen door, he couldn't hear any movement, but her truck was still there. She must have gone for a walk, either around the campground or back into the woods.

Disappointment surged through him, until he started the walk back to the store and heard Hannah calling his name. He turned and saw her walking down the hill toward him at a fast clip. She waved, and he reversed direction, meeting her at the front of her truck.

"Were you looking for me?"

If he said he was, he'd be put on the spot as to why and he'd prefer to ease into inviting her over to the house. If he said no and she'd seen him from the top of the hill coming out of her site, she'd wonder why he was denying it.

"I was around and figured I'd say hi." He figured that was a good compromise—yes, he'd stopped by, but he hadn't been seeking her out deliberately.

"I was up in the overflow parking, talking to my dad. They're doing a joint backyard barbecue for him and my sister's husband, so I wanted to call him before they started." She gave him a questioning look. "You and Brian didn't have to go south to see your dad?"

He chuckled. "There's no Father's Day brunch. Dad's

always been pretty chill about it, and with Mother's Day, we only had seasonal campers in, but he knows Sunday is our checkout day for weekenders. And we have to clean the cabins after they're vacated and all that. We called him this morning."

"Come sit if you have time," she said. "The log I usually sit on was still damp from the rain, so I was standing for the entire call."

"I can spare a few minutes."

Luckily, Hannah kept her camp chairs folded and leaned by her door, well under the awning, so they hadn't gotten wet during the overnight shower. Today would have been a good day to take the four-wheelers out. It wasn't actually raining, but the trails wouldn't be dusty and there would be some fun puddles to play in, but he'd gotten sidetracked by the calendar. And now he'd rather sit with Hannah, anyway.

They talked about the campground goings-on for a while. Oscar had slipped his collar last weekend and everybody had been too afraid of the little dog to help catch him.

"So Tony panicked," Rob said. "He was running back and forth in front of the store and pool to try to keep Oscar from running onto Route 3, and Barb was panicking and chasing him in circles."

"When was this? How did I miss the whole thing?"

"Saturday morning, I guess. Your truck was gone."

"Saturday morning…" She thought for a moment. "Oh, I saw a flyer at the market about a yard sale that listed old books, and I always like to check them out when I can."

"Find anything good?"

"Not this time. They didn't mean *old* as in antique or rare. They meant *old* as in bloated, smelly paperbacks from somebody's basement." She held up her hand. "I don't care about the books. What happened with Oscar?"

"Oh, so there was a lot of panicking and arm waving and yelling, which is totally how you want to calm a spooked dog. Then Connie went into her camper and got a slice of cheese. As soon as she crinkled that wrapper, Oscar was at her feet, sitting pretty."

Hannah laughed. "A happy ending, then. With bonus cheese."

"A happy ending for everybody except Connie, who had to listen to a lecture from Dave about giving people food to dogs."

"Have you considered finding some kind of super epoxy and sealing their doors closed so they can't get in and have to go home?"

"No, we haven't considered that, but Brian and I have both thought about hooking the tractor onto their camper and dragging it to the curb."

"You could pretend there's something wrong with their electrical system that requires them to pull their camper out."

He chuckled. "Okay, *that* we thought of, although Brian said the sewer lines."

"Oh, that's better. They can run on the battery and propane without electricity, but nobody wants to mess with sewer lines."

"My dad talked us out of just telling them to leave because they're jerks and we're tired of hearing them complain."

She made a questioning sound. "But isn't this supposed to be a fun place to relax?"

"Yeah, but they don't interact with the transients much, and most of the seasonal campers either avoid them or seem to actually like them for some reason. And like my dad said, it's not good to limit your business to only people you like."

"I guess, but it's not a regular transaction. This is also

a community of people you're spending the entire summer with."

Rob shrugged. There wasn't much they could do about Dave and Sheila. They weren't breaking any rules, since there was no personality clause in the agreement they'd signed.

"I have to get back because I've got a running to-do list and the longer I leave it unattended, the more stuff Brian adds to it."

"I have a load in the washer down at the bathhouse, so I should go switch it before I forget all about it."

Rob knew it was now or never. "Before I go, I have a question for you."

Something in her expression changed just enough to let him know she was apprehensive about what he might ask her. "Okay."

"Brian's going home for a couple of days. Stella has a vet appointment and he's got some other things to take care of." He paused, taking a deep breath and marshaling his courage. "Would you like to come over to the house for dinner Tuesday evening? And maybe a movie?"

Her expression cleared instantly, and then she laughed as she pointed toward the house. "Rob Kowalski, are you inviting me on a date to over there?"

"Hard to resist, I know."

"What movie?"

"You can pick." His pulse kicked up a notch. "Does that mean you'll come?"

"I would be happy to go on a date to over there with you," she said. "First Date of Doom?"

Rob chuckled. "Hopefully not in the burnt-dinner-and-disaster-flick kind of way."

"No, in an epic way." She slapped him on the arm. "And I guess it's not our first date, really. More like our third."

"Third?" He liked the sound of that. Good things tended to happen on third dates. "How do you figure?"

"You took me to see the waterfall. First kiss and all, so it must have been our first date. And then there was the Blanket Fort of Doom."

Rob laughed. "That was a date, huh?"

"It didn't start that way, but there were drinks, snacks, kissing, romantic music and more kissing, so definitely a second date."

"Granola bars we didn't eat and water, which isn't my best work, but there *was* music and kissing. And technically I invited you personally to the cookout."

"No." She shook her head, laughing. "Your mother *and* your grandmother were there."

"So not a date?"

"Definitely not a date."

"I'm looking forward to our third date, then."

"Me, too. And I'll walk with you as far as the bathhouse, I guess."

Rob always wanted to spend as much time as he could with her, but he realized the critical mistake too late— because they were right in the middle of the campground she just gave him a goodbye wave and they went their separate ways. No goodbye kiss.

There was heat in her eyes before they split, though, and a promise in the smile she gave him.

But in that moment between him saying he had a question for her and then telling her what the question was, Hannah had tensed up. She'd been anticipating a question she didn't want to hear, and all Rob could come up with as an explanation was that she'd been afraid he'd ask her to define their relationship or ask her about where she saw it going come the end of July.

That was a conversation she clearly didn't want to have, so if he wanted things to keep on as they were—which he very much did—he was going to have to keep his mouth shut.

On Tuesday evening, Hannah stood on the step of Rob's house, trying to calm her nerves.

Apparently, she was really doing this. If the butterflies in her stomach and the fact she hadn't been able to sit still for the last hour weren't confirmation enough, she'd shaved her legs. That was no easy feat in the tiny camper bathroom.

It was ridiculous to be nervous. Not only had they already had their hands all over each other, but he'd spent the night in her bed. And he'd been almost naked at the time. She would very much like for him to be in a bed with her *actually* naked.

"You know I can see you with my superspy doorbell, right?" His voice came out of the device with a slightly tinny note.

Startled, Hannah pressed her hand to her heart and laughed. "Don't sneak up on me like that."

"Were you planning to actually ring that doorbell or just come in or…?"

"I was just standing here to test how good your surveillance system is."

Rob pulled the door open. "It's not as effective as Stella, but I knew you were out here."

She looked at the device. "Even if I don't ring it?"

"I have a confession." He chuckled. "I actually knew you were out here because I've been looking out the window every two minutes for the last hour."

"I'm right on time."

"But today felt ninety hours long." He grinned and stepped back. "Are you coming in?"

As soon as Hannah crossed the threshold, Rob hauled her up against him and kicked the door closed. She was ready when his mouth claimed hers and she wrapped her arms around his neck. The kiss was hungry and she moaned as he backed her up against the door.

Only when she was melting in his arms and she wasn't sure if being pinned between his body and the door was the only thing holding her up did Rob break off the kiss. He smiled, the heat in his gaze almost as potent as the feel of his lips on hers.

"Wow," she said breathlessly. "Way better than a welcome mat."

"Wait until you see dinner."

She wouldn't say it out loud, but the last thing Hannah wanted to do right now was sit down and eat a meal, because food was the last thing on her mind. The first thing on her mind was stripping Rob's clothes off. But he'd invited her for a date night and dinner was part of it.

She toed off her shoes and kicked them toward the small pile of men's shoes next to the door, and then she followed him into the kitchen. From what she could see of the house from here, there wasn't much in the way of decor—which wasn't surprising since they'd been focused on the campground—and it was badly in need of updating. But it was clean, and not the kind of clean that spoke of a panicked surface cleaning because a date was arriving.

"It was hot today and we both eat a lot off the grill, so I hit my aunt up for her Cape Cod chicken salad recipe and made wraps, with a side salad," he said. "I hope that's okay. I do have some microwave pizzas as a backup."

"Sounds perfect," she said, and she smiled when he pulled her chair out for her. "The wraps, I mean, though I do like a good microwave pizza from time to time."

All the anxiety about this date that had built up over the last few hours melted away over dinner. They fell into easy conversation, and Hannah liked that they both seemed to be avoiding talking about anything that could circle back to their families or their jobs.

This night was just about them, as it should be, and the light meal was delicious. It also made for minimal cleanup, which was a bonus.

"What do you want to watch?" he asked while he dried the few dishes they'd used. She'd offered to wash since drying and putting away were hard when you didn't know where anything went.

"I don't know. I like most things, but I don't watch horror. I'm not a huge fan of movies about or set in space. And I should warn you it's really annoying to watch historical movies or true crime with me."

"I'll watch almost anything, but my warning, I guess, is that it's not a great idea to watch a movie with me if it's based on a book I've read."

She laughed. "Oh, that probably should have been on my list, too."

"I suspected that about you." He chuckled. "It might be fun to watch one based on a book we've both read and see which one of us is more annoying."

"We'd need a third party to judge objectively, and somehow I don't see people lining up for that job."

"If Stella was here, we could have her lie down between us and whoever's speaking when she sighs and leaves the room wins."

"I'm not sure Stella is impartial," she pointed out.

"I've seen her running off to visit your site."

Hannah pulled the plug in the sink and used the sponge to wipe around it while Rob dried and put away the last of the dishes she'd washed. Then she wiped down the table and called it good.

"How about a tour of the house?" he asked, running his palms over the sides of his jeans. "I mean, there's not much to see, but I guess it's something people do."

She shrugged. "I'm more of a point-out-where-the-bathroom-is-and-my-bedroom-is-none-of-your-business kind of a host, but it is something people do. And I want to see it. Maybe I can claim I was gathering counterintelligence if the paranoia crowd finds out I was in here."

"You can tell them you were on a mission to disable the spy doorbells."

Hannah laughed as she followed him down a hallway, past doors that were closed over enough so she couldn't see in.

"I guess we'll start at the end of the house and work our way back," he said, pushing open a door.

They walked into a small and plain but very neat bedroom. It had a queen bed and a dresser, and a small closet. There was a line of shoes—mostly of the rugged work boot variety—under the window, and a folded pile of sweatshirts on what looked to be an extra kitchen chair. On top of the dresser was a zipped case she assumed held toiletries, and there was one nightstand with a small lamp and a charging dock.

"Straight for the bedroom," she teased. "I like that. I thought you'd be messier, though."

"Confession—this is Brian's room. With fresh bedding, of course, but I, uh… I have a twin bed. Joey and I have twin beds in the other room. Also, hey! Why did you think I'd be messy?"

"Not messy. Just not this…neat. Did Brian claim this room because he's older?" She paused, running the list of brothers through her head. "Wait, Joey's older than Brian. How did Brian get the big bed?"

"Actually, Stella got the big bed." Rob shrugged. "And Brian's her human."

"And Brian's brothers didn't fight it because it's for Stella. You're all very sweet, you know."

"We really are, though wrangling a campground full of people is easier if that doesn't get around."

She didn't think Rob could hide the fact he was sweet. Sure, she was biased, but he was a nice guy no matter who he was talking to. He even managed to make friendly small talk with Dave and Sheila, which was no easy feat.

Those quiet alarm bells started going off in the back of her mind again. She was already swimming toward the deep end of the pool with Rob, and if she made love with him tonight, she was afraid she wouldn't be able to touch bottom anymore. Being able to tell herself the kisses were just a flirtation and that the night he spent in her camper was simply him being kind weren't much of a life vest, but the little white lies had kept her head above water.

Spending the night with him was the equivalent of tossing the life vest away.

When he gathered her hair and pulled it aside so he could kiss the back of her neck, every argument against getting naked with Rob in that bed became invalid. Or maybe not totally invalid, but something to worry about tomorrow.

His other hand skimmed down her ribs and side until he grasped her hip and pulled her back against his body. The rigid length of his erection pressed against her and she closed her eyes.

She'd definitely worry about tomorrow when tomorrow came.

Rob kissed his way down her neck, and then he released

her hair and turned her in his arms. She tilted her head back to meet his kiss and slid her hands under the hem of his T-shirt so she could run them over his naked back.

They kissed their way toward the bed, only pausing to peel his shirt off, and then hers. His hand cupped her breast and she arched into the touch as he deepened the kiss.

But when he popped the button of her shorts, she had a moment of clarity and leaned back. "Wait. We're in Brian's room."

"I changed all the bedding," he said, his hand sliding down to cup her ass. "We can go to my room if you want, but it's a twin bed and I can't guarantee we won't fall off."

Then he shifted his hand to the space between her thighs and she stopped caring whose bedroom it was.

By the time their clothing was scattered across the floor and she was naked on the bed, she didn't care about anything but the feel of his mouth and his hands. He explored her body, touching her and kissing her until her fingernails bit into his shoulders and a whimper escaped her lips.

Hannah heard the crinkle of a condom wrapper and then he covered her body with his, grinning down at her. She buried her hands in his hair and pulled his face down for a hard, thorough kiss as he reached down and guided himself into her.

Yes, she thought as she lifted her hips. He thrust into her, moving slowly at first as his tongue danced with hers, until he filled her completely. Hannah wrapped her legs around his, holding him there so she could savor the feeling.

His breath was hot against her neck as he dipped his head to close his mouth around her breast. He sucked hard on her taut nipple and she gasped, her legs releasing their hold.

Rob rocked his hips, and Hannah lost herself in the sweet friction. She ran her hands over his shoulders and down his arms. Then she stroked his back, reaching down to feel the curve of his ass. His fingertips bit into her hip until he slid his hand down to the back of her knee, lifting it so he could thrust harder and deeper.

The orgasm rocked Hannah and she might have sighed his name or she might have screamed it. She didn't know anything but the waves of pleasure that took her breath away as she gripped his shoulders.

His orgasm wasn't far behind, and she raked her nails over his back as he found his release. Then, when he collapsed on top of her, she wrapped her arms and legs around him, holding him close as they found their breath.

He buried his face in her neck, pressing kisses there as their breathing slowed and their bodies relaxed. Lifting himself onto his arm, Rob kissed her sweetly as he withdrew, and then he kissed the tip of her nipple.

"I'll be right back," he said, and then he slid out of bed, leaving her missing him already.

When he returned from the bathroom, she took a turn. And then she had a moment of hesitation, wondering if getting dressed, kissing him goodbye and then heading back to her camper was the right thing to do. Maybe if she could maintain the slight bit of distance of not actually *sleeping* with him, she could tell herself she wasn't in too deep.

Then Rob shifted, lifting his head to see where she was, and even in the dark room, she could feel the impact of his gaze on her. When he pulled back the covers, she climbed into bed and smiled when he drew the sheet over her before pulling her closer to his body.

"We never did watch a movie," he muttered against her hair.

She laughed softly. "I never intended to."

Chapter Eighteen

Rob woke slowly from one of the best night's sleep he'd had in a long time. Hannah's body was warm along his, and he smiled against her hair.

"You're awake," she mumbled, and then she stretched, which put a lot more of her body in contact with a lot more of *his* body.

He wanted to wake up like this more often. "You did *not* feel that smile in your hair."

"No, but I did hear you stop snoring."

He winced. "Sorry. It wasn't bad, was it?"

"Nope." She sighed a sleepy sigh. "I'm in the mood for French toast."

Rob thought about what he had not only in the house fridge, but in the store. He could throw that together, but it wasn't his best dish, by any means. If she'd said scrambled eggs, he'd be right on it. "Okay, but are you in the mood for *good* French toast or are you willing to settle for mediocre?"

She made a sound like she was actually thinking about it. "If you have the stuff, I can make it and split the difference to *decent* French toast."

He chuckled and then kissed the side of her neck. "Or we can get dressed and go to the Kitchen—Corinne's Kitchen, I mean—and have excellent French toast, and also real maple syrup and bacon without having to wash the dishes after."

"And magically refilling coffee cups." She rolled to face him, and he pushed her hair back from her face. "Don't you have to clean the bathhouses or be in the store or anything?"

Technically, yes. "No. There hasn't been enough traffic through the campground to worry about the bathhouses. I can spot-check them later. And I'll put a sign in the store window that I'll be back."

"I'm not sure your brothers would be okay with you running off for French toast."

"I don't care what they think."

"Yes, you do." She smiled sweetly, looking into his eyes. "You care very much what they think and I'm pretty sure together we could throw together a reasonably edible breakfast."

The understanding in her eyes squeezed Rob's heart. Yes, he cared what his brothers thought. He wanted them to know they could leave everything in his hands and he would handle it. But he also had a limited amount of time to spend with the woman in his arms.

"They won't care," he said sincerely. "We don't get enough Route 3 traffic stopping to worry about yet. And everybody around here knows the hours aren't set in stone. Think of the magically refilling coffee cups, Hannah."

"Mmm." She snuggled deeper under the blanket. "Five more minutes here. One cup of coffee. Then you give me a half hour to run back to my camper, and then we'll go get the good French toast. How does that sound?"

"Only five more minutes here?" He slid his hand up her side and then cupped her breast, brushing his thumb over her nipple. "That works for me, but I don't know if you'll be satisfied."

As it happened, five minutes was *not* enough time for Hannah and it was another twenty minutes before they rolled out of bed and headed for the coffeepot. And it was a full hour before she pulled up outside of the store to pick him up.

Thankfully, the restaurant wasn't as busy during the week, and they hit the gap between the very early morning crowd and the sleeping-in crowd. Kenzie smiled when they walked in together, her gaze bouncing between the two of them, before she nodded toward a small table in the corner.

"I know you both want coffee," she said with a chuckle. "I'll be right there."

Once they were seated, Hannah leaned across the table to keep her voice low. "It's a good thing Brian already got over the whole fraternizing-with-campers thing, because going to a small-town restaurant together is not stealthy."

"You've got that right."

"She didn't look very surprised."

Rob picked up the menu and gave her a sheepish grin. "Don't forget, she was a witness to me trying to get you into my book club the first time we met, when you were just 'passing through.' Also, I guess Danny comes here a lot whenever he's staying at the campground? I don't even want to think about what he might have said to her."

"I guess we weren't very good at being discreet."

"No. As a matter of fact, Dave and Sheila are concerned I'm giving you special treatment."

"To be fair, I got some pretty special treatment last night."

Before he could respond to that, Kenzie returned to the table with two mugs of coffee. "I also started another pot brewing because I know you'll go through it."

Rob looked at Hannah, eyebrow raised. "Come here often?"

"I've come here a few times, but I think she's talking to you."

"You're both overcaffeinated, to be honest."

"That's fair," Rob said.

"How's your brother doing? I haven't seen him in a while?" Before he could tell her she needed to be more specific—even though he could guess which one she was asking about—she held up her hand with a laugh. "Danny, I mean."

"He's good. Writing a lot, I guess, which means we won't see much of him. He said you helped him break through some writer's block, so I guess we have you to thank for the fact we're not listening to a clacking keyboard in the middle of the night or having to field really random questions, like how long it takes the average person to take a shower."

"That seems like an odd thing to want to know," Kenzie said.

"I know, but I guess something was happening in his book while one of the characters was in the shower and he needed to make sure there was enough time for the thing to happen." He shook his head. "He was so annoyed that none of us knew the answer, as if we timed ourselves regularly and kept notes."

Hannah looked up from her phone. "Eight minutes is the average, apparently."

"Eight minutes?" Rob shrugged. "Now I'm going to have to time myself to see if I'm average."

Kenzie laughed. "We open early and I like sleep, so I'm definitely faster than average. Anyway, what are you eating today?"

They both ordered the French toast, along with the upcharge for real maple syrup rather than the store-bought stuff. When Kenzie went to pass the order to her dad and do a coffee check of her other customers, Rob leaned back in his chair and looked at Hannah over the rim of his coffee cup.

She smiled back at him and lifted her coffee to her lips. He looked at her mouth, memories of last night flooding his mind, and he really wished something would come up to keep Brian down south for another day. Maybe even two. Nothing bad, of course. But he'd love a little more alone time with Hannah.

"Stop looking at me like that in public," she whispered.

When he stretched his leg out until it brushed hers, she didn't pull away, but she gave him a look that told him he better not even think about getting more adventurous. He grinned, thinking about it.

"You're distracting me from my coffee," she warned.

Rob laughed and held up his hands in surrender, though he didn't move his leg.

They chatted about nothing much while they ate their French toast, mostly arguing about which sitcoms weren't funny enough to merit the title. Considering how often they laughed together and seemed to have similar senses of humor, they *really* disagreed about funny television shows.

Like every conversation he had with Hannah, he enjoyed it and didn't want it to end.

"So do you have any regrets?" she asked, and when he looked at her—startled and confused—she barked out a laugh and shook her head. "I mean about buying the campground. Not about... Now that it's been open a couple of months, do you regret it? Is it going better or worse than you thought it would?"

"Better," he said instantly. "For the most part. I was afraid it would cause fights with the four of us—not arguments or just giving each other crap like usual, but the kind of fights that destroy relationships. But we're getting along for the most part and even though Joey isn't totally pulling his weight, it was always him and Danny and then Brian and me, so the two of us work together well enough without him."

"I think protecting relationships is hard when you go into business with family. The potential is always there for a big blowup."

"Were you worried about you and Erika?"

"That was a little different. We were casual friends when we started the podcast, but our relationship grew and strengthened over time. What we have now goes a lot deeper than when we started."

As she spoke, her eyes lost some of their sparkle and she slouched in her chair while drawing random patterns in the syrup on her plate with her fork—like a very sticky Zen garden.

Rob wasn't sure she wanted to talk about it, but he knew he'd be a jerk not to ask about one of the biggest things in her life at the moment. "Are you making any progress in your decision-making? About the podcast, I mean."

The sigh that sounded like it came from the depths of her soul told him she hadn't, but she shrugged. "Still working through it, I guess. It would probably be easier if I didn't love Erika so much."

"If you make a decision based solely on it making Erika happy, doesn't that mean it's not the right move for *you*?"

"Not necessarily." She shrugged. "Okay, maybe, but it's not that easy. We're partners and we built *Improbable Causes* together. I can't just turn my back on that."

Rob nodded. He wanted to keep pushing—to argue that if she only changed the format to please Erika, then Hannah wasn't going to be happy—but he kept his mouth shut.

He couldn't be objective because her and her business partner going their separate ways opened the door for even the slight possibility Hannah might be willing to consider relocating.

It wouldn't be fair of him to influence her—assuming he even could—based on what *he* wanted for her on top of everything else she had to consider.

Talking about her plans definitely dimmed the glow he'd woken up with, and it felt like the wrong time to have brought up a subject that would only remind him how temporary his relationship with Hannah had to be.

By the time Kenzie brought their check, he was ready to get out of there. They'd killed the vibe by turning the conversation from sitcoms to their families and businesses, and heading back to the campground would be a good reset. Maybe he'd spend some time outdoors, splitting wood or trimming weeds or anything that required physical effort.

Then, as she put the truck in gear and pulled out of the parking lot, she said the words that reeled him right back in.

"I want to see your photography portfolio."

"You just click through, like this…" Hannah smiled to herself, but leaned sideways so Rob could reach around her and show her how to click through the slideshow of photos as if she was new to computers.

They were in the store now, since he did actually have to open it, so she was in one of the chairs with his laptop on her lap. She'd been amused when he went through and tweaked his notification and do not disturb settings before handing it to her, though. She'd spent enough time around the family to suspect he was afraid embarrassing messages from his family would pop up.

Hannah looked at the first photo in the slideshow, which

was an action shot of Stella in the air, her body twisting to catch a stick. In the background, slightly out of focus, was Brian, his hands on his hips as he watched his dog.

"It's not a portfolio, exactly," Rob said, and she realized he was still standing over her. "Like, not a professional one. It's just some of my favorite photographs and the ones I think are the best."

"So it's a portfolio." She smiled at him. "Don't minimize your work, Rob. And stop hovering. Either pull up a chair and look at them with me, or go find something to do."

Rob hesitated, running his palms over his hips, and she realized he was actually nervous about her looking at the photographs. He cared what she thought of them, enough to doubt whether he wanted to be next to her while she clicked through them. But she also knew if he went and tried to find busywork to do, he'd still be focused on her reaction.

Finally, he dragged the other chair over so he could sit next to her. It was a lot better than having him staring at her face, trying to judge whether she liked each picture or not, and she clicked through to the next shot.

It was a close-up shot of an older woman's hand clutching an obviously well-loved wooden spoon, folding eggs into flour in a blue mixing bowl. The color adjustments were amazing, with the yellow yolks and the blue bowl popping against the glimpse of a battered butcher-block counter.

"That's Gram," he said simply.

He didn't have to say more. She recognized the photo for what it was—a simple moment in time that captured the essence of his grandmother so simply that hopefully many, many years in the future, when she was gone, the photo would evoke such strong memories of her, he'd almost be able to feel her presence.

She clicked again and there was a photo of a wooden covered bridge. It was artfully framed and the next two—different angles of the same bridge—were the same.

"New England Photography 101," he joked. "Covered bridges are mandatory. And loons."

"There's going to be a red barn and a moose in here, too, right?"

He chuckled. "Of course. Still chasing the elusive moose-standing-*next*-to-a-red-barn shot, though."

With each photograph that passed, Hannah grew more impressed by his talent. He not only had an eye for composition—which was vital, of course—but for capturing the feeling, and she was no photographer, but she assumed that was the hard part. He had an obvious gift and she was glad expanding his potential was a priority for him.

It also seemed very like him to not have them sorted into categorized folders. Whether family members or cool trees or animals or artsy takes, they were all mixed together and she never knew what was going to come up next.

Then she got to the photograph she hadn't even realized she'd been waiting for until it filled the screen. The foundation of the Elizabeth Whaley house, taken from the low vantage point with the gnarled trees in the background.

"Wow," she said. "I watched you take this one, and it was definitely worth lying on the ground for. It came out amazing."

"I'm pretty proud of that one, I have to admit."

"Because of the angle, the trees and the stones really frame the void where the house should be." She leaned closer to the screen. "I mean, that might not be what you were going for and I might lean that way because Elizabeth disappearing is the reason I was out there in the first place, but it really captures the feeling of lost history."

"Hold on to the laptop for a sec because I'm going to kiss you and I don't want it to fall on the floor."

She laughed, but then he did lean over and capture her mouth with his. Clutching the edges of the computer, she held on to it throughout the kiss, and maybe for a few seconds longer.

"Okay," he said. "You can keep going now."

There were several other photos of the foundation, and then she clicked through again and her hand froze over the touch pad.

It was a photo of her. This picture of the foundation was taken from a farther distance than the others, from the back, and she was the focal point. She was standing inside the rectangle of stones, taking note of the pile of smaller stones that were almost buried by earth and moss in the center. It was probably the fireplace and she'd imagined Elizabeth Whaley standing in that very spot, stirring a pot of stew or heating a pot of water to wash with.

And then the woman had simply vanished from history, without so much as a notation as to what happened to her.

Rob had captured that moment somehow. Hannah could see the awe and reverence she'd felt in that moment on her face, and yet her hands were balled into fists at her side by the frustration that across the years, women were so easily erased from history and forgotten.

"I hope you don't mind," Rob said softly, and Hannah realized she'd been staring at the photo for a while without saying anything.

She turned from the image to smile at him. "I love it. I really do. I was just... You captured everything I was feeling in that moment so well that I was sort of feeling it again."

His eyes widened, and a flush of pleasure pinkened his

cheeks. "Thanks. That's… I'm glad you like it. I can send it to you."

"Please do." Hannah could hear Erika's voice in her mind, urging her to go into her laptop files and find the paperwork Rob would have to sign to give her the rights to use the photo for commercial use. It would be an amazing photo for social media, but also for any print work or for articles about the podcast.

But she didn't want to. That moment and this photograph were intensely personal to her—almost raw, emotionally—and she didn't want to expose that to the world to comment on for a temporary uptick in engagement.

The next picture was a red barn, and the laughter popped the bubble of intensity the previous photo of her had trapped her in. Two more angles of the barn, and then there was a photo of his parents sitting on a couch, surrounded by the debris of a Christmas morning. There were boxes and wrapping paper strewed around them, and they were both sprawled against the couch cushions as if utterly exhausted. But there was something joyful about the way they looked at each other that made Hannah's eyes well up with tears. Mike and Lisa Kowalski clearly had the kind of love she could only hope to find someday.

"I was fourteen when I took that one," Rob told her.

"Fourteen?" She blinked back the tears and turned to him. "You were really only fourteen?"

"My grandparents had bought me a really nice digital camera for my birthday. I still have it, actually. It meant so much to me because it wasn't just a gift. It was…like an investment, I guess. They believed in me."

"They were right to." She clicked to the next picture and saw a teenage Brian holding up his middle finger to the camera.

"Yeah, the teen years were fun."

She laughed. "But you can see that he's amused and... I'm not sure how to explain it. There's affection. Like maybe even if I didn't know you were brothers, I'd guess it from the photo."

There were so many photos in the slideshow, and she loved all of them. He had so much talent, and she hoped his plan to use the freedom of owning the campground to further his photography worked out.

"So that's it," he said when she reached the end and it circled back to the photo of Stella catching the stick in mid-air. "What did you think?"

"They're amazing, Rob. Really. Obviously I love the pictures of your family because I can really feel your love for them and how well you know them." She tried not to think of the picture he'd taken of her during their work. He knew *her*, too. "But I can feel it in your landscape pictures, too. How well you know the land and how much you love it really shines through."

She could see the pleasure at her words in his eyes, but he just dipped his hand and lifted a shoulder as though embarrassed by the praise. "It's home, you know? It's almost as much a part of who I am as my family is."

Hannah felt a tightening in the pit of her stomach, and she had to clear her throat to speak past the lump of emotion. Rob really, truly belonged here. "You should find markets for these. Not all of them, obviously. Some are clearly personal, but you could sell any of them."

He nodded. "I was thinking this winter, when I'm not working on the house, I'd really go through them and make an actual professional portfolio of the ones with commercial potential."

It was on the tip of her tongue to offer to help, but obvi-

ously she'd be back in California and she wasn't sure how—
or even *if*—communication between them would work.

Rob looked at the clock on the wall—one that had actual
numbers and hands and was possibly as old as them—and
swore under his breath. "Brian will be back anytime now."

"Seriously? How long have we been sitting here?"

He laughed. "It's always like that with you. Time just
flies by when we're together. He didn't give me an ETA,
but I know he planned to be back by supper because he said
he'd pick up grinders at a place we like that's close enough
to want them, but too far away to actually grab them on a
whim. Damn, do you want me to call him and have him
get you something?"

Her initial urge was to say yes, but the word didn't come
out. She loved spending time with Rob, and she liked his brothers, but there was something so...serious relationship-y, for
want of a better word, about hanging out in the house and
eating with them.

"I can't. I have chicken thawed I need to throw on the
grill or I'll end up throwing it away," she said casually. "And
I should go now so you can at least cross a couple of things
off of whatever list you were supposed to be doing today."

His disappointed sigh echoed her feelings, but he walked
her to the door. "I wish he wasn't coming back for a few
more days. Or weeks."

Hannah smiled, nodding. She felt the same way, although
a tiny voice in her head was reminding her about six weeks
were all she had left here. "Me, too. But you know where
to find me."

Rob hauled her up against his body and kissed her until
she was breathless and could barely remember her own
name, never mind why she had to leave his arms right now.

Then he released her and gave her one of those grins

that was as potent as his kisses. "I absolutely know where to find you."

She left in a hurry, before she could wrap her arms around him and demand more. Brian coming home to find them naked on the floor of the store would be a funny story in ten or fifteen years, but awkward as hell in the moment.

It's always like that with you. Time just flies by when we're together.

As she walked, his words echoed through her mind. He'd been right. It *was* always like that when she was with him—it was so easy and right and time just flew by.

What had she done to herself?

As if there wasn't enough indecision about her future clouding her mind, she'd taken things with Rob to a whole new level. And it wasn't just the sex. That had been incredible and she'd very much like to do it again.

But him sharing his photographs with her felt even more intimate than being naked in his bed. It was as though he'd bared his soul to her and, though she knew that was what good photography felt like, it just deepened her awareness that this was a man she could love with her whole heart.

Love.

Hannah stopped walking, standing in the middle of the dirt road as the word really sank in, and it was like a heat sweeping over her skin that also chilled her to the bone. She was falling in love with Rob Kowalski.

Dammit.

That wasn't supposed to happen. Sure, she enjoyed his company. They laughed together and talked about anything and everything. They loved books and didn't love granola bars. His kisses made her toes curl and the sex was amazing.

But she wasn't supposed to fall in love with him. She was supposed to come to this campground and find clarity.

There were decisions to be made for *Improbable Causes* that would change not only her life, but Erika's, as well.

Maybe she could walk it back. Starting to fall in love with him didn't mean she had to tumble head over heels. She just needed to keep reminding herself over and over that she was leaving in a month, and that her life was in California.

And she would start by opening her laptop and really going through the deluge of information Erika had sent over the last two months. She'd sort it and make notes and really dig into how she felt about the possibilities.

She just needed to refocus herself, and the surge in her feelings for Rob would fade back to a summer infatuation.

Chapter Nineteen

When Brian and Stella pulled back into the campground that evening, Joey and Nora were right behind them. Apparently their brother felt guilty about not being around more, but his wife had plans, so he brought Nora with him.

Rob didn't bother to ask how he thought bringing a child who wasn't old enough to be unsupervised in the campground was helpful. At least Joey recognized he wasn't pulling his weight and he was trying to do something about it.

Unfortunately for Rob, it also meant sleeping on the ancient couch because Nora got his regular bed. Going from sharing the queen-size bed with Hannah to sleeping folded up on cushions that had lost their spring at least a decade ago was quite a downgrade, so he didn't sleep well. And that did nothing for his mood when he woke up the next morning.

While he ate the pancakes Joey made because that's what Nora wanted, he wished he could have woken up with Hannah in his arms again. And again and again and again.

When he was finally able to escape the house, he skimmed the pool and checked the chemical levels. After battling with it for so long, the chore had actually become soothing somehow. He assumed he got the same benefit from tending the pool as other people did from tending a garden, and it was the one job he didn't try to pawn off on Brian—or Joey, when he was around.

Then he opened the store, hoping to have more alone time. He wasn't in a bad mood often and he was trying like hell to shake it off, but he was low-key resenting his brothers for showing up and putting an end to his alone time with Hannah. It wasn't fair, but he still wasn't happy to see Joey walk in an hour later.

"Why aren't you helping Brian clear that fallen tree over by the northern fence?" he demanded with a little more attitude than was merited.

He wasn't surprised when his older brother pinned him with a questioning look before shaking his head. "He decided the two of you can do it next week."

"Oh, *Brian* decided we'd do the physical labor while you're not around?"

"I'm not sure where you got the hair across your ass today, but yes, Brian decided that it wasn't going to get done today because Nora's here and she wants to hang out with him and Stella. And it can't be done over the weekend because it's going to be loud and messy. Therefore, next week. If it's that big of a deal to you, I'll arrange to come back for it."

Rob scrubbed a hand over his face and blew out a long breath. "No. It doesn't make sense to do it while Nora's here *or* to have you come back for one fallen tree. I woke up on the wrong side of the couch this morning, I guess."

"I know it sucks, but I do appreciate you giving up your bed for Nora. She was so excited to come, I didn't have the heart to tell her no. I should have asked Gramps if I could borrow their RV. It doesn't even need a site. I could just park between the house and the store."

Rob chuckled. "When people say our parents and grandparents love us unconditionally, I think there's really tiny fine print that excludes scratching or dinging the RV."

"Or spilling drinks on the cushions." Joey shook his head. "And I'd probably have to take out a loan to fill the fuel tank."

"We'll figure it all out," Rob said. "We have to get through this first summer and then we'll start making improvements for our sakes and not just for the campers."

Joey nodded. "Since Brian's making up things to do that Nora's capable of helping with, I figured I'd do an inventory."

"Inventory of what?"

Joey gestured toward the shelves and coolers. "Of the stuff. We should be doing it regularly."

Rob rolled his eyes, but he didn't care enough to fight about it. It had probably been Danny's idea, anyway. Instead, he opened the campground's email account and started sorting through the bids they'd been collecting for personalized merchandise. At the very least, they needed to get some T-shirts made. The previous owner had left four boxes of them in the storage closet, but they all had the wrong telephone number on them.

It was tedious work because it wasn't just a matter of price. There was also the quality of the product and the screen printing process. And the one that had, hands-down, the best price also had a minimum order size of five hundred. Who the hell needed five hundred T-shirts for anything?

When the door opened and Rob saw Hannah walking in, his entire body lit up. Their gazes locked and the smile she gave him melted away the sour mood he'd been in since the last time he saw her.

Then she spotted Joey, who was actually counting individual bags of marshmallows. The smile stayed on her face, but the wattage dimmed slightly.

"Hi, Hannah," he said. "Good to see you again."

"You, too. You picked a good weekend to be here, I guess. The weather's supposed to be great."

"Hot enough for Nora to be in the pool, but not so hot and humid I die sitting poolside watching her is excellent weather."

"Oh, is Nora here, too?"

"Yeah, but she ran off with Brian and Stella. I'm sure you'll run into her at some point."

When Hannah finally made it to the counter, Rob cast a glance at Joey and found him still counting, so he leaned across the counter and Hannah met him halfway for a quick kiss.

"What can I do for you today?" he asked, trying to keep as much innuendo as possible out of his voice because they weren't alone. She caught it anyway, but other than raising her eyebrow, she didn't respond to it. "Fair warning, not a good weekend to shoplift."

"I don't think our campers are shoplifting," Joey protested loudly. "I think you and Brian are taking stuff off the shelves and not marking it down."

"Maybe a water here and there, but I promise Brian and I are not sitting around eating bags of marshmallows." After taking a breath, he gave all of his attention back to Hannah. "Sorry about that. What's up?"

"It says in the contract that any overnight visitors have to be approved by you." She cleared her throat, still looking down at her phone screen on which he could make out the seasonal agreement for her site. "So I guess I need to get you to approve an overnight guest for me."

Hell no, he didn't want to approve an overnight guest for Hannah—not if it was some guy, anyway.

Not that it was any of his business, of course. And, unless there was some giant red flag, he'd approve her visitor because that was his job. But if she'd invited a man to join her overnight in her camper? Rob wasn't sure what, if any, right he had to question her about it, but he was going to do a lot of tossing and turning and trying not to think about it if it was the case.

"Okay. I just need to write down the details and when your guest arrives, they should check in here." He flipped open a file and took out the guest form they'd put together.

"Name?" he asked, trying to sound as professional as possible.

"Erika Dawson."

His breath left him in a relieved rush before he could stop it, and then he gave her a sheepish grin. "Your podcast partner's coming to visit?"

"Yes, she is." She stabbed her finger at him. "You thought I invited a guy to sleep over."

"No, I didn't," he lied.

"Yes, you did." She put her hands on her hips. "And you were just going to approve that?"

"My job is to keep track of who's in the campground, not to judge your choices." He shrugged, struggling not to grin. "Even really, really bad ones."

Joey cleared his throat and Hannah's cheeks turned a cute shade of pink. She'd obviously forgotten he was there, and while she was comfortable with Brian, she didn't really know Joey.

"I'll just let you fill it out yourself," he said, spinning the paper around so it faced her and setting the pen on top.

While she was bent over the counter to write, Rob looked

at Joey over the top of her head. Then he jerked his head toward the door, trying to send the message he'd like for his brother to go away and leave him alone with Hannah.

Joey pulled out his phone, sat in the chair and started scrolling. Rob wanted to throw something at him, but that would only make it worse. Sometimes older brothers were like feral animals—it didn't pay to show weakness.

"I won't know her license plate number until she gets here. I offered to go get her, but she's renting a car."

"That's fine. Just write *rental* on that space." She did that and then slid the paper back to him. He skimmed the information and then looked up at her. "She's arriving *tomorrow*? How long have you known she's coming?"

"About two hours. She flew into Boston yesterday for a meeting today." She paused, her jaw tightening, and Rob got the impression she wasn't pleased about the meeting. "Then she decided since she'd come that far, she should check out where I'm staying. She'll spend a couple of nights and then drive back to Boston to get a flight home."

Rob ignored the pang in his chest when she said *home* like that. While it might be good for him to have regular reminders this woman lived in California and they were over halfway through her time in New Hampshire, it still got under his skin.

"It'll be interesting," she continued. "Erika's not really the outdoorsy type. Or the camping type. Or the woods and bugs and dirt roads type."

He chuckled. "Introduce her to Dave and Sheila. They can bond over their joy of Birch Brook Campground together."

"I can't think of anybody I dislike enough to do that to. Erika would never speak to me again."

"Decision made," he joked, but the quick glance she

sent his way told him it hadn't landed well. "I can steal a bag of marshmallows for you if you want to introduce her to s'mores."

That made her laugh, much to his relief. "I bought marsh-mallows for just that reason, but I appreciate your willing-ness to turn to a life of crime for our entertainment. The customer service here really is excellent."

It was her turn for the innuendo, he thought, and he winked at her. "Anything you need."

Muttering from Joey's direction caught their attention, though Rob couldn't make out what he said. Probably some-thing along the lines of telling them to get a room. Of course, he *had* a room, but his niece had stolen it.

Hannah had a room, though. She had an entire camper.

"I should let you get back to it," Hannah said. "Thanks for the guest approval."

"Anytime," he said. And then he grinned. "Some con-ditions apply, of course."

She laughed, and then waved goodbye to Joey on her way out. His brother returned the wave and then, as soon as the door closed behind her, he turned to Rob with a smug smile on his face. "Seems like Mom was right."

Rob shrugged. "She usually is, but about what specifi-cally?"

"We were still *at* the seasonals and family welcome cookout when she said you and Hannah were going to end up together. She didn't even wait until we got home to say it."

Rob spent enough time thinking about it. He didn't want to *talk* about it. "Hannah's going to end up back in Califor-nia next month."

"Plans change."

Not when those plans also affected one's family and

business partner. He knew all about that since he couldn't change *his* plans without disappointing *his* family and business partners. "I hate to burst anybody's bubble, but Mom's wrong on this one."

If she'd said Rob was going to fall for Hannah, she would have been right. Or if she'd said they'd end up breaking that no-fraternization rule. Or almost anything except that they'd *end up* together.

They were together now. But he couldn't see any way for them to have a happy ending.

Hannah woke at an indecently early hour the next morning, despite having tossed and turned for what felt like half the night. Erika was coming today. Sometime in the early afternoon, Erika was going to drive into this campground and throw her arms around Hannah, hugging her so hard she wouldn't be able to breathe.

And even though she was still somewhat mad, Hannah couldn't wait.

When Erika had called to tell her she was in New England to meet with a potential sponsor and wanted to see her, Hannah had let her business partner know in no uncertain terms that not only had she overstepped her boundaries, but she'd essentially set them on fire. Erika had insisted it was for good reason and that it would be better to talk in person, so she was going to join her at the campground. Hannah was tempted to tell her not to bother and go ahead and get an earlier flight home, but she didn't.

Yes, there were going to be some tough conversations in their future, but she missed her family and she'd missed her best friend. Video chats and text messages weren't always enough, and she was looking forward to some in-person time.

She'd even cleaned the camper, not that it really needed much. And she'd done a rushed grocery shopping trip to stock up on some of the things Erika liked. She'd also gotten a few things Erika might *not* like, like the makings for s'mores and some bug repellent lotion that was supposed to be all-natural, and which Hannah happened to know smelled so bad it was more of a people repellent. There was no reason she couldn't have some fun with it.

Just when she was starting to wonder if Erika had taken a wrong turn somewhere and ended up in Vermont, her phone chimed.

I'm heeere!

Hannah smiled and headed toward the office, tucking her phone in her pocket. They could talk about the heavy stuff later. For now, her best friend was actually here and she couldn't wait to see her.

The rental car was empty when she got there, so she went into the store. All four of the Kowalski brothers were in there, and Stella immediately trotted over for some pets.

Erika turned away from the desk and Brian when she heard the door open, and her face lit up when she saw Hannah. Her high-pitched squeal of excitement startled the dog and made the men wince, but Hannah just laughed and met her friend halfway across the store, wrapping her in a tight hug.

"I can't believe you're here," she said, surprised when her vision got a little blurry from tears. She really had missed her.

"I can't believe I'm here, either," Erika exclaimed. "Did you see that monster machine?"

Hannah frowned, shaking her head while she ran through

the possibilities. The tractor? The UTV? Brian's truck? "Monster machine?"

When she looked to the guys for a hint, Rob tipped his head toward the window that faced the house. When she went over to look, she saw one of the big, sporty side-by-sides that she'd been watching go by since the ATV trails opened, but this one had two seats in the front and two in the back.

"Oh." She had to admit it fit the description of monster machine. "I haven't seen that one in the campground before, I don't think."

"It just arrived," Danny said. "Our cousins in Maine own a lodge and campground on ATV trails and they were selling it, so we bought it and paid a guy to go get it because everybody's busy. It arrived this morning."

Joey shook his head. "Still think it's not a great idea to buy a vehicle driven by Kowalskis."

They all laughed, and there was some brotherly shoving. Erika leaned close and looped her arm through Hannah's. "Can we go for a ride in it?"

"I don't think so," Hannah said at the exact same time Rob said, "Hell yeah."

Erika looked back and forth between them a few times and then pointed at Rob. "I'm listening to him."

Joey shrugged. "There's no reason Bobby can't take you both for a ride. We've got all those helmets in the garage."

Rob nodded, and Hannah could tell by that cheeky sparkle in his eyes when he looked at her that he was really enjoying this. "What do you say, Hannah? Want to give Erika the full Birch Brook Campground experience?"

She wasn't sure she *did* want to do that, but Erika was practically bouncing on her toes. "You realize you'll get dirty, right?"

"That's part of the fun," her friend who didn't even eat wings or ribs because she couldn't stand her fingers being dirty actually said out loud, and Hannah rolled her eyes.

"How's eleven tomorrow sound?" Rob asked, his look practically daring Hannah to back out.

That wasn't going to happen. Erika had gotten them into this, so she was going to enjoy watching her friend trying to brush dirt out of her hair. "Sounds good to me."

His eyes widened in surprise, but he grinned. "I'll be ready."

"I can't wait," Erika said. "Okay, time to see your home away from home, Hannah."

"You've seen my parents' camper before."

"Sure, but not its parking spot."

On her way out, Hannah glanced over her shoulder to see if Rob was watching her leave. He was, and he didn't look the slightest bit guilty about staring at her ass while everybody watched him watching her.

It was strange for all four of them to be in the store. As far as she knew, there was nothing going on to indicate this would be a busier than usual weekend, so maybe they'd all shown up to see the side-by-side they'd bought from their cousins.

She got in the passenger side of Erika's rental and guided her through the campground. There was plenty of room for her to park next to the truck, and since Erika only had one carry-on and her tote, it didn't take long to get her settled.

Hannah brewed them each a mug of coffee. "Do you want to sit outside?"

Erika's nose wrinkled. "With the bugs? I'd rather sit here at the table."

"You do realize you signed us up to be outside for most of the day tomorrow, right?"

"Yeah, but we'll be moving, so the bugs won't be able to catch us." She grinned and leaned closer. "You didn't mention the campground is owned by four very attractive men. Seriously, Hannah. There are *four* of them."

"I didn't mention it because I don't care." But of course, there was that image of Rob laughing that seemed permanently imprinted on her brain. And because she was talking to Erika and not a random person, the slight deception made her cheeks feel warm.

And her friend didn't miss it. She leaned closer. "Which one is it?"

There was no sense in trying to lie. "Rob."

Erika frowned. "Rob?"

"His brothers call him Bobby to annoy him."

"Oh." After a few seconds, her eyes widened. "*Oh.* He's the one taking us out for a ride tomorrow."

"Yes, and you will *not* embarrass me."

"Define that."

Hannah sighed. "You know what I'm talking about. No winks or nudges when you think he's not looking. No innuendo. We're just hanging out and I don't want you to make it awkward."

"Are you hanging out in bed?"

"We have…hung out in bed, yes." She waved her hand. "It's not a big deal."

That was a lie. Rob was a very big deal, but confessing that would just muddy the waters. While Erika might think it was fun to tease Hannah about a guy she liked, she wouldn't be so cavalier about it if she realized he was a guy who might factor into Hannah's thoughts about her future— a future which impacted Erika's in a big way.

"Is it serious?" Erika asked in an unusually quiet voice, and Hannah could see that awareness was setting in already.

"No, it's not serious." Saying the words out loud felt wrong somehow. "How can I be serious about a guy I'm only going to know for a few more weeks?"

"Okay, so a campground affair. A summer fling." Erika brightened immediately, and she didn't notice Hannah didn't do the same. "For the record, I one hundred percent approve of that. Have a little fun and then come home and get back to work."

"Speaking of work," Hannah said, because it was time to address the elephant in the room. "You didn't tell me you were flying to Boston."

Guilt flashed in Erika's eyes. "I met with a potential sponsor. They submitted an offer I couldn't ignore, but I wanted to talk to them first to make sure their vision and sense of ethics around true crime aligned with ours. Yours mostly, I guess."

"And yet, you went without me? And you flew all the way to Boston for what could have been a Zoom meeting?"

"Your expression right now and your tone are exactly why I wanted to vet them first. If I didn't think you'd like them, there was no sense in wasting everybody's time," Erika said. "It's a lot of money, and the CEO hates virtual meetings. Plus, they paid for my flight and hotel."

Hannah frowned, trying to make sense of it. "The sponsor paid for all of that?"

Erika tapped her fingers on the dinette, her anxiety showing. "Maybe not so much a sponsor as a production partner. They want to work with us to take *Improbable Causes* to the next level, with a full research staff and merch and so much stuff, Hannah. You wouldn't believe it."

"No, I don't believe it." Hannah paused, taking a few breaths to keep her temper under control. "I'm the research staff, and do they want *Improbable Causes* as it is, or your new and allegedly improved version of it?"

"Well, growth requires change, so—"

"Erika." She shook her head. "You agreed to give me time off to consider what I want to do, and yet you're flying across the country to take secret meetings?"

"Yes, I agreed to put my life on hold for three months while *you* make a decision about *our* business. But that doesn't mean I can't start putting pieces in place while I wait. They know there's no guarantee we'll change the format of the show. I didn't make them a single promise. It was a fact-finding mission and you can add that data into whatever mental algorithm you're running while you're out here in the middle of nowhere."

Hannah forced herself not to answer right away. She loved this woman, and she needed to consider how she'd feel if Erika took off for three months with their business's future in her hands. "I'm sorry. I know it's hard for you."

"And I know if your heart isn't in a new format, it's best to know *before* we're in bed with some soulless corporation." Erika covered her hand. "I'm not trying to undermine you. I'm trying to find a compromise, and I just want the pieces in place no matter which way we go so we can hit the ground running."

Hannah nodded and even managed a smile, but the pressure was like a weight on her chest, making it hard to breathe. She had no doubt when she looked over the new information Erika had sent her, the potential income was going to be that much higher, which meant her decision would be that much harder.

"I didn't come here to pressure you into committing," Erika continued. "I've never been camping and I missed you and I honestly just want some girl time. In the woods, I guess."

"Fine. I'll go easy on you today because you did a lot of driving, but tomorrow when we get back from this four-wheeling adventure of yours, you're going to sit outside at my campfire and make s'mores with me."

Her nose wrinkled again, but then Erika mustered a game smile. "It's a deal."

Chapter Twenty

Today was going to be fun, Rob thought while he waited by the big, four-passenger side-by-side. And by fun, he meant torturous and agonizing. But also wonderful. Apparently that's how days spent with a woman one was falling in love with but would have to let go next month went.

The small cooler strapped in one of the back seats was stocked with cold drinks and snacks. There was a line of helmets on the picnic table, waiting to be tried on. His camera was in its ruggedized case and stowed in a bag hung between the front seats, as safe as he could make it. It wasn't his best camera, which was still in the house, but it hadn't been cheap. All he needed now were his guests.

"You look like you're waiting for your prom date to come down the stairs," Brian told him as he paused on his way to the tractor. "And like maybe you're afraid she stood you up."

He chuckled. "I think I'm fifty-fifty on getting stood up. Hannah would back out in a heartbeat because she prefers walking to the machines. And Erika was very excited about it, but I got the impression from Hannah that the outdoors isn't really her thing. It wouldn't surprise me at all to get a text message canceling."

"That machine's bigger than you're used to," Brian said. "Do *not* roll it up in a ball with guests inside of it, please."

"If it's got wheels, I can drive it."

"Pretty sure Dad's riding lawn mower had wheels. And Joey's dirt bike."

Rob snorted. "Yeah, remember how Mom and Dad bought that old compact pickup for all of us to learn to drive in and to use until the next kid's time to learn and by then we had to have our own? I seem to recall you wrecked it right before I started driver's ed class, so you have no room to talk. It was supposed to go to me and I would have gotten to keep it, being the youngest."

"I wrecked it because the wheel fell off because it was a piece of crap when they bought it, and by the time it went from Danny to Joey to me, it was held together by duct tape and zip ties. You should be thanking me."

When Hannah and Erika finally emerged from the tree line where the dirt roads intersected, Rob's pulse kicked up a notch.

"Huh," Brian said. "My money was on you being stood up. I'll leave you to it. But seriously, Bobby. That four-seater's obviously longer, but it's also wider, so watch the corners. I don't want any of you getting hurt."

Usually when one of his brothers called him Bobby, Rob bristled, but this time he could hear what Hannah was talking about. *The people who really love you call you Bobby sometimes.*

Sometimes they did it to annoy him, but this time, he felt as if Brian used it because to him, the little brother of their formative years and the one he shared all those memories with would always be Bobby. It was Bobby that Brian helped right the riding lawn mower and fix the mower deck the best they could. Then when Brian jumped in to keep Joey from actually hurting him when he crashed the dirt bike he wasn't supposed to be riding, he was doing it for Bobby.

It was a perspective he hadn't wrapped his head around until Hannah pointed it out, but now he could see it and he clapped his hand on Brian's shoulder. "I'll be careful, especially in the corners."

"I'll leave you to it, then."

Brian didn't actually walk away, though, because Stella wanted to say hello to Hannah and her friend. Erika was tentative about petting her, which confused the dog, but Hannah dropped to one knee in the dirt road to give Stella a good thorough belly rub.

When Stella got up and shook—sending dust from the road flying—Erika made a squeaking sound and stepped back, and Brian's snicker drowned out Rob's groan.

"Yeah, you have fun with this," Brian said. "Come on, Stella."

It took them almost fifteen minutes to find a helmet for each of them, but he finally found two that would work. Most of the helmets belonged to the women in the family, and they'd all been thrilled to have another garage to store stuff in. Since they primarily rode in that part of the state, they'd dumped ATV stuff off on the campground.

"I've never worn a helmet like this," Hannah said. "I don't know if I can figure out the buckle."

"I'll help you," Rob told her, trying to sound nonchalant. Being so close to her made him feel anything but nonchalant, but he had to fake it because he wasn't sure what—if anything—she'd told Erika about him.

He did notice, however, that Erika's helmet was already fastened, which meant she'd figured out the buckle. And yet she made no move to help Hannah, but left it for Rob to do.

Interesting.

He had to pop the door panels open because they couldn't figure out how and then Erika climbed in the back seat.

"You should sit in the front," Hannah protested. "It's your adventure."

"I might be too scared in the front. You sit up there."

Rob pointed at the cooler. "I can move that to the front seat if you want to sit in the back together."

"Hannah gets carsick if she rides in the back seat," Erika said before Hannah could speak.

He looked at her and she nodded, so he stood back to let her climb into the front seat. That was something he hadn't known about her, and he added it to the *Hannah* files in his brain. Not that it was a piece of information he'd ever use, in all likelihood, but he wanted to know everything about her.

Once they were in and had figured out the seat belts, he checked to make sure they'd fastened them correctly. It was slightly awkward—especially with Erika—but he wasn't going to take any chances with their safety.

"Okay," he said once that was done. He pointed to the door panels, which had an opening at the bottom. They were going to order nets or the full door panels for it, but hadn't yet. "Don't, for any reason, stick your arms or legs out of the side-by-side. There's a bar in front of you called the *oh shit* bar. If you hear me say *oh shit* or some variation of that, you grab that bar with both hands and don't let go. That's to keep your arms from flailing and possibly being outside the vehicle if it rolls over."

"That sounds…not fun," Hannah said.

"You don't have to worry about it. I won't be tearing it up today. But if something on the machine breaks or just a random accident, hold that bar and trust in the roll cage. It's pretty rugged."

"I was wondering why we had to wear helmets even though it's like a car," Erika said.

Rob sighed. "Definitely not a car."

Hannah touched his fingers, getting his attention, though she withdrew her hand quickly. "Drive it like your mom and gran are in it, okay?"

He laughed. "You don't want that, sweetheart. They may be Kowalskis by marriage, but they keep up. And if they're in a mood, they lead."

Hannah's eyes sparkled with amusement and she looked like she was going to say something else, but Erika shifted in her seat. "It's too hot in this helmet."

"It won't be once we start moving."

Rob walked around to the driver's side and, after putting on his helmet and buckling his seat belt, he hit the button to fire the engine. It roared to life, making the entire machine vibrate, and he glanced over to find Hannah staring at him with wide eyes.

He gave her a reassuring smile and put it in gear. Thanks to the speed limit in the campground and on the narrow trail that connected it to the main system, they had time to get used to the feel of it. A glance over his shoulder told him Erika wasn't waiting for something to happen—she had both hands on the grab bar at all times. If they went over a rock or hit ruts, Hannah would reach for it, but otherwise, she kept her hands in her lap.

When he finally hit open trail and could punch it a little, Erika squealed and Hannah laughed. That was all the encouragement he needed. He'd been riding this trail system for most of his life—from the small 90cc ATV he'd learned on, to the ATVs with major horsepower, to the side-by-sides—and he knew where to be extra cautious and where he could play a little.

It was hard to keep his attention fully on the trail in front of them, though, because he just wanted to watch Hannah. He knew she'd only agreed to this because her friend seemed so excited about it, but she was having a good time. He could see it on her face when he looked over, and every time she got nervous enough to grab the bar, he could hear her laugh.

He'd decided to take them up to the scenic overlook his family had visited every summer. It offered some shade, picnic tables and a breathtaking view that stretched into Vermont.

When they'd made it up the rocky hill and he parked, he could tell he'd made the right choice. They both hurried to get their helmets and seat belts off, though it didn't do them any good because they still couldn't figure out the door latches without his help.

As soon as he freed them, though, they went immediately to the edge of the clearing to look at the view. Rob grabbed his camera and went in the opposite direction, toward a cluster of boulders that had gathered earth and debris over the many years and had become something of a second lookout.

His intention in walking to the higher vantage point was to take some photos of Hannah and Erika with the view behind them so Hannah would have them. But he only took a few shots before lowering the camera and just watching them.

He couldn't hear what they were talking about, but they were clearly having a good time. There was a lot of grinning and laughing and, on one hand, he loved to see it. This was why he'd brought them out to have the experience together.

But on the other hand, it was painful. For almost two months, he'd had Hannah all to himself, as if she existed in a vacuum. In theory, he knew she had family and friends and her career in California, but in reality, she'd just been a captivating, amazing woman who was alone on site twenty-nine.

Seeing her with Erika really drove home that Hannah had a full life somewhere else that he knew nothing about.

Then Hannah turned, clearly looking for him. He waved so the movement would catch her eye, and he knew the moment she spotted him because of the smile. Even from a distance, it took his breath away.

They sat at the picnic table and ate trail mix and chocolate. He gave them bottles of water, which they both started guzzling.

"Um, so one thing I didn't mention," he said. "There's a roll of toilet paper in a plastic bag in the side-by-side's storage box if you need it."

They both lowered their drinks, staring at him.

"Why do we need a roll of toilet paper?" Erika asked in a higher-than-usual voice.

Hannah screwed the top back on her bottle. "We haven't really passed any bathrooms in the woods, have we?"

If Erika shook her head any harder, she probably would have fallen off the picnic table bench. "I'm pretty sure you and I *very recently* had a conversation about how we don't pee with our butts hanging over logs to get bitten by bugs. It was a hard no, Hannah."

She held up her hands, laughing. "I didn't choose this adventure. You did."

"How much longer is the ride?" Erika asked Rob.

He shrugged. "If we head back now, it'll be the same amount of time it took us to get here. Just in reverse."

"Okay." She appeared to do some mental calculations

and then took a long swig of the water before putting the cap back on. "I can hold it that long."

"Unless we hit a bump really hard," Hannah said, and Rob laughed when Erika threw a nut from the trail mix at her.

"I'm going to go take a quick walk through the woods," he said. "Then I'll be ready to go when you are."

"Show off," Hannah shouted as he disappeared into the trees.

"Hopefully not," he called back, and he could hear her laughing as he looked for a discreet spot to water a tree.

When he got back, the women had stowed the bottles and snacks, and they both had their helmets on, though Hannah's wasn't buckled. She was a pretty quick study, so he was starting to think she wasn't even trying to figure it out because she wanted a reason for him to touch her.

He definitely approved.

While he didn't want to switch the seating around, Rob knew how to be a good host. And being one of four kids, he was a veteran of the who-gets-the-front-seat wars—which he never won, of course, being the youngest. "Hey, Erika, I think it's your turn to ride in the front now."

She tipped her head toward Hannah. "Carsick, remember?"

"Right." Once Erika was in, he walked over to help Hannah buckle her helmet. "Sorry, I forgot you have to sit in the front."

She tipped her head back so he could get to the buckle, and he took his time grazing his knuckles along her jawline. "Yeah, about that. It's not true, but nobody's ever caught on to the fact it comes and goes depending on the situation. I want to sit in front with you, so yeah—I'll get carsick in the back seat."

"I like the way you think." He finished with the buckle and sighed. "Maybe I should have tried that when I was a kid."

"I've met your brothers and I'm pretty sure they would have just put a bucket in your lap and turned the radio up."

They were still chuckling over that visual when Erika yelled at them to hurry up because not being able to pee was making her have to pee.

When Rob pulled the side-by-side alongside the store and cut off the engine, Hannah had mixed feelings. On the one hand, she'd been having a great time and would have been happy to stay out longer. But on the other hand, she was going to have to pee soon and she was glad to be out of the woods.

He helped them climb out of the machine, and they both took their helmets off. She looked at Erika and burst into laughter. "Is my face as dirty as yours?"

"Totally. And this is the dirtiest I've ever been in my life. I think I even have dirt in my mouth." She grimaced and then pulled out the neck of her shirt, looking down. "Yeah, there's dirt in my bra. In my *bra*, Hannah. I have dirty boobs right now."

Hannah laughed, not only at her friend's distress, but because Rob was trying so hard not to react to what Erika was saying. His lips were pressed together, but she could see the tilt at the corners, and his eyes were sparkling when their gazes locked.

"Are your boobs dirty, Hannah?" Erika demanded, and Rob covered his mouth as his shoulders jerked with the effort to stifle a laugh. He turned away, suddenly very busy doing something with the side-by-side.

"We were on the same ride, so probably. I'm not going to show you right now, though."

"Why not? He's seen your boobs already."

Rob's head whipped around and Hannah cringed. So much for Erika not embarrassing her.

"Sorry," Erika said, noticing Rob's reaction. "She told me you guys are having a summer fling, but I'm her bestie, so it's okay. I won't tell anybody else."

Hannah wanted this conversation to take a hard turn away from her relationship with Rob. "I'm not going to show you right now because you never know when a campground might have doorbells that spy on you."

Erika frowned. "Doesn't everybody have those door-bells now?"

Hannah laughed, her hand on her stomach because she couldn't remember the last time she'd laughed until tears streamed down her cheeks and her stomach muscles ached, but she had all afternoon. The way Erika screamed when Rob drifted the machine around a mud corner or plowed through a puddle, sending up sprays of mud and water, had cracked her up. Of course, that only encouraged Rob.

"No laughing," Erika said sternly. "I have to pee."

"Me, too." Hannah turned to Rob. "Do you need help cleaning this stuff and putting it away? Where do the hel-mets go?"

"I've got it."

"Thank you for today. I didn't think I was going to like it very much, but it was really fun. And that view was spe-cial. That's where you used to have picnics with your whole family when you were a kid, right?"

His smile was full of happy nostalgia. "Yeah, with one of those little grills and everything. I thought you might like it up there."

"I have to pee," Erika reminded her in a voice that told Hannah it was no longer a theoretical problem.

She wanted to tell her to just use the bathroom in the store, but they were filthy. And she knew other people used it anyway, but she didn't want them making a mess the guys would have to clean up, especially after Rob had taken them for a ride.

"Go," Rob said. "Get cleaned up and relax. I'll see you around."

When they reached her site, Hannah realized they were way too dirty to go in the camper. If it belonged to her, she might have done it, but it belonged to her parents. And she knew neither of them were going to strip down to their underwear outside. So they went to the bathhouse on the hill because she knew there was a broom in the corner and she'd be able to sweep up the dirt they tracked in.

After they'd both used the bathroom, Hannah took the broom outside and they brushed as much of the loose dirt and mud off of each other as they could.

"These are going to make a mess of my carry-on," Erika said, looking down at herself. "My little laundry bag wasn't designed for this."

"After we shower and change, we can do a load of laundry."

Several hours later, with the laundry done and dinner eaten, Hannah held Erika to her promise of sitting by the campfire, making s'mores.

Hannah had already eaten two by the time Erika managed to toast a marshmallow. Her first attempt turned into a flaming ball of blackened sugar that she barely refrained from flinging into the side of the camper. Her second was almost perfect when it slid off the stick and into the fire.

"This shouldn't be so hard," she muttered.

"Worth it, though," Hannah said, licking melted marshmallow from her fingers. "Once in a while. They're a lot of work and usually I just eat the chocolate bar and leave the rest."

She heard rustling in the area of the rental and some familiar whispers. "Boys, do you want to make s'mores? If you do, ask your mom if it's okay."

In her mind, the boys would go to their mother and ask permission. In reality, they bellowed the question at the same time and Melissa yelled back that they could if they were invited, but only one each or she'd have to duct-tape them to their beds.

When the Scott boys arrived at the fire, Hannah introduced them by name and by nickname, and then gave them each a marshmallow stick. This was the third time they'd been over for s'mores and they had a lot of experience making them, so other than ensuring they didn't get too close to the fire, Hannah could just sit back and watch.

And once they were done eating them, she was very grateful they'd be going in their own camper and not hers. How two boys could get so much marshmallow and chocolate on themselves from one s'more each was a mystery.

"Do you guys ever swap colors, just to mess with people?" Erika asked. When both boys shook their heads, she gave them a skeptical look. "Really? Isn't that a thing twins do?"

"Mom said we better not," Blue replied. "Because the only way to tell us apart is the birthmark on my private parts, and she said if she ever even *thinks* we switched, she'll drop our drawers right then and there."

"Oh." Erika nodded. "You definitely don't want to try that prank, then."

They heard Melissa call for the boys, who took off at

a run yelling thank-yous over their shoulders. Hannah watched them go, wishing she had a fraction of their energy right now.

"So they put a family with kids next to a woman camping alone?" Erika asked, fortunately in a low voice that wouldn't carry. "There should be, like, a family section and an adults-only section."

Hannah laughed. "Trust me, I've got it good here. I remember some campgrounds we went to as a family that were overrun with kids and they had no boundaries. My mom got in a huge argument with another mom one day because some kids unhooked our water hose and stole our marshmallow sticks."

"I think I'm a hotel kind of person."

"You definitely are," Hannah agreed, and they both laughed. "But they're good kids. High energy, for sure, but I like them. The whole family, actually. Trust me, I could have ended up with worse neighbors in this place."

"But twins. Can you imagine? I mean, I can't even imagine having kids at all yet, but when it's time, I hope they come one at a time. You know how I am at multitasking."

Hannah chuckled because it was rare for Erika to admit that while she rarely focused on one thing—or even five— at a time, multitasking wasn't one of her stronger skills.

"Can you imagine us with kids, Hannah?"

An image of a little boy with dark hair and Kowalski blue eyes filled Hannah's mind, and she shook her head while managing a weak smile.

"Anyway, I can't wait for you to get back to California so we can get back to work and work toward whatever goals we decide on before it's time to settle down."

Chapter Twenty-One

Somehow Rob ended up alone in the store when it was time for Hannah's guest to go. He'd been hoping to be anywhere else, even scrubbing bathhouse toilets if he had to, because he was still nursing the bad mood he'd fallen into after mulling over what was said after their ride yesterday.

Summer fling.

Those were the words Erika had used, which meant that was probably how Hannah had defined their relationship to her. A summer fling—hot, fun and very temporary. Knowing it was possible and having to be reminded it was actually probable were two different things.

But Danny was writing, and Brian and Joey were changing the oil in the UTV. He would have done that, but it was a beautiful day and neither of them wanted to be stuck in the store. As usual, Rob got the job nobody else wanted.

When the two women walked into the store and his gaze fell on Hannah, he felt better. Her face lit up when she saw him, as it always did, and he realized it didn't matter what anybody called what they had together. They had what they had, and it made him happy.

"It's time for me to head out," Erika said, and she almost managed to look sad about it. "But I'm going to get snacks for the drive, and for the flight."

"Feel free to look around and see what we have. I wouldn't recommend ice cream, though."

She laughed, but then she froze for a second before un-zipping and rummaging through her tote. "Oh crap, I forgot my phone charger. It's plugged in by the sink."

"I'll run and get it while you pick out your snacks," Hannah said. "Is that the only thing you forgot?"

"It's the only thing I remember that I forgot," Erika said, and Rob chuckled softly.

"I'll do a final sweep."

"I had so much fun yesterday," Erika said as soon as the door closed behind Hannah. "You have a really great job."

He nodded. "It is a pretty great job, though we don't get too much riding in. Not as much as you'd think, anyway. I'm glad you had fun, and I apologize for the dirty laundry."

"Oh, we washed it last night. If I'd checked a bag, I might have thrown the muddy clothes in a plastic bag, but I flew carry-on only."

"It's great that you got to visit. I know Hannah's missed you."

She gave a wistful sigh. "I can't wait until she comes home. Three months is *forever*, and this place is great, but she needs to get her butt back to California."

Rob nodded, but he couldn't fake even a sorry excuse for a smile. He wanted Hannah's butt to stay right there in New Hampshire, thank you very much. But he knew that wasn't the plan, and her best friend certainly wasn't going to agree with him, so he kept his mouth shut.

When Hannah returned, she was slightly out of breath and looking slightly annoyed. She gave Erika a handful of things, only one of which was a phone charger. "I also grabbed your brush, your earplugs and those disgusting mints you like."

"They're *great* mints. You just have no taste."

"Mints should be minty," Hannah argued. "Cinnamon that sears your taste buds and makes your eyes water is not minty."

After tucking the items in her bag, Erika selected her snacks and paid for them at the counter. Then, after thanking him again for taking them out in the side-by-side, they left. Hannah looked over her shoulder and gave him a little wave before she walked out the door, and he waved back.

When the rental car pulled out and headed south a little while later, Rob waited expectantly, but Hannah didn't come back into the store. He'd been hoping she would, because he always wanted to see her, but it wasn't a big camper and Erika had a big personality. Maybe she needed some alone time.

When the door *did* open, Danny walked in. He was scruffy and looked tired, but at least he was clean. When he was deep in writing mode, he sometimes didn't bother taking the time to shave, but he *almost* always showered.

"How's it going?" he asked when Danny sank into one of the chairs with a sigh.

"That kitchen table is not ergonomically awesome," his brother answered, wincing slightly as he shifted his position. "And neither is the chair or the couch, but I keep bouncing around, writing until I can't sit there anymore, and then I move to the next. Worst musical chairs ever."

"You have a nice desk at home. And a chair that cost more than my first car. Why come up here and wreck your back?"

"Because I get in my head and sometimes it takes a change of scenery to get out of it."

Rob snorted. "And because you can go to the Kitchen for breakfast and see Kenzie."

Danny's head was leaned against the back of the chair, but he swiveled it to face him. "She says she has no interest in writing anything, but she has an amazing grasp of story elements."

"Maybe she could be an editor, like Aunt Keri." When she'd given up her job to marry their uncle Joe, she'd become an editor and, though she refused to edit *his* books, she liked it and was well respected.

"She'll never leave that restaurant."

Rob knew what that sentence really meant, even though neither of them said it out loud. Kenzie couldn't leave the restaurant as long as her dad worked there. And maybe not even after he was gone, because it was her mother's legacy. He liked Kenzie a lot and hated seeing it, but he also knew what family meant and he respected her for staying.

The door opened again, and again it wasn't Hannah. This time it was Brian and Joey, with Stella at their heels. Drinks were taken out of the cooler—and noted down after being reminded to by Joey—and the four of them had a few minutes to relax together. Stella, probably overheated after being outside, slurped up half the fresh water Brian poured in her bowl and then sprawled on the cool tile floor.

"Since we're all here," Joey said, and he was met with groans. That opening usually led to serious discussions. "This isn't public knowledge yet, but Ellie and I want you three to know because it affects—"

He didn't even have the words out before all three of them were on their feet. Even Danny, who winced a little, pushed himself out of the chair.

"We're having a baby," he said, unable to keep the grin off his face.

There was a round of hugs and backslapping and congratulations, all of which disturbed Stella's peaceful slumber. But finally they all settled back in their seats, though they were all still smiling.

"Just to be clear," Brian said. "Mom and Dad *don't* know yet?"

"No. It's still early to be telling people."

Danny held up his hand. "And you decided to punish us by making us keep this a secret from the family *why*?"

"Ellie and I wanted you to know because…" He paused, then gestured around the store. "I know I haven't held up my end of the work. I know that. But even with Nora out of school there's a lot going on and I keep telling myself I'll just take the time to come up and here we are with the summer half-over. But once the baby comes, it's going to be even harder. The money I did put in can be a loss and I know you can't buy me out or whatever, but I think it's time we rework the company so I'm not getting any of the profits."

"No," all three of them said at the same time, and Rob felt a flood of relief that Danny and Brian felt the same way he did. Sure, they'd been annoyed by his absence, but cutting him out? Rob wanted no part of that.

"Kowalski Brothers, LLC is not getting hacked up," Brian said. "Did you pull your weight this summer? Not really. But you have a new wife and a cute-as-hell kid. And you're going to have a baby."

"I'm going to pull even less weight with Ellie pregnant and then an infant," Joey pointed out.

"Yeah. But you'll be around when you can. Maybe when the kid's past the helpless infant stage, you can bring them up when there's something big going on."

"It's not fair to you guys."

"Maybe not at first," Danny said. "Right now, you've got a lot going on. But at some point, it'll be somebody else's turn. Hopefully we're all going to find what you've got and then maybe that guy gets to take a step back and you're ready to step up."

"Unless we all find it at the same time," Joey said.

"Not likely," Brian grumbled, and though he kept quiet, Rob felt the same. After Hannah left, it was going to be a very long time before he was interested in dating again.

"We've got you, Joey," Rob said. "And at some point, you'll be there for one of us."

He nodded and sniffed a couple of times before chuckling. "Considering you're all a pain in my ass, I'm feeling pretty blessed right now."

"That's what brothers are all about," Danny said. "That and getting me another soda from the cooler because if I try to get up right now, I might fall on the floor and you guys would just leave me there with Stella."

Hannah woke the next morning feeling restless before she even got out of bed. Even though she'd stayed up too late two nights in a row with Erika, she hadn't slept well.

Despite sticking to her promise to have a fun girls' weekend and leave the podcast out of it, just having Erika around had brought the pressure of her decision bubbling to the surface. She'd allowed herself to be distracted by Rob and the goings-on of the campground, but she needed to focus on the rest of her life.

She owed it to Erika, and to the podcast, to make it a priority. They'd both poured money and their hearts and souls into it, and they'd gotten a decent return on their investments. Now she had to figure out where to draw the line, as far as her personal sense of ethics, and decide if that line could be swayed by the financial figures Erika had sent.

She'd even dragged out the notebook again, sorting her

thoughts and writing things down because numbers and concepts seemed more concrete to her that way. But no matter how great the pivot looked on paper—and it was *really* great, moneywise—she knew her decision was made.

Perhaps it had been made before she'd even come. The excuse for being in New Hampshire was to give herself the space to think about what she wanted, but maybe it had been an excuse to put off the inevitable. She wasn't comfortable with the format Erika envisioned for the future of *Improbable Causes*, so she was going to have to tell her friend it either stayed the same or Erika would move on without Hannah.

Sighing, she flung open the screen door of the camper with the intention of going for a walk, but she jumped slightly when the door bounced off of Rob and rebounded back at her.

He laughed, and the sound was like a balm to her ragged nerves. Pushing the screen door open more gently, she stepped outside and smiled at him. "Sorry about that."

"Am I interrupting something? You seemed like you might be leaving with a serious purpose in mind."

"No, I just…" Hannah let the response die away because Erika had been consuming her time and energy for days. She wanted to focus on Rob right now. "I just got a little enthusiastic about being outside, I guess."

"Did Erika make her flight okay? I know traffic was bad down south yesterday."

"Yeah, she factored all that in, luckily, so she had no travel woes." She gestured toward the chairs. "Do you want to sit?"

He looked like he was going to say something, but then he stopped. After another moment, he shook his head. "I don't have time. I have to deal with a pool situation."

"That sounds ominous." She knew how much pride he took in the pool.

"Yeah, very late last night—or technically this morning, I guess—one of the campers had way too much to drink and decided to jump the fence because he wanted to swim. He stripped down to his underwear before trying it, though, so when his thigh caught on the top of the chain-link fence and gave him a nice cut, he flailed and fell on the cement and hit his head, though not horribly, thankfully."

"That's awful." No wonder he looked so tired.

"Oh, he wasn't done. He got up, staggered and fell in the pool. Luckily Stella alerted Brian because the guy's friend was hollering, but was too drunk to even try to jump the fence. Brian cleared the fence and dived in after the guy, who was panicking and tried to drown my brother to save himself. So Brian punched him in the face and then hauled him to the steps, but the guy vomited the entire way there."

"Oh, Rob." Hannah covered her mouth with her hand. "I'm so sorry."

"So those campers are gone and will never, *ever* be here again, but we had to post the pool is closed and now I have a bunch of stuff I have to do to the water before it can be reopened."

"And the Fourth of July weekend is coming," she added.

"Yes, or the Fourth of July *week*, actually. Everybody will come early." He shoved a hand through his hair and blew out a breath. "I'm sorry. I didn't mean to dump all that on you. I just wanted to see you."

"You can always talk to me." She smiled and moved forward. "I give good hugs, you know."

When she wrapped her arms around his waist, Rob buried his face in her neck and squeezed her with an intensity that seemed out of character for him. She knew he was tired and pissed off about the pool, but of all four of them, he was the one who seemed the most able to roll with those kinds of punches.

She held him until she could feel the tension ease from his body. His hold loosened and his breathing felt lighter somehow. And when he finally released her and stepped back, he looked a little more like himself. He even managed to give her a grin.

"I haven't had a chance to look at the footage yet, but I'm really hoping the superspy doorbell caught Brian clocking that guy."

"Stella must have been beside herself."

"She can't get over the fence and thankfully didn't try, but she did scare the other guy into climbing on a picnic table. I'm surprised you didn't hear her bark, even from here."

"I was so exhausted from Erika's visit I had the white noise cranked. I'm not sure even a thunderstorm could have woken me up." When heat flared in his eyes, she knew he was remembering the Blanket Fort of Doom, and she smiled. "It's been a while since we've had a storm."

"Technically we don't need a storm to blanket fort, you know. It's like buying a birthday cake. Nobody checks your ID. You can just buy one and eat it whenever you want."

They laughed together and she was relieved to have Rob back to himself again. Even when he looked at his watch and scowled, the annoyance didn't reach his eyes.

"I should go. The propane company's coming out to change out a valve, and I have to get started on that pool." He tucked a strand of hair behind her ear. "I'm glad I stopped by, though."

"Me, too. I hope you'll stop by again soon."

"As soon as I can," he promised, and then he kissed her. Not a quick goodbye kiss, but the kind of kiss that went on and on, until all she could feel was a desperate yearning for more.

Then she watched him walk down the road before she sank into her chair and tipped her head back to look at the sky. She had so much to think about.

She was still sitting there an hour later when Stella trotted into her site.

"Out doing the rounds?" she asked as the dog propped her chin on Hannah's knee and gazed up at her with adoring eyes that eased some of the turmoil in her mind. Dogs really were the best.

Especially since she was feeling particularly lonely at the moment. Erika had a big personality, so she'd left a silent void in her wake when she left yesterday. And Jenn was busy with work and her kids' activities, and their parents were on a short trip with friends. Because she had so much on her mind and wanted a distraction, she was more keenly aware she didn't really have any at the moment.

And then there was Rob. She hadn't seen him out and about much since Erika left, and today when he'd stopped by, he'd seemed out of sorts. Her gut told her it wasn't just the pool. Something was going on with him, but he wasn't telling her what. Maybe he'd had a falling-out with one or all of his brothers. Though he'd seemed better when he left, she didn't know if it would stick.

When she heard footsteps in the gravel near her truck, she thought it was Rob and leaned forward in her chair, already smiling. Stella's tail was wagging so hard her back wiggled under Hannah's hand as Brian came around the corner.

She did her best to hide her disappointment, but judging by the wry smile he gave her, she didn't do a great job.

"Didn't mean to bother you," he said. "Just looking for my dog and I figured I'd save time and start here."

"She likes to stop by and say hi from time to time, don't you, Stella?" The dog licked her hand before wiggling back under it for more scratching.

"We had some campers who were *not* great about food and trash, so we've become a popular dining destination for the local wildlife. We haven't seen any bear yet—and hopefully won't—but I'd rather she not tangle with a skunk or raccoon, either."

She winced. "Yeah. I don't know if she'd try to fight them, but she's always on the lookout for new best friends."

He shifted his weight from foot to foot, his jaw flexing for a moment. "Is there something going on between you and Rob?"

Hannah frowned. Since, as far as she knew, Brian was aware that she and Rob had been spending time together, this felt like more than him being a jerk about their ridiculous fraternization rule. "That sounds like a question for your brother."

He looked at her for a long time and then sighed. "Sorry. That was out of bounds. He just seems off and I wasn't sure if you guys had a fight or something. This might come as a shock to you, but I'm usually the grumpy, brooding brother."

Hannah put her hand over her chest, gasping in exaggerated shock. "You? No."

His grin was so like his brother's, it made her heart ache. "I know. And I also know I should mind my own business, but you have a sister. You know how it is."

"Even though my sister's older than I am, I do know how it is. But I'm not sure what's up with Rob. Maybe he's just tired? And also that guy who got super drunk and threw up in the pool didn't help. I'm glad he didn't actually drown you."

He shook his head. "That was not fun. But whatever's

bugging Rob started before the pool thing happened. But whatever. Everybody has bad days, I guess."

Hannah made a noncommittal sound, but it seemed her hunch that something other than the pool situation was bugging Rob was correct.

"You know," Brian said. "Maybe it was because we were young when we came here on a regular basis, but I don't remember there being so much alcohol involved in camping. Or vomit, for that matter. Except that one time the coleslaw got left out way too long and my mom was going to throw it away but she got distracted and Danny wolfed it down."

Hannah's stomach twinged in sympathy. Over the years of staying at campgrounds with her family, she'd seen more than one person succumb to the fundamental truth that food shouldn't sit out in the heat for hours and then still be eaten.

"I'd better get Stella back to the house. Once I get her back in the yard, she'll stay there if I tell her to, but only if she's already in it." He smiled at the dog, who was gazing up at him. "She finds all the loopholes."

After they left, Hannah pushed herself out of her chair and stretched. With Rob in a mood and so much on her mind she might just sit in the chair and stare at the sky all night, she decided getting out of the campground was the thing to do.

She'd go for a drive with the music cranked loud just to clear her head. Then she'd treat herself to dinner and dessert at the restaurant. She'd just finished reading a book so she'd pick whatever she had left in the pile that looked like something she could lose herself in.

There was almost no mood a good meal and a good book couldn't lift.

Chapter Twenty-Two

The long Fourth of July weekend was forecast to be hot as balls, and since it was only Wednesday and his brothers were cranky already, Rob knew it was going to feel a month long.

The campground was already half-full in the middle of the week. The rest of their reservations would be arriving sometime between noon and midnight the next day. Half of the seasonal campers were staying the full week, and quite a few of them had guests or family staying with them for the holiday. And the air-conditioning in the house was definitely not up to the task of keeping it even reasonably cool.

So far the only positive to this day was the fact he'd started the morning in Hannah's bed. They'd made love before falling asleep nestled together, and then they'd made love again this morning. And because her camper's AC was top-notch, they'd done it all without getting too sweaty.

It wasn't the first time they'd made love in her camper since Erika left, but it was the first time he'd spent the night there. It had been wonderful, but he could feel the void in their relationship now—the space where the conversations about the future were supposed to be, but weren't because they both knew there wasn't one. He tried not to focus on that space, but to enjoy every day he *did* have with her. It wasn't always easy.

Joey was at the counter, doing the tedious task of emailing each seasonal site their electric bill for the previous month. He'd come up to take care of that and to help check people in, but he was going home tomorrow night. While he'd offered to stay for the entire weekend, it would be his first Independence Day with Ellie and Nora, and the little girl was obsessed with seeing the fireworks. They didn't want him to miss it, but there simply wasn't space for them to join Joey at the campground that week. For the moment, though, he was spending his time muttering about automating some of their systems someday.

And when Brian walked in, Rob could tell from the way he swung the door closed behind him that his mood had gotten even worse since the last time he saw him. Stella went to her water dish, but Brian walked the width of the store, looking down both aisles to ensure there were no campers present. They'd already learned that lesson.

Then he pointed at Rob. "If the guy from site eight goes in the pool without hosing off the trail dirt first one more time, I'm going to hold him under until the bubbles stop."

"Okay," Rob said. "I'm calling *not it* for explaining that to the insurance company, though."

It wasn't a good sign that the group from site eight were only on day three of a weeklong stay and Brian already wanted to drown one of them. It hadn't even *really* gotten hot yet. They were going to see the heat index breaking triple digits on Friday and Saturday, but it was only ninety right now. *Only.*

"Danny's calling again," Joey said, holding up his cell phone.

Rob sighed. Danny hadn't come up for the busy weekend because of his book, and it was the right decision—

he'd never been expected to be there—but he felt guilty so he kept checking in to see if they needed him, after all.

Brian cursed and took the phone from Joey, sliding the bar to answer it. "What now?"

Rob gestured for him to put it on speakerphone so he and Joey could hear both ends of the conversation, but Brian wasn't looking at him.

"Yes, we're busy. No, we're not busy enough to need you even though you keep interrupting us to ask if we're busy." He listened for a moment and then snorted. "What you can actually do to help us is finish that book and then sell another book, and when you get that shiny advance, buy us some air conditioners that actually blow cold air."

Then he hung up and took a deep breath. "Okay, I feel a little better."

Joey gave him a dry look. "That'll be a big comfort to me while I'm fielding pissed-off texts from Danny all day. Use your own phone next time."

"I'll drive down there and smash *his* phone if he doesn't stop," Brian said. Then he chuckled. "I almost hope I have to do that because my truck has great AC and it's a long drive."

When Brian sank into a chair and put his feet up on the table, Rob saw his opening. "All three of us don't need to be in here generating body heat for the AC to blow back at us. I'm going to get some fresh air, even if it feels like I'm in a sauna."

"Tell her we said hi," Joey said, and Brian snickered.

He took his time walking through the campground so he wouldn't show up at Hannah's door drenched with sweat. People waved to him and he waved back, happy that everybody seemed to be in a good mood. Luckily, they seemed to have more families than groups of adults here for the holiday. There was usually less alcohol involved—or at least it was consumed more responsibly.

Hannah's truck was there, so he assumed the door was closed because the AC was on. He knocked on it, and faintly heard her asking who it was. When he called back to her, she told him to come in.

He stepped up into the blessed cool air and yanked the door closed behind him before any could escape. She didn't keep it chilled, by any means, because she didn't like the sound of it running, but it was a blessed relief for him.

"I'll be right out," she called from behind the closed bathroom door. "I just got out of the shower."

Rob was about to answer when his gaze landed on a notebook on the dinette. He shouldn't be reading it, but Hannah had left it out. He hadn't touched it at all. It was just there, drawing his attention.

The page was a mess, but he could see it was some kind of decision tree, with lots of arrows and annotations. Pros and cons. Going with her gut as to leaving her podcast the way it was or changing it obviously hadn't brought her to a conclusion, so now she was trying to use logic and data.

The projected income data was interesting. She'd potentially be leaving a lot of money on the table—for both her *and* Erika—if she chose not to introduce current true crime to her podcast. He also noted the figures in the bottom corner included office and recording space. Up until now, he'd assumed a podcast could be done from anywhere, and he'd wondered more than once if they boosted their internet, if she could do her part from here.

But nowhere on the page was his name—either as a pro or a con. There were no doodles about how he factored into the equation. There weren't any notations about loving New

England and it being rich in historical fodder. There was nothing at all to indicate she'd even considered staying.

Summer fling.

No matter how many times those two words had echoed through his mind, he could tell they hadn't really stuck. If they had, it wouldn't hurt so much to look at the plans Hannah was making that didn't include even thinking about him.

Because she'd meant them. Erika had used the words because Hannah had, and that's all he was to her. The last two months had been about having fun while she was in New Hampshire, and he wondered if she'd even glance in her rearview mirror when it was time to go.

The pain was so intense he could barely take a full breath, but he clenched his hands into fists and did his best to push it down. She'd made him no promises. On the contrary, it had been clear to him the entire time that she was going back to California, and she'd never given him a sign she was wavering.

He couldn't do this for another month. Every single day since they'd met he'd fallen further and further in love with her. Every time they kissed. Every time they laughed. Every time she gave him that sizzling smile that was only for him. There were a lot of days between now and the end of July.

There was no sense in putting his feelings on her. She clearly had enough on her mind and since he wasn't a factor, what good would it do to pile his emotions on top of it all. All he could do was make as clean a cut as possible now so she could spend the rest of her time here focused on what mattered to her and he could…miss her.

The bathroom door opened, releasing the scent of her soap and shampoo into the main cabin of the camper. He closed his eyes briefly, inhaling the smell of her, and then he braced himself and turned to face her.

Hannah was in shorts and a tank top, her wet hair piled on her head and held with one of those puffy elastics. Her skin glowed and her smile was bright, but it faded quickly. It only took her a few seconds to see something was wrong.

"Hey," she said with a nervous smile. "What's going on?"

"Not much." He touched his fingertips to the notebook, turning it slightly. "You've got a lot of planning going on."

She sighed, scowling at the notebook. "Can't make an informed decision without being informed, but that woman is *really* into information."

"I see that."

When her gaze returned to his face, the frown smoothed out, except for a tiny crinkle between her eyebrows. "Are you coming over later tonight? I can turn the AC up a little. You look flushed."

"No, I'm not coming." They were some of the hardest words he'd ever said, and it was only going to get harder.

"What's going on, Rob?" she asked in a quiet voice, that crinkle between her eyebrows deepening. "Just tell me."

"Look," he said, because the only way to do this was to rip the bandage off and hope he didn't emotionally bleed to death in front of her. "We're busy right now and I haven't been giving my brothers one hundred percent. And you have a lot on your plate and some big decisions to make before you go home."

"What are you saying?"

Rob looked into her eyes and forced himself to say the words. "We had a fun summer fling, but I think it's run its course. I need to focus on the business and I can't have any more distractions."

He wasn't sure what he expected her to do. Had their

fling even meant enough to her so she'd cry? Or rage and throw things at him? Curse him out?

Hannah looked at him, the crinkle smoothing out as her face lost all expression. It was as though she turned to stone in front of him, cold and hard. It was so much worse, and he silently begged her to call him names—to pick that heavy pottery mug up off the counter and hurl it at his head.

Anything but look at him with her chin up and her shoulders back, and nothing but disappointment and dismay in those eyes.

"Okay," she said, and her voice was so quiet he could barely hear her over the hum of the air conditioner. "I guess we're done distracting each other, then. You should get back to your job. You don't want your brothers to think you're slacking."

"I'm sorry," Rob said, because he couldn't wrap his head around her reaction—did she care or not—but he was definitely sorry to be ending their relationship.

"Nothing to be sorry about." She gestured toward the notebook. "I have work to do, too."

Rob nodded because there was nothing else to say and then left her camper for the last time. Tears stung his eyes and he wasn't sure how he managed to walk out of her site without walking into a tree, and then up the hill to the woods where he could be alone to mourn what could have been.

Hannah hated humidity. Heat, she could roll with, but she wanted nothing to do with the outside while the air was just this side of being actual liquid. She was afraid if she left her camper, she'd instantly be sticky. Then some of the never-ending parade of ATVs would go by, throwing up dust, and she'd look and feel like she'd rolled in the middle of the dirt road.

But mostly, she was hiding. It was Saturday, and she'd been hiding from the world and all the happy people running around the campground for days. She was hiding from Rob and anybody else with the Kowalski last name.

She wasn't hiding from the pain, though. There was no escaping the broken heart she hadn't seen coming. Burrowed into her nest, she cried and then got angry, and then she cried some more.

Under both emotions was a constant confusion, though. She'd had her heart broken before—though never like this. It wasn't the first time she'd been more invested in a relationship than the man and not realized it until he walked away.

But that wasn't what had happened here. She wasn't sure why he'd said those words—*we had a fun summer fling, but I think it's run its course*—but he hadn't meant them. What they'd had was real, and she believed down to her very soul that Rob felt the same way.

With a sound that was part angry growl and part painful crying out, Hannah threw back the blanket and climbed out of her bed. Then she adjusted the AC, which she'd cranked to make it cold enough so she could nest properly. It took her a few minutes to wash her face and brush her hair into some semblance of a ponytail.

Hannah was tired of feeling sorry for herself. And she was *absolutely* tired of thinking. She didn't want to think anymore. She wanted to act.

After unplugging her phone from the charger, she opened the door of her camper and stepped out into the soup that was passing for air this week. Then she turned and walked up the hill. Even though there was a sense of urgency humming through her, she took her time because after being in a chilly camper, pushing herself in this heat would be a bad idea.

When she got to the fallen log, she pulled out her phone and pulled up Erika's number. Then she took a deep breath and hit the FaceTime button.

Her friend answered on the second ring, looking her usual cheerful, put-together self. When she focused on Hannah's face, she did a double take. "Holy hell, Hannah. What's wrong?"

She barked out a mirthless laugh. "I thought I did a good job of scrubbing away the evidence."

"How long were you crying?"

"Three days, I think?" She sniffed, determined to get through all of it without breaking down. "So, confession— my summer fling wasn't a fling for me. It was real, but apparently it was only a fling for him and it's over. So I've been crying."

"Oh, Hannah." Erika's face crumpled in sympathy. "I don't understand. He was *super* into you. Even though you guys were trying to play it cool, it was so obvious."

"Yeah, I thought so, too. We were wrong." She took a deep breath and blew it out. "That's not why I called."

Erika gave her a sad smile. "Listen, before you say anything, I want you to know I love you no matter what."

"You already know my answer, don't you?"

"I do." She sighed. "I tried. I mean, I tried *hard*, which you definitely know, because we were talking about a lot of money. But right from the start I knew you wouldn't be comfortable with it and we'd have this conversation eventually. I'm sorry I pushed so hard."

"I love you no matter what, too. And you wouldn't be you if you didn't push. I'm sorry I'm letting you down."

"I have options, Hannah. But you're my number one."

Hannah smiled through yet another round of tears. "I want you to take the option that gets *you* where you want to go. You bring your podcast magic to a producer with deep pockets, and I'll keep being a historian who tells quiet stories about true crimes that happened before our grandparents were born."

"And we'll still be best friends."

"We'll *definitely* still be best friends."

They were quiet for a long moment, both of them breathing without the pressure of this decision hanging over them. Their gazes were virtually locked and as the anxiety faded and their pulses slowed, they smiled.

"When are you coming home?" Erika asked. "We'll get a massive tub of ice cream and watch movies about handsome guys who get murdered."

Hannah actually laughed, which she hadn't been sure she'd ever do again. "I'm not sure yet. I'll text you as soon as I have a date. And you better keep me updated on your meetings, okay? Don't agree to anything or jump at big numbers without running them past me."

"Why, Hannah Shelby, are you implying I'm impulsive?"

"Implying? No." She smiled. "Look, it's so hot and humid right now I can barely breathe, and I didn't bring water with me on my trek to the cell signal. I'm going to go, but I'll talk to you soon."

"Okay. And, Hannah? He never deserved you."

Hannah disconnected and stood, relieved to have that call behind her. She wasn't sure what the future held for either of them, but at least they'd still be friends. Right now, she didn't have the emotional strength to lose anybody else she loved.

The sound of male laughter drifted to her, and she closed

her eyes, trying to pick out Rob's. It was impossible, she knew. All four of the Kowalski brothers had laughs that were similar enough so even their mother might have trouble telling them apart.

It hurt to think he might be somewhere in the campground right now, sharing jokes and laughing so freely.

It hurt to think of Rob at all, and maybe it was time for more action.

As far as she could tell, she had two options. She could stay here for another few weeks and leave on the date in the agreement. She'd be miserable and lonely, and her heart would probably break all over again every time she saw Rob—which would probably be from a distance because she had a hunch he'd avoid her. Brian would probably take care of anything in her part of the campground.

Or she could pack up and leave early. She wouldn't get a refund on the site, but she wouldn't be stuck living in Rob's world without Rob.

She didn't want to be here without him.

Chapter Twenty-Three

After a long holiday weekend of working his ass off in what felt like record heat in a futile attempt to wear himself out enough to sleep without dreaming of Hannah, Rob was done. Her camper had been closed up since the last time he was there, just like everybody else's because the air conditioners were on. By midday on Monday, he hadn't had so much as a glimpse of her, which was both a blessing and a curse.

He skipped the store and went straight to the house after fixing a fire ring some guys had tried to move, hoping he'd be alone. It was just his luck that Brian had the same idea and was sitting on the couch with an old rickety fan they'd found in the basement blowing on him. Stella was stretched out on the floor, trying to soak up the barely cool air from the AC in the window.

Rob stopped, not wanting to lock himself in the hot oversize closet that was his room, but not wanting to stay here. He didn't want to go in the store. He was about to grab his truck keys when Brian looked at him and did a double take.

"You look like your..." Brian paused and looked at Stella. "Like your cat just died."

Rob shook his head, unable to manage even a weak smile at the joke. He sank into the chair, and Stella immediately trotted to him and rested her chin on his thigh despite the heat. Usually scratching behind her ears and giving her a good belly rub made him feel better, but he wasn't sure even Stella's love could help today.

"What happened, Bobby?"

"You were right the whole time. Fraternizing with our campers is a really bad idea."

"She's not leaving until the end of the month. I don't… What happened?"

"I knew that by the end of the month, I'd be so damned in love with her I wouldn't be able to stop myself from asking her to stay. I thought it would be easier to just break off our summer fling now, so we'd already have some distance and separation between us when she pulls out, so I told her it was over."

Brian let his feet fall to the floor with a thump. "It was too late like a month ago."

"Yeah."

"You said you wouldn't be able to stop yourself from asking her to stay. Why can't you?"

"Because she can't stay. And I can't go. It's that simple."

Brian made a really annoying *but is it, though* sound. "People move. It's a thing that's possible. People even did it before trucks were invented and they had to carry their shit on their backs."

"Erika has all this data and growth projections and business plans. Hannah's been going through it and sorting into pros and cons and comparisons and all that. They're making plans—big ones—and based on what I saw, not the kind of plans you just toss out the window on a whim."

"But Hannah doesn't have all the data, does she? You can't feel like she's leaving you out of the decision if she doesn't even know you're part of it."

Rob's hand—the one not rubbing Stella's head—was

balled into a fist so tightly his knuckles ached, and he forced himself to open it and rest his palm on his thigh. "She told Erika I'm a summer fling. That's the data *I'm* working with."

"I'm sorry, Bobby." Brian blew out a breath. Then he leaned forward and rested his elbows on his knees. "But have you thought—"

Rob pushed to his feet and turned his back on his brother. He wanted to walk out the door, but he had nowhere to go. "I've done nothing *but* think about this for weeks."

Brian stood and put his hand on Rob's shoulder to spin him back to face him. "I'm going to finish my sentence."

"Why? Shouldn't you be the last person to be fighting for love?" As soon as the words left his mouth, Rob regretted them. "I'm sorry."

Brian was quiet for a long moment, his eyes sad in a way that battered at Rob's broken heart. "I don't even know what went wrong with Kelly. One day she just decided she didn't want to be married to me anymore. But that doesn't mean I don't believe in love, Bobby. Do you really think I can look at our family—at our parents and our grandparents—and not believe in it?"

Unable to meet his brother's eyes, Rob looked down and gave Stella a sad smile. She cocked her head, probably trying to figure out why her favorite humans were upset with each other.

"Joey found it," Brian continued. "I want it for all of us. I want it for you. I even want it for myself again someday. If you really love her—if she's the one—you can't just let her leave without telling her."

"I'm not sure if I can survive Hannah telling me she doesn't love me enough to stay."

"Sit back down," Brian demanded, and since Rob had no

idea what else to do with himself, he listened. "You can't frame it like that, man. She either stays or she doesn't love you. It's not like her family lives a few hours away, so that's not fair. She might love you, but *also* love her family and her home and the life she's built."

"I know." Rob dropped his face to his hands, giving it a good scrub.

"Do you love *her* enough to go with her to California?"

Rob froze except for a tremor deep in his muscles as the emotions his brother's question evoked threatened to overwhelm him. "I can't do that."

"Why?" Brian sat back in his chair and held up his hand. "Do you not love *her* enough?"

Heat prickled over his skin, and Rob looked down at his hands because he couldn't bring himself to meet his brother's eyes. Yes, he loved Hannah. But even if he could be happy so far away from New Hampshire, how could he leave his family? Would he get to see them once a year? Twice if he was lucky?

And there was no way he could bail on this campground before the first summer was over. He'd come into this hoping to earn his brothers' respect so they'd take him seriously. That would never happen if he took off.

How did he end up in this place—having to choose between the woman he loved and everybody else he loved?

"Yeah, that shit you're feeling right now?" Brian said. "If she loves *you*, she's feeling the same thing. And because neither of you want to say it out loud because it looks too hard, you both might walk away from the best thing to ever happen to you."

"I can't leave," Rob insisted in a hoarse voice. "I made a commitment to you guys. An even bigger commitment now because Joey's having a baby and we're going to take up his slack. You're my brothers, and we're in this together."

"That means we'll figure it out together." Brian shoved a hand through his hair. "And if we don't… Bobby, come on. There's no business—no amount of money—that's worth you throwing away your chance at a future with the woman you love. We'd walk away from it and let it go bankrupt and all of us go back to rebuilding the lives we had before the campground before we asked you to do that."

Rob wasn't sure he could speak even if he'd any idea of what to say to that. He looked at his brother, looking for annoyance or even anger. All he saw was concern and sincerity.

"I don't know what to do," he whispered.

Brian shook his head. "You already did it, dumbass. You shouldn't have told her it was over. You should have told her you love her."

"It's too late now."

"I'm pretty sure if Dad was here he'd say it's never too late," Brian said. "So would Mom. And literally everybody."

"Don't you dare tell Mom. Or Dad. Or literally anybody."

"You know I won't." He sighed and leaned back against the couch cushion. Then he grimaced and leaned forward again because it was an awful fake-leather material that was highly unpleasant when it was hot. It was almost enough to make Rob smile. "You need to think long and hard about this, Bobby. I know it's hard to imagine not living here surrounded by your incredibly handsome and funny family, but I like her for you. There's something real between you and even if you do go your separate ways, you need to tell her how you feel."

"I don't know if I can. I saw those notes and I told her

our summer fling was over *because* I don't think I can take the pain of telling her I love her and having it rejected."

"That pain will heal. But I think the pain of wondering will haunt you."

Rob looked sideways at him. "I know older brothers are supposed to be wiser and all, but you're treading really close to the self-help book line."

"It's the heat," Brian said. "I'm suffocating and under-oxygenated."

"I'm getting a beer."

"Get me one, too. It won't help, but maybe it'll make me care less."

When Rob retrieved two and bent to hand him the ice-cold bottle, Brian captured his fingers along with the beer so he had no choice but to stay and look at him. "Think about it, Bobby. No matter where you are, we're your family and we've got your back. We're always here. You need to ask yourself if you're ready to spend the rest of your life without Hannah because you were scared."

It wasn't until he nodded that his brother released his hand, sliding the bottle out of his grasp.

Rob sat and twisted the cap off, but he paused before taking a sip. "I don't want to spend the rest of my life without Hannah."

"Then you better start thinking about what you're going to say, little brother, because winning a woman back is always harder than finding her in the first place."

"Okay, we definitely need better air-conditioning if this is what heat does to you. A few more degrees and you'll have us all doing yoga."

Hannah heard the footsteps in the gravel, but she was in the process of trying to stow the two camp chairs in the storage compartment and they didn't want to fit beside the small grill. Since she didn't care who was coming into her site, she didn't bother to turn around.

"Hannah."

She closed her eyes, allowing the pain of hearing her name from Rob's lips to wash over her. Then, when she was fairly confident she could see his face without bursting into tears, she straightened and turned to face him.

Rob looked like hell. His face was puffy and the dark circles under his eyes spoke to a serious lack of quality sleep. He looked a lot like she felt, actually.

"What can I do for you?" she asked, surprised and pleased that her voice sounded steady.

"You're leaving."

"Yes." She'd sent the notice to the main campground email address, neither knowing nor caring which of them would read it. "I made my decision so there's nothing left to keep me here."

He flinched as if she'd struck him, but then he took a deep breath. "I'm glad you made the decision."

"I'm not going to change the format and Erika's probably going to leave the podcast for greener pastures." She waved her hand. "Not that you care."

"I care." He shoved his hands in his pockets and looked at the ground for a long time. When he lifted his head again, his eyes were full of raw emotion. "I lied."

The look on his face was shredding her heart, even though she didn't know what he was talking about. "What did you lie about?"

"I lied when I said we were a summer fling that had run its course. I used those words because Erika did and they hurt me. So I used them to hurt you."

Tears welled in her eyes and she shook her head. "I don't understand."

"I love you." He said the words with certainty, looking her in the eye, and they were like a punch to her chest. "I didn't want to tell you that because you had so much on your plate already and I didn't want to add to it because it would be hard. My family and my job are here. Your family and your job are all the way across the country. But those plans... I couldn't ask you to stay. But now you're leaving and I didn't want you to go thinking I didn't care because that's a lie. I love you, Hannah. That's the truth and I just wanted you to know it before you go."

He gave her a sad look, and then turned to leave. Hannah ran his words through her head over and over, trying to understand—trying to take in the one thing that made sense.

He loved her.

And she loved him. That was also the truth.

"Rob, wait." He did *not* wait. With his hands shoved in his pockets and his shoulders bowed, he kept walking. "Rob!"

He paused for the space of a breath, and then with a small shake of his head that shouldn't have had the power to break Hannah's heart in two, he took another step. Then another.

She was afraid if he turned that corner and disappeared behind the trees, nothing would ever be okay again.

"Bobby!" she cried. And then in little more than a whisper, "Please wait."

When he stopped walking, she sucked in a breath and held it, practically willing him to stop—to understand what she was trying to say. And more than anything, to turn around.

And then he did, and she saw the hope burning in his eyes. "People who really love me call me Bobby."

"I love you." Tears streamed over her cheeks, but she didn't care because Rob was walking back to her. "That's the truth. I was afraid to tell you because I didn't know… I was a mess and wasn't sure what I was doing with my life, but I was sure I loved you."

He cupped her face in his hands. "When I was in your camper, I saw your notebook. You had plans and pros and cons and things to consider and I didn't factor in anywhere. My name wasn't on that page and it broke my heart."

"I was using that page to sort how I felt about things and I didn't write your name down because I didn't need to sort my feelings about you." She smiled through her tears. "That was all noise, but under it all, there was you. I didn't need to write your name for it to be imprinted on my heart."

He kissed her, fiercely, and she clutched his shoulders as his arms slid around her and tightened as if he was never going to let her go again.

Then he rested his forehead against hers. "I'll go to California with you if you ask me."

A sob escaped her and she curled her fingers into his T-shirt. Helping his brothers make this campground a success meant the world to him, and she couldn't take that away from him. "You can't leave your brothers."

"I can't leave *you*."

"I love you so much," she said, her heart filled with the joy of saying it out loud. "But I was drawn here for college. I was drawn here when I was at a crossroads in my life. I was drawn to *you*, and I want to be here with you."

"But your family. I don't want to take you from them."

She stroked his cheek. "We're going to make our own family, and mine will be there whenever I need them. We can talk on the phone. FaceTime. There are planes. Campers. They'll be happy for me, Rob."

He picked her up off her feet, swinging her around while she laughed. He was laughing, too, when he set her back on her feet. "Do you forgive me for not telling you I love you like a month ago and saving us the heartache?"

"Do you forgive *me* for not telling you a month ago?" She threw her arms around his neck and kissed him again.

What could have been one minute or ten minutes later, when the kiss ended, he looked into her eyes. "What's next?"

She looked over her shoulder at the camper she'd been preparing for the road. "Do you think they can live without you for two or three weeks?"

"As much as it pains my ego to admit it, I think they could keep things together without me for that long."

Hannah leaned back enough so she could tilt her head back and see his face. "How do you feel about a road trip?"

"I'm up for anything as long as we're doing it together." He brushed a strand of hair from her cheek, his thumb lingering on her skin.

"We can take our time heading west and maybe see a few things along the way. You can meet my family." She chuckled when he made a mock-terrified face. "Then we can pack what I absolutely need into my car, sweet-talk my mom and sister into shipping the rest to me and then head east again. We'll be back in plenty of time to help get the campground ready for Steph's wedding."

"Road Trip of Doom," he said, giving her that Kowalski grin. "Let's do it."

Epilogue

"You know my mother's going to want to throw us an engagement party."

Hannah nodded, flipping on her turn signal to indicate she was going to pass the car that was doing five under the speed limit. The closer they got to New Hampshire—to *home*—the faster she wanted to drive.

"She can throw us any kind of party she wants as long as Gram makes the blond brownies," she said. "And I'm sure my mom and your mom are already talking about it."

"They really did take the news well. About you moving all the way across the country, I mean."

"Better than I expected, actually. I must look as happy as I feel." She smiled when he reached over and squeezed her thigh. "Plus, my parents are once again in possession of their truck and camper, and you and your brothers own a campground. I'm sure you can see where this is going."

"I think if we added up your family and my family, we could almost fill that place."

"If we do that, can we get rid of Dave and Sheila?"

He laughed and rummaged in the bag at his feet for snacks. "Brian almost threw them out while we were in California, you know. Dave had some strong feelings about them moving the horseshoe pit and Brian had some strong feelings about what he wanted to do with the horseshoes. Joey really earned his keep that day, from what I hear."

"Every day's an adventure."

"You're sure you want to do this?"

She laughed. "We just drove all the way to California, packed this poor car full of what it could hold, sweet-talked my mother and sister into packing and shipping the rest, and now we're driving all the way back. I'm pretty sure."

"You're just in it for the road snacks," he teased, pulling an emergency Snickers out of the door pocket.

After he opened the wrapper, she took it from him, but didn't take a bite. "I kind of miss the camper."

"I kind of miss the legroom in the truck, but this gets way better gas mileage."

"But with the camper, we could pull into a nice shady spot and climb in the back and make love. We can't do that in my car."

"Not without pulling some muscles and possibly getting arrested. Also, you're insatiable. I thought it was going to take us four days to get across Nebraska."

Hannah gave him a smile that promised more of that in the near future, and then took a bite of her candy bar.

By tonight, they'd be back at Birch Brook Campground and as much as she'd enjoyed their road trip, she couldn't wait. They'd be staying on site twenty-nine, in an RV borrowed from his family.

There was a lot to sort out. Maybe they'd stay in the house during the winter and in an RV in the summer. Joey had pointed out there were plenty of Kowalskis who were good with a hammer, so maybe they'd add a second story to the house.

In their spare time, she and Rob would work on a coffee table book of forgotten places and stories in northern

New Hampshire. It would be a joint effort, with her doing the research and writing, and him taking the photos. The book might even tie into her podcast, which she'd keep in a format that would probably lose a massive chunk of audience, but she didn't care. She might even help Kenzie out at Corinne's Kitchen if she wanted to get out of the campground now and then. She'd waited tables to help pay for college and she was sure it would come back to her.

She wasn't sure yet what else her future held, career-wise. But she knew with absolute certainty that Rob would be at her side, and they'd build that future together. And hopefully, before too long, they'd add some more kids to the family tree.

Once she was finished with her candy bar, she took a long swig of the coffee from the center console. Then she reached out and took his hand, weaving their fingers together.

"Do you want me to drive for a while," he asked, squeezing her hand.

"Not yet. Have I told you in this state that I love you yet?"

"You did in New York, but we're in Vermont now."

"I love you."

He lifted their joined hands and kissed the back of hers. "I love you, too."

They were almost halfway to the New Hampshire border when Rob's phone chimed. In the time it took him to fish it out from under their snack stockpile and extra napkins in the door pocket, it chimed six more times. And Hannah realized her phone was vibrating in the center console. She'd been added to the family group chat before they left for California and, to be honest, she loved Rob's family, but she had some regrets about sharing her contact info.

"The wedding planning group chat is blowing up," he said, scrolling down his screen.

"If it's the tie versus bow tie thing again, I already voted."

"It's not. Also, I thought the tie versus bow tie argument got walked back to suit versus casual."

"Sure, because every bride in a gown and heels wants to exchange vows with a guy in cargo shorts and a Patriots T-shirt."

"Hey, better than a guy in a Jets T-shirt."

"My phone is still buzzing," she pointed out. "Even the blowup when Joey suggested white crepe paper strung around and Steph was mad because that was just a fancy way of saying he wanted to TP her wedding wasn't this bad."

"Oh," he said as he stopped scrolling. "Damn."

"What?" If they called off the wedding after all the text messages that had gone into it, she was going to delete every Kowalski in her contact list. Except Rob, of course. And Brian because he sent her funny pictures of Stella when he was bored.

"Steph's maid of honor can't make it, so her friend Siobhan is stepping in."

"And that's bad why?"

"Siobhan used to be Brian's sister-in-law." He winced. "They didn't like each other much *before* Kelly left him. Things got heated during the divorce and…let's just say Steph's wedding just got a *lot* more interesting."

* * * * *

HARLEQUIN
Reader Service

Enjoyed your book?

Try the perfect subscription for Romance readers and get more great books like this delivered right to your door.

See why over 10+ million readers have tried Harlequin Reader Service.

Start with a Free Welcome Collection with free books and a gift—valued over $20.

Choose any series in print or ebook. See website for details and order today:

TryReaderService.com/subscriptions